NOT RIGHT NOW

K. THOMAS

Cover Art by **Ana Ristovska** at.ARBookCoverDesign

Many thanks to the editing team: **Grace Heneks, PhD**, for content, **Paul Martin Editorial** for content and copy editing services, and **Scout Dawson** for proofreading of those last minute content changes.

ISBN: 978-1-66781-382-0
ISBN eBook: 978-1-66780-432-3

Dedicated to my legally bound human,

for being the only reason there is any actual romance in these pages.

I love you.

CHAPTER 1

I WATCHED as Hunter pulled the dagger out of the man's side. A pained cry dragged from the lord's mouth, which Hunter quickly took to covering with his hand to muffle the sound. Hearing the disturbance, Jonah rushed into the room.

Finding Hunter restraining the other man, Jonah let out a reprimanding growl. "What have you done?" he asked.

"I found I could not bear your plan," Hunter said, his voice calm and unruffled by Jonah's temper. He wiped the blade clean using the sleeve of his captive. "You will need to find another puppet."

With irritation dripping from his voice, Jonah said, "We had an agreement on this, and you allowed your jealousy to best you." He then snatched the weapon from Hunter.

"Oh, have your feed and be satisfied, Jonah." Hunter gestured at the bleeding man who continued to struggle, unsuccessfully, in his arms. The man was angry and fearful, and the smell of it all filled the room. Jonah flicked his eyes to our victim, then returned his glare to Hunter. He wouldn't allow the spirit to go to waste, and we all knew it. Ripping the man from Hunter, Jonah tore into his throat and fed.

I wrinkled my nose at the action. I found it perverse that he still engaged in drinking the lifeblood of strangers. It was wholly unnecessary but for his preferences.

Hunter sauntered over to me and drew me into his arms. "My apologies for the interference."

"It is Jonah's forgiveness you should seek," I said.

"I have no concern for his temper, so long as I haven't displeased you."

"You haven't." I kissed him gently. Content with my response, I felt him smile against my lips as he tightened his embrace.

Letting his finished meal sink to the floor, Jonah interrupted us. "It took months to get this in order, and you could not bring yourself to allow the game to play out. You are being greedy with her."

"Et je vais continuer d'etre," Hunter whispered and kissed the palm of my hand. "I did not want her touched by that filthy creature. You would not have acquired my consent if I had known the details of his disposition."

"Well, now you'll have to endure her sweet tongue persuading the constable when they find his corpse. Does that bring you more pleasure?" Jonah asked, causing Hunter to look away, clenching his jaw. "As I thought," Jonah continued. He crossed an arm over his waist, holding his chin with his other hand in contemplation. Eyeing the lifeless body, he mused, "This may work in our favor. The château and estate shall pass to his younger brother, and he will make a much easier mark for your persuasions."

I let my breath out slowly. "Jonah, I'm weary of this. We're comfortable enough, are we not?" I did not have the energy, nor desire, for another disagreement between them.

"This is simply what we do; comfort is not the point," he said as he kicked at the limp leg sprawled in front of his feet. "And I shall not be made to sit, twiddling my thumbs in boredom, at Hunter's command." Jonah's eternal petulance made him an entertaining companion, both in an enjoyable and exhausting way. At this moment, he was leaning heavily into my exhaustion.

"Hand me the dagger then, so as I can release you of your current station. Then you may choose a child of the blood in your next cycle and save us all the machinations of your rise to power," I challenged, holding my hand out for him to surrender his weapon to me.

"Oh, but the rise is the enjoyable part," he said, smiling as he came to stand at my side. He pulled at one of the meticulously placed curls upon my neck. "Not all of us can have your attention as our distraction from this dullness."

"I would dare to say your jealousy is now presenting itself, Jonah," I said.

"I am not jealous."

Hunter's laugh rolled from him. "So quick with your deceptions," he said. "You forget yourself and your company." Hunter then placed his lips on my temple as he traced a hand along my back and the skin of my shoulders. He was taking enjoyment not only from the feel of me but also from the ability to vex his friend with such little effort.

Jonah narrowed his eyes at Hunter as he addressed me. "You well know, you could temper him by employing some of that demure restraint that has come into fashion."

It was my turn to laugh. "And deny my raison d'ê·tre? Ridiculous, Jonah."

Jonah permitted a smile to spread across his face. Using Hunter's confiscated dagger, he reached up and nicked my shoulder. Startled by his action, I jumped, then swatted him. He let out a deep chuckle, enjoying my half-hearted retaliation as he lowered his mouth to where the blood began *to well on my skin. He closed his eyes as I allowed him to take the small price he exacted for our deviation from his plan. I stroked his cheek gently. Jonah was made to feed on the harshest emotions amongst us, and I posed the rare opportunity for him to taste something else. I did not begrudge him that occasional ask. He took a deep breath, inhaling my skin, lingering although the wound had already closed.*

"Ça suffit, Jonah," Hunter said in a quiet warning.

Jonah retreated from me slowly, ignoring the threat in Hunter's tone. I stared back into his steel-blue eyes as he regarded me. They were cold and intense—a contrast to the warm midday sky of Hunter's. "If you are done, I will not demand it of you," he said softly to me, "but I would require your assistance at least long enough to clean up the mess he made."

Before Hunter could protest, I put a hand on his chest, urging him to control his mouth. I turned back to Jonah. "I won't break my promise to help you."

Jonah nodded at my acceptance. He then paused, his gaze darting between us before adding, "You are wasted on him, truly."

I rolled onto my side and groaned, the sound of Jonah's voice still lingering in my head as I escaped my dream. I felt Hunter leaving soft kisses down my bare shoulder. Taking a deep breath, I turned, barely opening my eyes as I smiled at him. My nose filled with his aftershave and that constant hint of vanilla from his skin. "What time is it?" I asked.

"Almost four. Don't get up," he whispered.

"Where are you going?" I asked, my voice raspy with sleep.

"Us adults have important work things we have to do," he teased.

"At this time of the morning?" I didn't even know Hunter had a job. I mean, I assumed he did, but he'd never mentioned what it was. I couldn't comprehend one that required early mornings. Plus, we'd only been asleep a few hours.

He smiled and brushed my hair back from my face, kissing me on the mouth this time. Just a soft touch of his lips before he pulled away. "Go back to sleep. I'll be back before you're up for the day."

I made a small protesting sound as I reached for him, pulling him back to the bed with me. Laughing, he leaned over me, bracing himself on his elbows. I kissed him, softly at first, then arching up to press the length of my body against him. I ran my hands under his shirt and up his back, pulling him down. He lowered his body, his mouth pressed firmly against me as I opened to let his tongue find mine. I curled my fingers into his hair and held him against my mouth, my movements demanding.

He lost control of his carefully placed shields, and his spirit poured into me as he kissed back. It was hot and needy, forcing me to pull away from him gasping for air. Nuzzling down his neck, I left soft fluttering kisses in a line to the crook of his shoulder, where I flicked my tongue out, licking along his skin before biting down gently.

His body trembled above me, and he let out a quiet moan, then pushed himself up and away from my mouth. "Sen, I'm sorry, but I just spent the past few hours pressed against you in bed." He lowered back down to kiss my cheek softly, then whispered in my ear, "My willpower is not this good. So, unless you've changed your mind about certain boundaries, I need to leave for work." He hesitated, hovering over me, waiting for my response.

My heart was racing. I wanted to press against him and roll him under the covers with me. I now knew it was natural for me to absorb energy and emotions as a Nephilim; it was not natural that I wasn't able to control when or how much I took. It was especially difficult on me when it was Hunter's spirit that was involved. Once we started kissing, I couldn't tell where my desire ended and his took over. Not being able to stop my soul from feeding off his made the whole physical part of our relationship complicated for me—almost as complicated as the thousands of years' worth of memories that he had of us being together, but I didn't.

I pulled my arms away and nodded. "Go on, before you're late."

His shoulders shifted, giving away his disappointment in my answer. "Are you sure you want me to go?" he asked as he kissed my neck and along my shoulder, pulling the strap of my tank top down and out of the way.

"No," I said, "but you had better anyway."

He bowed his head against the pillow. "I was really hoping for a different answer," he replied with a laugh.

I smiled. "Sorry."

He moved down to place a kiss over my heart. "Don't apologize," he said, then smiled back as he crawled out of the bed. "I'll be back soon." He leaned forward and left one last, quick peck on my lips before grabbing his jacket and helmet off the floor by the bed.

I watched him leave. When I finally heard the front door close, I pulled the pillow over my head and groaned into it.

Benny still hadn't forgiven me for refusing to call off my relationship with Hunter. When it finally came out that he wasn't just Benny the ghost, but *my* Benny, he'd expected me to march Hunter out the front door—preferably hitting him with it on the way. Since that wasn't my reaction, to say he was angry would be an understatement. Livid? Enraged? Possessed? Yeah, let's go with that last one. Ultimately, I did have to rush Hunter from the house, but only to keep Benny from trying to physically hurt him. Surprisingly, we didn't draw attention from the neighbors during his celestial meltdown. That was something I could probably thank Katie's parents for as the neighborhood had grown accustomed to their nightly yelling. It's possible they didn't even suspect the disturbance was coming from my house that time.

Benny moped and refused to acknowledge me for a week. We eventually came to a sort of truce. He tolerated me in the evenings, as long as there was no reference or interaction with Hunter in his presence. I'd been alternating staying overnight with Hunter, so I didn't have to deal with

Benny's attitude over leaving or returning from his company. He seemed less agitated if he could altogether ignore the nights I wasn't there. It felt a bit like being stuck in a custody battle. If Benny could have bought me a pony to win me over, I think he would have attempted it.

It wasn't for the best reason, but I enjoyed the excuse to stay near Hunter. I wanted Benny to forgive me, so I kept going home, but those nights were harder than I expected. It was getting to the point I couldn't sleep without hearing Hunter breathing beside me. The nightmares of Jonah weren't helping there, either. For better or worse, everything that had happened seemed to trigger my memories in a pretty steady flow. Unfortunately, most of what was resurfacing was dominated by Jonah's presence, and it was taking its toll.

I'd accepted Hunter's offer to share his memories since he could control them, hoping it would bring more positive events back to me. It didn't work. What it did do was result in a heated kissing session that led to me putting up a very defined line we couldn't cross. Not until I could figure out how to put my barriers up and keep them there—which brings me full circle to my predicament right now, burying myself in his sheets and questioning why the hell I'd let him leave this morning. I pulled the covers over my head, knowing my dreams were going to continue to drag me through my past, but I was too tired to start the day. This was my normal bedtime, and my body was not okay with the idea of skipping sleep altogether.

CHAPTER 2

"WAKE *up. Please, wake up," Hunter begged.*

I woke again as Hunter slid under the blanket and wrapped his arms around me, curling against my back. The sunlight coming through his window helped push away the haze from my dreams. "Hey, beautiful. Did you sleep okay?"

I wrapped my arms around his and smiled. "Yeah," I lied. I was itching to ask him more about what my dreams meant, but I was worried about how he would react if he found out Jonah was the subject of most of them. I opened my eyes to see a to-go cup sitting on the nightstand.

"You brought me tea?" I asked.

"Brought *you* tea? No, that's mine…Did you want caffeine?" I elbowed him gently as he laughed. "Yes, I brought you tea," he admitted.

I rolled over to smile at him. "Thank you."

"You're welcome." He smiled back, pressing his forehead to mine and closing his eyes.

"Tired?" I asked.

He nodded. "You're wearing me out with your nocturnal schedule," he said softly.

"How was I supposed to know you're a morning person?" I asked.

"Anyone is a morning person compared to you."

I grinned. "That's fair."

I traced my hand down his temple and cheek, and his lips curved in a smile at my touch. He had shaved this morning, leaving his face smooth, the dimple in his right cheek fully visible. I couldn't decide if the usual stubble he kept complimented his cheekbones or distracted from them. Enjoying the opportunity to admire him while his eyes were closed, I ran my thumb along his jaw. His upper lip was full enough he didn't have much of a cupid's bow, and the lower lip tucked ever so slightly under it, giving him a permanent pout. It was especially prominent when he was deep in thought or asleep. Without his eyes open to distract you, it was easier to notice how nice the shape of his mouth was. I listened as his breathing started to take a consistent rhythm.

"Need to sleep for a bit?" I asked in a whisper.

"Mmm," he confirmed. I kissed his forehead before cuddling against him, my head on his arm. It felt so good just being wrapped in the warmth of him, the soft electric hum of his spirit swirling against my skin. It was calm and comforting. His sleep was obviously not as disturbed as mine.

My phone started vibrating across the nightstand. I reached out fast to stop it from waking Hunter. Answering, I whispered, "Hold on," as I slowly crawled out of the bed and tucked the blanket around him.

Once I was in the hallway, I greeted Vincent, "Hey, how are you?"

"Are you coming over today?" he asked, his voice tense.

"Yeah, I need to do a few things first, but I was planning on it. Every-thing okay?" I asked.

"I just really need to show you something."

"Okay, I'll head straight there."

"Good. See you soon." He hung up before I had a chance to say goodbye. I took a deep breath and shook my head before going to gather up my stuff. I had hoped to go home and do some laundry first, but I had more strips for him to prepare for the site anyway. I pushed myself to finish weeks' worth of panels for the comic, hoping to put Vincent in a good mood with all my hard work. After dressing, I sent Hunter a text, letting him know I was running by Vincent's, then heading to my house, and I would be back later. He was so deeply asleep he hadn't even moved. I was going to have to figure out an easier schedule for him.

When I finally arrived at Vincent's and knocked on his door, he didn't answer. I rang the doorbell, pressing it repeatedly to get his atten-tion, but to no avail. Deciding to use my spare key and just barge in on him, I shifted to pull my keyring from my bag. But as I reached up to unlock it, the door swung open.

Vincent stood there, squinting from the sun as he raised his hand up to shield his eyes. He was in a black T-shirt and grey sweats, and his hair was uncharacteristically messy. It looked like he had just woken up, but it was almost two in the afternoon.

"What took so long?" he asked.

"I think that's my line… Good afternoon to you, too." I pushed past him with my box of pastries, wiggling it at him. "I brought your favorite, and I have more work for you."

His mouth twitched into a smirk as he grabbed the box from me. "Alright, you know where to set up the laptop."

"Oh, you're allowing me near the command station?" I asked, caus-ing him to roll his eyes. I wiggled my eyebrows at him and went to his computer desk to hook up. A glass desk lined the wall, with two black computer towers and a large monitor perched in the center. It sprawled behind a chair that looked like it belonged on a sci-fi battleship. It was attached to a metal frame that held six more monitors towering over a metal tray. The set-up was connected to an obnoxiously large keyboard. Naturally, everything was covered in lights he had installed himself because every male in my life was obsessed with neon backlighting. There's no way I could have sat at this desk for long periods of time and accomplished anything. My focus was not strong enough.

"You haven't been streaming lately," I said.

"Surprised you noticed."

I held a hand over my heart and made a pained face. "Ouch."

"I used to have to force you to check your own site. Don't act like you were waiting with bated breath for me to post," he said.

"Accurate." I laughed.

He gave me a small smile and a head shake as he pulled a scone from the box and took a bite. He then carried the box to the coffee table and proceeded to sit on the sofa, folding one leg under himself and sinking back against the arm. He kept one hand on his side, protectively over the spot he'd received the worst wound from his fight with Nathan, and I took a seat next to him, mirroring his posture and then grabbing an apple tart.

"How are you feeling?" I asked, nodding at his midsection.

He looked down and dropped his hand, sitting up a little straighter. "I'm alright." He put the half-eaten pastry down on the box lid. Then he leaned forward, resting on his knees. "You don't have to keep asking, you know."

I put my food down next to his. "I don't do it out of obligation."

He looked over at me. His dark eyes scanned over my face and then down before settling on his hands clasped between his knees. "Yeah, I know," he said.

I reached out to touch his arm. As my hand met his skin, he jumped into a standing position, quickly moving out of my reach and over to my computer. "You don't need to do that."

"Do what?"

He waved a hand at me as he started clicking around on the trackpad, transferring the files from my computer to his. "You know. I'm healing fine; you don't need to worry about it."

"I was just trying to comfort you… But I do worry."

"I'm fine, Sen." Vincent had been very understanding in the hospital. He wasn't even angry that I'd kept what I was from him for so long. It had been a relief to share everything. And I had thoroughly enjoyed his reactions as he relived every weird incident from high school with sudden comprehension. But not long after he was released back home, he shifted. He didn't come right out and say it, but it seemed like he was upset with me after all. Since he won't talk to me about it, it's been a real treat trying to navigate restoring our relationship on my own.

I watched him work, his back to me as he took what he needed from my laptop and closed it. The tattoos on his arms were all visible in his short-sleeved T-shirt. A light scar remained in only one place: running along one of the angel wings on his forearm. Everywhere else the art was intact, and the skin had healed completely.

He turned and held the computer out to me. "All done," he said.

I stood, taking the laptop from him but not moving away. "You need to let me help more, Vincent. If you don't heal perfectly, you could have some long-term side effects." I looked up into his face and pleaded. "Please. It's my fault this happened, and I can't stand it if you won't let me do what I can."

He stood there for a minute, his mouth tight as he battled with my request. Standing this close I could tell he was angry, but I didn't understand it. Maybe he agreed it was my fault. I couldn't blame him if he did.

I'd nearly gotten him killed—not just because Jonah was after me, but also because I hadn't shared what was really going on with him. I'd withheld information and put him in danger. He had every right to be angry with me. "Please," I whispered again.

He closed his eyes and took a deep breath, then nodded.

I went to lift his shirt, to reach for the scar on his side, but he grabbed my wrist. "What are you doing?" he asked. His skin was warm, warmer than Katie's spirit for sure, but even warmer than I remembered him being in the past.

Afraid of what I'd see in his face if I looked up, I stared at his hand. "If I touch closer to the injury, I can heal it faster. I'll be out of your way quicker that way."

I tried to slow my pulse as he held my arm, willing myself not to cry from all the frustration burning under the surface of his skin. He released me gently, then pulled his shirt up. The scar was still an angry pink despite the amount of energy I'd fed him over the last month. I'd been mostly focusing on his internal injuries up to this point and hadn't wasted much on the surface damage.

I pressed my fingers tenderly against the smoothness of his side, trying to not hurt him as I pushed against his skin. As delicately as I could, I fed him the energy I had spooled, running my fingers along the rough texture of the scar tissue. He sucked in a breath as my spirit spread under his skin. The sound made me look up to see he had closed his eyes and was swallowing hard at the pain. I tried to be as gentle as possible, but no matter what I did, it always seemed to cause him discomfort.

I took my hand away when I was done, watching him as he stood there, not moving or opening his eyes. "All done," I said quietly.

He didn't even bother to look at the scar to search for improvements, he just pulled his shirt down and turned his back to me. "Thanks."

I nodded. When he didn't say anything else, I threw out, "I guess I should get going."

"Wait, I need to show you what I found," he said, but he didn't turn around to face me. He was pulling news articles up on several of the monitors quickly as he spoke. "I came across this last night."

"What is it?" I stepped up next to him, careful to not come in contact with his body. I didn't want to feel his displeasure with me again so soon.

The article on the screen was talking about a young man waking up in a hospital room and attacking the attendant. He had been hospitalized after a climbing accident. While being monitored in the ICU, he woke suddenly, disoriented and violent. He somehow escaped the hospital and was on the run. Although, given our experience over the summer, that didn't seem all that surprising. The hospital security wasn't exactly a SWAT team.

"That's pretty crazy," I said, "but why do I need to see it?"

"Look at what he did when he attacked the attendant, Sen." Vincent pointed to one of the paragraphs in the article. The victim suffered a puncture wound and blood loss from the patient biting his neck.

"Again, weird, but I don't get it?"

Letting out an annoyed growl, Vincent made a sharp motion at the screen again. "It's Jonah."

I looked at him then, my eyes wide. "Vincent, Jonah's dead."

"You don't die, Sen. You reincarnate. This man attacked three people on his way out of the hospital. They all have bite marks. I don't know how, but I know it's Jonah."

I wanted to wrap my arms around him. Vincent was obviously not okay. Hugging him right now was likely to send him running from me though. So instead, I asked, "Did you tell Will?"

Grinding his teeth, he said, "Yes. He said the same thing, that Jonah's dead."

"Maybe it's another Nephilim. Or maybe the person was on drugs and the biting is a coincidence."

"No." He shook his head. "This is him. I can feel it."

"When Jonah comes back, he'll be a baby. It will be years before we have to worry about him." I paused, softening my voice, "Vincent, you've been through a lot, and it's hard to just forget and move on —"

He cut me off. "You know what? Just forget it." He crossed his arms over his chest and leaned back against the desk, looking up at the ceiling as he tried to contain his temper.

I chewed my lip for a minute. I wanted to be supportive, but as far as I knew, what Vincent was suggesting wasn't possible; however, I wasn't an expert. I was just starting to get my memories back, and they were still coming in bits like they weren't really mine. I wasn't truly remembering myself the way Hunter and Ryder described it. "I'll ask Hunter about it and see if he has ever heard of something like this," I offered.

Vincent didn't respond. After a minute, I let out a sigh. As I turned to leave, he reached out and grabbed my arm again. Startled, I looked at him, my eyebrows wrinkled in a question.

"I know I'm dealing with some stuff. I get that. But in case I'm right, you need to be careful. Okay?" he said.

"Okay," I whispered.

"Come here." He tugged me toward him, enveloping me in a hug and burying his face against my hair.

I was so surprised by the action I just stood there awkwardly, trying to not cry. But my voice cracked as I spoke into his shoulder, "I'm sorry all this happened."

"Stop. It's not your fault." He gave me a squeeze, then released me. "You reek of Hunter. Are you still avoiding Benny?"

Laughing and blinking back my tears, I nodded. "Yeah, he's still angry." I didn't add "too" but it was implied.

I wish I'd thought to have my phone out and record when Katie introduced Vincent to Benny. Mind you, Benny had seen him before, but he'd been unusually compliant with my requests to stay hidden whenever Vincent had been there after dark. It was safe to say Benny liked Vincent a lot more than Hunter. Not that it was saying much since he absolutely hated Hunter. It set a pretty low bar to hurdle.

"You know, you aren't going to fix things by staying away from him."

I wrinkled my nose. "I know."

Vincent chuckled then. "Are you liking the morning sex so much you can't even skip it one day for Benny?"

"I am not having morning sex." I glared at him.

"Oh, no? Are you just spraying yourself with Hunter's cologne because you like the smell?"

I felt the heat rising to my cheeks. "No! It's from sleeping in his bed. *Sleeping*, Vincent."

"Uh-huh," he said, giving me one of his usual smirks. This was the one that meant he knew he was getting away with something.

"I don't have to convince you of anything." I shook my head at him and put my laptop back in my bag.

He watched me shuffle my bag onto my shoulder tersely, then his face lit up with realization. "Wait, you're serious?"

"Yes, I'm serious," I said.

He was staring at me, his mouth half-open, then asked, "Is Hunter sleeping on the couch or something?"

"What? No." I scowled. "Why would you ask that?"

"You've been sleeping over his house the better part of three weeks, and you're telling me the two of you aren't…" He motioned his hand up and down at me.

I squinted my eyes at him. "Yes."

"You both have a pulse, right? Or did I miss something?" He reached for my wrist and pretended to check for one.

I felt my nostrils flare. "It's complicated."

"Nothing is that complicated." He laughed.

I snatched my arm back. "This is."

Before, I probably would have told Vincent all about it. How I couldn't keep my barriers in place, so I couldn't stop myself from feeding on Hunter when things started getting heated. How feeding off him made me completely out of control, unable to tell if the emotions were mine or his, and I didn't want to make any decisions that I'd wake up regretting. Vincent would make lewd jokes in encouragement to make me feel better. But now...

He was being more himself now, but I didn't feel completely safe opening up, knowing that deep down he was still angry with me. Maybe once I had gotten him to forgive me, things could go back to normal.

He shook his head. "If you say so." Even though he was letting the conversation go, his eyes were twinkling. He was just as amused by his internal dialogue as he would have been if he let it out.

I scrunched my face up at him. "I'm leaving."

"Be careful, okay? Call me if you need me?" He was still smiling even though his voice had turned serious.

I nodded. "I'll see you in a few days?"

He walked me out, watching me get into my car. As much as he didn't want me to do it, I could tell from his body language he was in less pain than before I healed him. At least that was something.

CHAPTER 3

I LET out a breath as I stepped into my favorite coffee shop, Not Right Now. I could hardly wait for the hordes of teens and college students to be swallowed up by their school schedules, so I could reclaim my corner table. Carol saw me enter and smiled. She raised a large cup to let me know she was getting my tea started. Carol, the bringer of caffeine, and the only consistent, unchanging person in my life. The chalkboard behind her had the words "How about you try NOT interrupting, instead of apologizing for it *after*?" written on it.

"Hey, Carol." I smiled as I approached the counter.

"How are you doing?" she asked.

"Good, you?"

"Looking forward to next week!"

I guess I wasn't the only one excited for a break from the crowd. I nodded and looked around at the groups of meandering customers. All of the cute little sofas and chairs were full of students enjoying the last days of summer. Even the barstools were taken, forcing several individuals to stand and lean against the large window tabletop. At least most of the conversations were hushed today and not competing with the background music.

"On the house," Carol said as she handed me my London Fog.

I turned and took it from her. "Why?"

She smiled. "Hunter's orders."

"Why would you listen to Hunter?"

She just laughed and shook her head at me. "He took your table if you want to yell at him about it." She motioned to my usual spot in the corner by the window. Hunter's back was turned to us, but the messy curls were a giveaway. He had one hand dug into his hair as he leaned on an elbow, and he was tapping a pen against the table, staring at a laptop screen.

"Thanks!" I waved at her as I headed toward him. I snuck up behind Hunter and put my hand over his eyes. "Guess who?"

I felt him smile as he reached for my hand. "Sorry, miss, but my girlfriend won't like a stranger touching me," he said, tilting his head back to look at me.

I raised my eyebrow at him. "Oh, you're telling people I'm your girlfriend now?"

He kissed the palm of my hand. "I use a few monikers, but I think the others would make you blush."

I felt a grin spread across my face and didn't even bother to hide it.

"I thought you were going to Vincent's?" he asked.

I took a seat, then looked over at the empty chair next to me, where Vincent usually sat. "Yeah, I did," I said, failing to hide the disappointment in my voice.

"Done so soon?"

"Yeah. He's still 'dealing with some stuff'." I made quotation marks with my fingers.

Hunter's eyebrows furrowed as the corner of his mouth tucked in. "Sorry."

"It's my own fault. I should have told him about everything sooner. I knew this was a possible consequence when it came out later, too. I don't know why I lied to him for so long."

"I didn't think Vincent was the type to hold that against you. Are you sure that's what he's upset about?" He was looking down at my hand as he rubbed his thumb over my knuckles.

I shrugged. "I guess I don't since he hasn't really admitted anything to me, but it's the only thing that makes sense."

Hunter scooted his chair over to me, as close as the furniture would allow, and put his arm around me. Then he leaned in, nuzzling against my cheek. "Maybe there's something I could do to cheer you up?" he asked.

"Presumptuous." I smiled.

He laughed in response. "Fine. Maybe it's to make me feel better."

"And what do you need to feel better about?" I asked.

"I woke up all alone after my nap."

"Sounds like a horrifying experience."

"It was scarring." He smiled and kissed my cheek. "What are you planning to do to make up for it?"

"Absolutely nothing." I kept my expression flat and took a sip of my tea.

He chuckled and pulled away. "So cold."

"You love it."

"That, I do," he said, smiling at me.

I cleared my throat and nodded at his computer. "What are you doing?"

He let out a tired breath and leaned back in his chair, running his fingers through his hair. "I came back to get some more work done. I thought you'd be tied up longer. Figured I'd try to finish some of the paperwork, so we could sleep in tomorrow."

"What kind of paperwork?"

"I finished inventory this morning. I was setting up the orders for the month and processing the invoices from last week."

"Inventory? For what?" I asked.

He gave me a lopsided smirk. "I have to make sure we don't run out of lavender syrup. One of the customers has an unhealthy addiction to our London Fog."

I just stared at him. When his comment started to sink in, I looked over at Carol. "Oh my god, that's what she meant. You work here." Carol was chatting away with another customer as she made their drink, oblivious to our conversation.

"I own here," he corrected. His tone gave away his amusement at my revelation.

"What?" I exclaimed, my attention back on him.

"Technically, our parents' trust owns it, but that's basically me and Ryder now."

"Why didn't you tell me?" I asked.

"I didn't think about it. Katie knows."

"Yeah, I'll take that up with her later." I narrowed my eyes at him. "That's why Carol ratted me out and told you when I was here before."

Hunter shrugged. "Maybe. She likes you, though. It didn't take much coaxing when I told her why I wanted to know. I think she would have done it even if I wasn't her employer."

"She's a traitor."

"You don't seem too disappointed with the outcome," he said.

"Not the point."

He grinned again and leaned back toward me, reaching up and brushing my hair over my shoulder before running his fingers along the opening in my shirt. I could feel his spirit thrumming hot against my skin, his shield barely stopping it from spilling into me. "I think it's precisely the point," he whispered. Then he kissed me, gently touching his lips to mine. I sucked in a soft breath at the feel of him, closing my eyes as another wave hit me.

"It's precisely the point, Jonah." Hunter's tone was cold. I watched him stalk around the circle, glass crunching under his feet as he paced against the barrier. Jonah held me tight against his body, one hand encircling my throat. I was trying to control my breathing as they argued, but my pulse was racing. With so much of him in contact with my skin, Jonah's spirit was enhancing the normal anxiety welling in my stomach, sending me to near hysteria in his arms. I clutched the piece of glass in the pocket of my dress, feeling it cut into my hand. The pain helped steady me by giving me something to focus on.

Jonah regarded him coolly. "You're so convinced that you know her. That she will still want you when she wakes up."

"I know she doesn't want you." Hunter's voice was low and confident as he glared.

Jonah snarled at him and tightened his arm around my waist. "If you were sure of that you wouldn't have been so afraid to share her." I felt Jonah's breath on my neck. "Part of her was always mine, and you know it."

The anger in him washed through me, making me feel sick. I closed my eyes and leaned my head against him to try to keep the room from spinning. "See. She's not even fighting me," he said.

Jonah moved his hand from my throat, sliding it down my arm as he pressed his lips against me. I couldn't stop the small whimper that escaped, but when he didn't immediately tear into my flesh, I let out a deep breath. Mistaking my response as encouragement, he kissed along my neck, moving his lips over my pulse.

I opened my eyes to see Hunter watching, he frowned as he fought to ignore Jonah's words, but he was faltering in his resolve as he watched us. "I don't belong to either of you," I said. My hand was shaking as I pulled the piece of glass from my pocket and pressed it to my neck.

I gasped. Hunter's blue eyes were staring into mine as he held my face in his hands. "Are you okay?"

I nodded. Pulling away from him, I looked around to see if anyone had noticed my momentary lapse of consciousness.

"No one saw, don't worry," Hunter assured me. "Have you been getting memories during the day?"

"Sometimes."

"Why didn't you say anything?" he asked.

"It's not a big deal," I said. I reached for my drink and wrapped my hands around it, trying to warm myself. My hands were shaking from the vision and the fear still coursing through me. A lot of anger starts out as fear. Based on my memories, Jonah had honed the relationship between those two emotions in particular. Practice makes perfect, I guess.

"It's a huge deal. You shouldn't be driving around town if you're getting flashes like this. You need to make sure you're with someone for a while," he lectured.

"I'm fine. It doesn't happen when I'm concentrating." Not that often anyway. They usually came while I was sleeping, or when I let my mind wander as I tried to sketch panels for the comic. Never when I was actively engaged in something. "Something triggered this one. That's not typical."

Hunter shook his head. "Could you just listen and trust me for once?"

"I'm not a child, Hunter," I snapped.

"Hey." He touched my face, turning me back to him again. "I know that, but you don't remember what this is like. I don't want you to get hurt."

I clenched my jaw. I know it was another lifetime, and knowing Jonah, it wasn't really Hunter's fault, but I was angry at him. He never wanted me to get hurt, and yet he seemed to always be there when I was. "I need to go home."

"Aren't you coming back to my place tonight?" he asked softly.

"No. I really need to spend some time with Benny." I stood before he could stop me.

"Sen, you can't just drive yourself home right now. Look at you." He motioned to my still unsteady hands.

"Alright." I pulled my keys out of my bag and threw them on the table. "I'll walk."

I left him staring after me as I stormed out of the coffee shop. At least he was smart enough not to follow.

I sent Katie a text. *Free to come over?*

Yes! I'm on my way.

I'm walking back from Not Right Now. Be there soon.

Addict.

I laughed.

CHAPTER 4

I WAS greeted by a dozen red roses laying on the steps to my front door. There was no card attached, but I had just walked out on the only person who gave me flowers. Was it fair that I ran out on Hunter like that? If he had been at fault in my memory, he hadn't done anything today.

Jonah's voice in my mind repeated, *"You are wasted on him, truly."*

I shook my head. Maybe I needed to try sleeping pills to drown out my nightmares. I wanted my memories back, but a night or two of reprieve would be nice. I took a deep breath. I was tired. It was causing me to be unreasonably angry at Hunter, and even I could tell my temper wasn't grounded in anything. I was going to have to apologize to him.

Just thinking that made me grumpier.

I heard Katie's voice carrying across the street. "Why don't you have another drink? Bet that would help!" she yelled, slamming the door behind her, and running her hands through her hair in frustration. She had switched from just the bangs being purple this summer to an all-over periwinkle color. It was a very soft style that seemed to match her sweet, bubbly personality—although, Periwinkle was a death flower, so maybe it was a fine match for the murderous look on her face right now, too.

I watched her huff and storm across the street toward me in her black shorts and hoodie. Her cheeks flushed with anger as she approached. "Hey," she said, sounding a bit out of breath.

"Heeey…" I dragged out my greeting, raising my eyebrow at her. "You okay?"

"Fine." Without elaborating, she followed me inside.

I tossed my bag and keys on the sofa, heading straight into the kitchen. I started opening cabinets, desperate for something to put my roses in. How did I make it to adulthood without owning a single vase? Giving up, I pulled a pitcher from the cabinet and filled it with water.

"I thought your stepdad was doing better?" I asked over my shoulder.

"Yeah. He was sober for a bit. He does this though. He'll screw up, go too far, then apologize with gifts. He'll be great for a while, but he always relapses. It doesn't help that Mom just nags and fights with him constantly, even when he's sober. I swear, some days I think the two of them deserve each other." The frustration and anger coming off her were intense for Katie. When she saw me dropping the roses in the container, she wiggled her eyebrows, her mood shifting only slightly. "Ooh, you got upgraded to red roses."

The roses were beautiful—as far as that sort of thing went. "I guess so," I said. "The caffeine Hunter brought me this morning was more impressive though. I should probably tell him I don't really like flowers." I was eyeing her as I responded, trying to make sense of what was going on inside her.

"Oh, don't do that. He likes giving them to you. You'll ruin something that makes him feel good." Katie leaned on the kitchen counter, swooning over the petals. It didn't bother her one bit that the flowers were standing awkwardly out of something originally intended for juice.

Despite her pleasant interest in the roses, her aura was swirling. Her temper had subsided, but it was floating just under the surface. What was I supposed to do with this bitter, depressed version of my friend? She needed to get rid of some of it before it carved a more permanent space in her soul.

"I haven't been sleeping great. Would you mind?" I held my hand out to her, indicating I could use a little energy boost, which wasn't a lie, I did need it—not as much as she clearly needed to offload some of that toxicity. I didn't want to upset her further by sharing that though. It was kind of like telling someone they don't look like they feel well. You're meaning to be empathetic, but really, you're just being insulting.

"Sure." She grabbed my hand without hesitating. Katie and I could pass energy at this point with no effort at all. I could pull it from her as easily as I could block from Vincent. If only I had this level of control with everyone else in my life. I closed my eyes as my spirit filled with the wonderful coolness of her. It didn't matter what her mood, Katie's energy was never hot or uncomfortable. She wasn't a Nephilim, but she had enough of the DNA to make her something in-between me and human. Her brother, Will, had the same cold energy. According to Will, the purpose of their existence was to offset ours. Knowing that, it made a sort of sense that their spirit would feel like the polar opposite of the fiery spark of a Nephilim. It was an almost canceling effect, to match the balance they brought. Will referred to beings like him and Katie as descendants. When I asked Hunter what the proper term was, he said, "Spawn." I couldn't really tell if he was joking or not.

I carefully tugged as much as I could at the negativity pooled inside her. I took a good bit of it before pulling away.

Katie let out a relaxed breath.

Pausing after I'd released her hand, she squinted at me. She immediately realized what I had done. I hunched my shoulders, bracing for her reaction, but she just smiled. "Thanks."

"Feel better?" I asked, relaxing at the sign of her happier disposition.

She nodded. "Yeah, I've been stuck in the house with the two of them too much this week. It was really getting to me."

"You should have said something," I scolded.

"You're busy. I didn't want to be a burden."

"Katie, you're not a burden. I would have happily rescued you. I'm sure Jessie would have too. Did you ask her?"

She shook her head. "She's been busy helping Vincent. I didn't want to—"

I interrupted her. "Please, don't say 'be a burden' again."

Losing her sister to Jonah's killing spree had taken a toll on Jessie. She and Ashley were close, and Jessie idolized her older sister. When Jessie caught Vincent failing to teach me how to manage his site at the hospital, she threw herself into working with him on his streams. Jessie was stoic as ever, but Vincent said her therapist was doing wonders to help her cope. I was glad she had Vincent to help distract her from her grief. Though I hadn't thought what that would mean for Katie, with Jessie being her usual escape route from home.

"I'm sorry. I'm staying here tonight. Want to sleep over?" I asked.

"Is the sky blue?"

I pretended to think about her answer before replying, "Not technically..."

Katie made an exaggerated eye roll. "Why aren't you staying with Hunter tonight?" she asked.

"Thanks for the segue. When were you going to tell me that Hunter owns Not Right Now?"

Her eyes widened. "You didn't know?"

"Why on Earth would I have known that?"

"He makes you tea all the time."

"I make you tea all the time," I countered.

"Okay, fine, but didn't you wonder why he was always there?"

I shook my head. "Until today, I had only seen him there a couple of times when we first met." After this morning, that made sense. I hadn't left my house before noon since moving in. If Hunter worked early shifts, I would have missed him. I also had no idea how many times he had snuck out the last month while I was sleeping, and it was a little embarrassing.

"Still, I just thought you knew. Everyone knows." She bit her lip. "Ryder said it was kind of a big thing when their parents died. Their mom opened the coffee shop Hunter's freshman year of high school. Everybody knew her. She gave jobs to a lot of kids that needed hours after school. That's part of why it's still so popular."

I winced at her explanation. Hunter never talked about their parents. Now, I was feeling extra guilty for being angry with him earlier. I had ruffled because I immediately took it as him keeping something from me. Really, it probably just hurt to talk about.

"That has to be pretty rough on Ryder," I said. He was an introvert, to begin with. I didn't imagine he loved having the entire school know such personal information about him.

Katie shrugged. "I think it was for a while. He seems to handle it okay now."

I nodded.

We stood there quietly staring at the flowers. I finally pulled out my phone.

"Who are you messaging?" Katie asked.

"Hunter."

She made a pouting face. "You're not ditching me, are you?"

"No. I was just a jerk earlier, and I owe him an apology."

"Okay. Good! I get Benny and Hunter are fighting over you right now, but I miss you too!"

I laughed as I sent Hunter a text.

Sorry. I shouldn't have blown up on you.

I started to put my phone away but saw the indicator that he was already typing back. If I wasn't apologizing, I would have teased him and asked if he had been staring at his phone, waiting for me to message.

I know this is hard. Can I come by? I'll bring your car.

Can you bring it tomorrow? I already promised Katie I'd spend time with her and Benny tonight.

Sure. Since Benny gets you tonight, does that mean you're mine tomorrow?

Guess you'll have to wait and see.

"You get the goofiest smile when you're texting him, you know that?" Katie laughed.

Grinning, I looked up at her. "Just what do you think you look like when you're talking to Ryder?"

Her face sobered. "Hopefully, not like that."

Laughing, I threw one of my dishtowels at her.

"How's your memory doing anyway?" She giggled as she dodged my throw. "Do you think you're close to remembering everything?"

"I don't know. They still feel like I'm watching someone else's life. None of it makes sense, and they seem to come out of order, which isn't helping."

"Are you still seeing Jonah a lot?"

I nodded, then walked to the fridge. "I'm going to make us something to eat." If we were going to get into this topic, I needed comfort food. Nothing but pasta could make talking about Jonah tolerable.

The sun had set a few hours ago, and I was sprawled on the sofa, staring up at the ceiling, thinking I really needed to paint the room soon, when a card hit the side of my cheek.

"Ouch. Benny!" I turned my head to face where he and Katie were sitting on the floor in front of the sofa. "I didn't say hit me," I complained as I fished the card out from where it had fallen.

"We're not playing twenty-one. And…you touched the card, so now you have to keep it." Katie shrugged at me, a small smile on her face.

"Ugh." I held it up. "I'm out." I tossed all my cards at Benny, and he let out a triumphant chime. He would let Katie win all night, but he was taking extreme amounts of pleasure out of beating me every hand. It would be working more like the punishment he intended if I cared at all about the game.

"I'm going to make more popcorn. Katie, do you need another drink?"

"I'll take more tea if you're making some."

I nodded, then stood to head toward the kitchen.

Benny made an insulted gargling sound at me.

"Why would I offer to get you anything? You can't eat."

The lights flickered, and he chirped angrily. I made a rude hand gesture at him as I walked into the kitchen. Yes, that hand gesture.

I heard Katie squeal with delight behind me. "I win!" Sure, she did. Benny probably folded once he knew I had lost. I shook my head. Katie's presence made Benny happier than I think he'd ever been before I met her but certainly more than he'd been with me lately. Once the air popper was going, I leaned against the counter and watched the water begin to boil in the electric kettle.

I wondered if Benny had once doted on me the way he did Katie. Part of me already knew the answer. His death aside, I don't think Benny would have been so angry still if he didn't believe I needed his protection from Hunter. I knew from conversations with Hunter that Benny had been taking care of me when he got sick. Some fever took over, weakening his heart. I was terrified of losing him and came up with the brilliant idea to heal him. I filled myself with as much energy as possible and poured it into Benny, along with part of my own soul to boot.

Benny had meant so much to me I didn't even care, but Hunter did. I didn't fully understand what it all meant, or why Hunter reacted the way he did, trying to bind us all in a ritual. Not yet anyway. Because of the accompanying headaches, I had made the decision to wait for my memories to unfold themselves, rather than have Hunter fill me in crash course style. Even though it was my choice, I was growing impatient with my lack of insight.

My phone vibrated from a text. *Are you okay?* Chris asked.

All good. Just hanging out with Katie.

Hunter seemed worried earlier. He's high maintenance when you're away.

I laughed at the text. Chris was Hunter's version of Vincent. If he wasn't hanging with me, Hunter defaulted to Chris's company. Unlike Vincent, who would keep my secrets to the grave, Chris always tattled to me on Hunter. I told myself it's because Chris liked me more.

He's high maintenance when I'm there too. Trust me.

They sent back, *Truth*, followed immediately by another text. *Tell me if you need anything. If I need to smack Hunter around for you, I will.*

Yup. Definitely liked me more. I really needed to spend more time with Chris. They still felt a little like "Hunter's" friend; it rarely occurred to me that I could hang out with them independently from him. The more I thought about it, the more I liked the idea. Chris was fun and calming. I would have invited Chris over tonight, but they didn't know about Benny. Benny was not behaving well enough to bring innocent humans into the house right now. I replied, *Thanks. I might take you up on the offer another time. Next time Katie and I have a movie night, do you want to join?*

I'd love to!

You'll have to watch horror movies. It's all she consumes.

Sounds fun. I like ghost stories.

I laughed abruptly. If they came over at night, I might get a chance to test just how true that statement really was.

I filled a tray with the popcorn, our cups, the teapot, and a cream and sugar container, then headed back to the living room. Benny and Katie had moved to the sofa to watch their horror shows. After setting up the tea on the coffee table, I curled up under a blanket next to them.

"What is this episode supposed to be about?" I asked.

Benny made another snide chirp.

"I wouldn't have asked if I didn't care," I said.

Katie hushed us as she reached for some popcorn, then whispered, "They're in a haunted asylum, and the spirits are possessing the inmates."

I watched as a room full of people on the screen reacted in horror to the apparition that appeared in the corner. They all screamed and scrambled to get away. The ghost was a poorly done projection, and its face stretched out in a grotesque howl for the sake of scaring the audience.

"Benny, I don't understand how you can watch this and not mock how inaccurate it is," I said.

Benny's choir of voices gargled out in a curt retort as he waved at the stack of movies Katie had brought over—most of which we had made it through already. The last two had been horrible vampire movies that Katie insisted were classics.

"I am not a vampire, and I mocked those movies plenty."

We were all quiet for several minutes as we watched the screen, then Katie broke the silence. "Are you both going to pretend like everything's okay, or are we going to talk about the tension in the room?"

I turned to look at Benny, perched between us on the sofa. "I'm good pretending. You?" I asked.

Benny made a short trill in agreement, turning back to his show. The image of him was wavering just enough to let me know he wasn't being entirely honest.

Katie let out of huff at the two of us, crossing her arms over her chest as she stared at the television. "This is silly. Benny, she loves Hunter. You're being selfish." She turned to me then. "Benny's your family. You can't just walk away when things get tough. I can't believe I'm the one having to say this, but you're both being childish." When she finished her chastising, she turned back to the show, her face screwed up with frustration.

Benny and I stared at her. My mouth was open a little in surprise from her outburst and also at the assumption that I "loved" Hunter. I wasn't sure I was there yet, but Katie was dropping it like it was an indisputable fact.

Benny turned to me. Making a low chiming noise, he patted my leg.

I narrowed my eyes at him. "I do not have bad taste in men."

He shrugged in response, then turned back to the show.

A laugh bubbled out of Katie's lips as she shrugged at me. "Well, I tried."

"Thanks for the help," I said, sarcastically.

She tossed a piece of popcorn at me. Catching it, I raised my eyebrow at her and popped it into my mouth. "Don't waste perfectly good food." No sooner did the order leave my lips, Benny threw a handful of popcorn at my face, causing Katie to break into a full belly laugh.

I glared at Benny. He was facing the television like nothing had happened. His posture and the energy coming from him made a smile spread across my face. I flicked my blanket playfully at him, making it land on his head. He made a grunting noise, then tugged it from his face and curled up under it. The three of us settled in together. Katie looked only marginally smug, but I guess she deserved it.

CHAPTER 5

I **WAS** in that strange place between sleep and waking, where you're still dreaming but you know it. *"Won't this be fun?" Jonah laughed as I felt him tug at my ankle.* The feeling jolted me awake. Squinting, I rubbed my eyes and looked around the living room. I must have fallen asleep watching the TV last night. I looked at the other end of the sofa, expecting to see Katie curled up asleep. Instead, Vincent was sitting near my feet, scrolling through something on his phone. He was absentmindedly rubbing my ankle through the blanket.

"Hey," I said as I sat up.

He looked up at me, a small smile spreading across his face. "Hey, Katie let me in," he said. I smiled back at him. He seemed so at ease lounging there. It made me aware of just how tense things had really been between us lately.

"Where'd she go?" I asked.

"Ran across the street to change."

I nodded, running my hands over my face and through my hair to wake myself up. It had to be at least late morning based on the amount of light coming through the windows. "I wasn't expecting you to come by today," I said. "How did you know I was home?"

He smirked. "Chris sent a text that they were worried about you. Sounds like Hunter was crying to them about you running off yesterday. You two okay?"

"Yeah. I was just being moody with him."

"Sounds like you," Vincent said.

I kicked him gently with my foot, making him laugh. "Alright, give me a few minutes to make myself reasonably presentable?" I asked him.

"Sure." He patted my leg, then went back to his phone as I dragged myself to the shower. I pulled my hair up. I didn't want to take the time to wash it and leave Vincent waiting. I was excited to see him when I woke up. He felt so peaceful and calm. It was like having my old Vincent sitting in the other room. I was almost afraid to blink and have him disappear.

After I stepped out of the shower, I wrapped the towel around myself before opening the door to dash to my room. Vincent was leaning in the hallway outside my bedroom door. His legs stretched across the narrow hall as his back braced against the wall, hands behind his head. His hair was styled today, and he had ditched the sweats for jeans, making him look more himself. He looked lost in thought as he stared at my ceiling.

"We should paint," he said.

I laughed and tapped gently at his leg with my foot. "You're in the way."

He looked down at me and blinked. "What are you doing?" he asked, staring at my towel.

"Trying to get into my bedroom for some clothing?" I motioned at the door.

He stood up straight to let me by, his head turning away as I walked past him. "Why didn't you take clothes with you to the bathroom?"

"I don't know. Probably because I just woke up, and I wasn't thinking that clearly?" I called through the mostly closed door. I had left it open a crack so I could talk to him. "What's the big deal?"

He was quiet on the other side of the door, then I heard him say, "No big deal." He let out a heavy breath. "Sen, we really need to talk."

I rushed to pull on jeans and a tank before I opened the door to find Vincent standing in the doorway. He had moved to brace himself against the frame, his head bowed. He usually stood back in the hall, staring at the ceiling when I was dressing.

"Are you feeling okay?" I asked and reached up to touch his forehead. He felt as warm as he had yesterday, but it wasn't feverish.

"I'm fine," he said, but he didn't pull away from me, for once. Instead, he just stood there watching me as I stared up at him with my eyebrows furrowed.

"Let me see your side." I reach down to lift his shirt. He didn't seem like he was running a fever, but he'd been so strange lately, I was worried maybe he had an infection. With his arms lifted up by his head, it left the muscles in his stomach and back stretched, giving a clear view of the scar. When he didn't complain or try to stop me, I leaned down and inspected it. It already looked much better than yesterday and didn't seem agitated at all. Without asking, I pressed my hand to it and felt Vincent tense under my touch. It didn't feel hot—at least, no more than the rest of his skin.

"I'm sorry. I know it hurts, but one or two more times of healing and you'll be in good enough shape that we can stop," I promised.

He let out an abrupt laughed. "You think that's why I don't want you doing it? Because you think it hurts?"

I blinked at him. Yeah, that was exactly what I thought.

He laughed again as he pulled the sleeve back from his arm. He bared his tattoos to me as if I didn't know they were there. "I can handle a little sting, love."

"Then why are you being so stubborn about it?" I scoffed.

As he opened his mouth to say something, I heard someone clear their throat. I peered around Vincent. Hunter was standing in the hall. His fist was balled around the stem of a pink rose, and he stood completely still, holding his breath.

"Hi." I smiled at him.

"Hi," he said, stretching the word out. His eyes roamed over both of us before he added, "Alright. I am not going to overreact."

"Good?" I said, a question in my voice as to what exactly he thought he wasn't overreacting to.

Vincent looked over his shoulder at Hunter. "Hey, man. How are you?"

"I'm fine." Hunter flicked his eyes from me to Vincent, then down to where my hand still rested against Vincent's side. "Are you almost done groping him?" he asked.

I frowned. "I am not groping him."

Shaking my head, I went back to inspecting Vincent. I released some of the energy I had stored up from Katie into Vincent's side. A little annoyed with his revelation that it hadn't hurt as badly as I thought, I wasn't nearly as gentle this time as I shoved the energy through him in a quick burst.

Vincent sucked in a breath and bit his lower lip. "Umph." He grabbed my hand and pulled it from his side in reflex. "Why did you do that?"

"Just trying to get it over quicker. Sorry if it hurt, but you can handle a little sting, right?" I asked.

Vincent shook his head at me and pushed his shirt back in place.

I turned to Hunter. His eyebrows pulled together as he narrowed his eyes at Vincent. He seemed confused over Vincent's response, but at least his posture was more relaxed.

"Let's go put that with the others," I said, motioning to the flower in Hunter's hand. I walked past him toward the kitchen, patting his shoulder as I passed.

"I'm coming," he said, not taking his eyes off Vincent. I heard them murmur as they exchanged a few quiet words in the hallway. I was glad to be out of the way if they were going to get into an argument.

I opened the fridge and pulled out ingredients to make omelets. Katie should be back soon, and I doubted anyone made her anything to eat at home. I put everything out on the counter, turned on the burner, and reached down for my favorite pan. Yes, I have a favorite egg pan. Everyone does. If not, it's because they don't cook them nearly enough.

Hunter came up behind me, wrapping his arms around my waist. He held the rose in front of me as he pressed his cheek to mine. "This was how I was planning to greet you," he said. "I'm sorry about yesterday. I wasn't trying to be controlling or upset you."

I smiled and took the flower from him, leaning back against his chest. "I was the one who stormed off like a child. I owe you the apology."

"None needed." He kissed my cheek before pulling away to let me cook, adding, "I brought your car."

Smiling, I reached over and tucked the soft pink flower into the center of the bouquet of red roses he'd left for me yesterday. At least he wasn't going to make me grovel over my behavior.

Hunter looked at the flowers as if he was just noticing them, then he let out an annoyed sigh. "Vincent," he called out, "if you're going to give flowers to people, you need to work on understanding their meaning."

"What are you babbling about?" Vincent asked as he strolled into the kitchen. He hopped up on one of the kitchen stools at the breakfast nook. "I will accept food as your apology for the unnecessary medical intervention," he said to me, smiling.

"Eavesdropper," I accused, and Vincent smirked.

Hunter pointed to the roses. "Red roses mean love and possession. You don't give them to a friend you aren't pursuing."

Not ruffled by Hunter's tone, Vincent raised his eyebrows and replied, "I'll take that into consideration next time I decide to do something as monotonous as giving flowers to a woman."

I looked up from the pan, registering what Hunter was implying. "Wait, Hunter, I thought the roses were from you?" I asked.

"No." He shook his head.

"They were on the steps when I got home yesterday. Who else would leave me flowers?" I asked.

Hunter looked at Vincent, and his eyes narrowed with suspicion.

Vincent put his hands up. "It wasn't me." Then, grinning at Hunter, he added, "Besides, I know her well enough to know she prefers donuts."

Hunter leaned back against the counter, crossing his arms over his chest. "She loves pink roses."

"Oh, is that so?" Vincent asked. He raised his eyebrows and then cocked his head to the side at me, his smile growing wider.

Avoiding him ratting me out, I changed the subject. "That's strange. I wonder if someone left them at the wrong house?"

We all stared at the bouquet. Our pondering was interrupted by the sound of a door slamming and screaming coming from across the street. Katie's parents were in top form today. I heard her stepdad's truck engine start, the sound drowning out her mom's voice as she screamed at him. As I pulled out my phone to text Katie, Hunter's phone started ringing from his pocket.

He answered with, "Everything okay over there?"

His brother's voice was elevated on the other end. All I could make out from where I was standing was, "You need to get here. Now."

Before I could ask where Ryder was, Hunter was already rushing out of the house. Vincent was hot on his trail as I worked to shut off the stove.

"Where are you going?" I yelled. Hunter was already out the front door when I followed after them. He and Vincent were running across the street toward Katie's house.

CHAPTER 6

K ATIE'S mom was on the porch. Her arms were wrapped around her stomach, holding her robe closed. Their truck was gone, presumably with her husband in it. She gestured toward the inside of the house as Hunter approached. She seemed more distraught than normal as she followed him inside.

Vincent reached back for my hand as I entered the house. He held it as we approached the sound of Ryder and Hunter's panicked voices coming up the stairs that lead to the basement. When I walked through the doorway to the staircase, I looked down to see Katie, a puddle of blood starting to seep into the carpet near her head as she lay sprawled at the bottom. Ryder was on the ground next to her, his hands covered in blood as he tried to put pressure on the injury.

"Oh my god," I said, dropping Vincent's hand as I ran down the steps toward her. "What happened?" I asked.

Katie's mom followed behind me. "It was an accident. John didn't mean to. She came up the stairs right as we were arguing, and he knocked her down. It was an accident." She was rambling as she paced the floor.

I knelt down next to Ryder and put my hand on Katie's neck. She was still breathing and had a pulse, but her eyes were closed, and her face was slack from being unconscious. One side of her face was red and swollen. It didn't seem from the fall. It must be where she was hit when she was pushed down the stairs. I tried to stay calm and focus on what to do next. Panicking made me no good to anyone, least of all Katie.

"Call the police," I said to her mom.

"It was an accident," she repeated.

I looked up. Her face was white as a sheet, and I knew she was probably in shock. But I didn't care. "Call the police. Now!" I shouted at her. She blinked back at me and nodded, wandering up the stairs.

"You have to heal her." Ryder looked up at me, his face wet from tears. "Please, Sen, you have to."

My heart pounded inside my chest. I had no idea what injuries she had besides an obviously cracked skull. I could heal some of it, but she was likely going to end up in the hospital anyway. I felt over her body, using my spirit to check for damage. Her head was in bad shape. She had a fracture and bad gash on the side of her skull and another fracture to her right shoulder, probably where she took the most impact when she hit the ground. I was going to need more than just me to do any good.

"Help me," I whispered to Ryder.

Ryder nodded. He let me grab his left hand and placed it on the bare skin of her shoulder, just inside her shirt. I left his right hand to cradle the back of her head and placed my hands over his.

"I'm going to push as much energy as I can through you and into her. Pay attention to what I'm doing so you can imitate me," I instructed.

Without saying anything, Hunter moved from beside Ryder to crouch behind me. He reached around me and pressed his arms around mine, circling his hands over my wrists. Enough to press against my skin but not restrict my movements.

Following Hunter's lead, Vincent took a step towards us. I shook my head. "No, you can't help with this. I just healed you, and it could reverse the progress."

"And I care about that, why?" he asked.

"Vincent." My voice was harsher than I meant, but I didn't have time to fight with him.

His nostrils flared as he clenched his jaw. Then he pulled out his phone, tapping away on the screen as he turned to stand guard on the bottom step. Whatever he needed to keep him busy was fine by me. Hopefully, he could keep Katie's mom from interfering, should she decide to come back down to the basement.

I closed my eyes and felt Hunter's energy thrumming against me. We both let down our shields. His spirit crashed like a wave of angry heat inside me, but under the anger was fear. We were both upset and frightened over what was happening. It wasn't ideal as far as emotions went, but they were strong, and that's what mattered most at the moment. I let it curl up inside my chest, then used my hands to guide it through Ryder.

Ryder sucked in a sharp breath as it flowed past him and into Katie. Our energy swirled around inside her, against the coolness of her spirit, and I coaxed it toward her injuries. I didn't consciously know if Ryder could share his spirit with her without me holding him, but something inside me said no—the same part of me that knew exactly what to do right now, and I was trusting it. It didn't take long for Ryder to understand what was happening and follow suit. Once he did, he started to pour energy into Katie like he was going to empty himself.

The panic in his energy was painful to touch, and I wasn't the only one to notice how much it hurt. Katie let out a cry under us as it filled her.

"Ryder, enough. That's too much, too fast," I said. Katie whimpered and curled up on her side in pain, but he didn't pull back.

"Ryder…" Hunter's voice was low with warning behind me, trying to get his brother's attention. "Stop."

"I don't know how," Ryder's voice cracked as his anxiety spiked even higher.

Before I could say anything to help him, I felt it. All our energy inside Katie had moved like water and oil mixing moments before, swaying and pushing against itself as it healed her. Suddenly, her spirit seemed to soak up what Ryder was sharing. Her soul was doing the pulling now, clinging to him, and he didn't have any barriers in place to stop her.

"Shit," was all Hunter said from behind me.

I had a breath to think, *"Huh, he doesn't usually swear."* Then, like a piece of fabric tearing, I felt Ryder's soul begin to rip. As I realized what was happening, I yanked his hands away from her, but it did nothing to stop the link between them.

"Fuck!" I whispered.

"What the hell is that?" Vincent asked as he dropped down to reach for Katie. Without hesitating, Vincent gathered her in his arms, swatting at Ryder's energy pooling around her as if it were a physical thing. As soon as Vincent came in contact with her skin, it felt like a sonic pop as Ryder's spirit broke free.

Ryder gasped. His hands were shaking in mine as I stared into his face. He looked back at me, his brown eyes wide and hollow, dark lines under them from all his tears.

And from splitting his soul in half.

CHAPTER 7

"**A**RE you okay?" I asked Ryder.

"I don't know." He shook his head, running his hand through his hair. It was still wet and sticky from Katie's blood, which he managed to smear all over himself. When he pulled his hand away and looked at it, he seemed to suddenly remember Katie. Vincent didn't stop him when Ryder reached to pull her into his lap.

"Katie?" Ryder spoke to her gently as he touched her face, trying to wake her. She was breathing evenly, and her face looked healed. She made a small whimpering noise, turning her head, then coughed and spat blood out onto the floor. I reached out, touched her cheek, and let out a relieved breath. The blood must have been pooled in her mouth. It was just a remnant of the injuries that were now healed.

I looked over my shoulder at Hunter. He was silent behind me as he continued to hold onto my arms. He had put his shield back in place, protecting me from his emotions—for all the good it did. When our eyes locked, I saw the panic he was swallowing in his stillness. Ryder healed Katie, but he paid a significant price for it. No one knew that more than me. Hunter leaned forward and placed his lips to my forehead, drawing me into a hug.

"We'll figure it out," he whispered against my skin.

I turned back to Katie and Ryder. She was blinking and rubbing her eyes, but her motions were sluggish. Her muscles were probably sore from all of the energy coursing inside her. Ryder was cradling her and running his hands through her hair. He kissed the top of her head. He was whispering in her ear, coaxing her more awake. I reached out and moved some hair from her face, causing her to squint up at me.

"Sen?" she croaked.

"Hey, kiddo."

"What are you doing?" she asked.

Ryder and I both laughed. It was an awkward, tired sound coming from both of us, but it was also full of relief. "We'll get to that later. Just rest for a bit, okay?"

She nodded and closed her eyes, nestling her cheek against Ryder's leg.

I squeezed his arm and felt a sharp spark pass between us when my skin came in contact with his. Ryder was usually very good at keeping his barriers up, especially around me. With neither of us having our spirit intact, my energy danced across his arm and under his skin like an electric current that already knew its path. He winced, causing me to yank my arm back.

"Sorry," I said, quietly, not entirely sure what all I was apologizing for. My energy not behaving itself? Helping him destroy his soul? All of the above?

The sound of feet running down the stairs filled the air around us, and I looked up to see Will rushing toward Katie. "A paramedic is on the way," he said, his voice calm and his face void of emotion as he crouched down to gently inspect Katie.

"Did her mom call you?" I asked.

Will shook his head as Vincent answered, "I sent him a text." Figures. What the hell was that woman doing upstairs if she hadn't even called anyone for help?

Will's eyebrows furrowed as he looked Katie over, then his head snapped up to look at me. "Did you do this?" he asked.

I winced. "We healed her," I said, looking over at Ryder.

Feeling my reaction, Hunter tightened his arms around me protectively. Will's eyes scanned me, then Hunter, before finally, they landed on Ryder. Will's mouth opened, making a silent, "Oh," as he stared at Ryder, no doubt recognizing the condition he was in.

"I feel like I'm missing something," Vincent chimed in.

"Part of Ryder's soul is now attached to Katie's," Will said very casually like he was sharing the weather, but he didn't take his eyes off Ryder. Will was usually calm, but this seemed extreme, even for him.

Vincent looked at me, his eyebrows raised as if he too had expected more emotion with that revelation. "Is he being literal?" he asked.

Hunter laughed abruptly behind me, then answered, "Yes."

Vincent looked back at Ryder like he was seeing him for the first time. "Did you know that was going to happen?"

Ryder nodded. "Pretty much."

Vincent gave Ryder an approving nod. "Right on, little man."

I raised my eyebrows at Ryder. I was surprised he had taken that risk knowingly. It probably should have occurred to me it could happen, but I had assumed I did something wrong when I tried to heal Benny. Feeling how Katie's soul had latched on to Ryder, I was beginning to think it didn't have anything to do with how much we fed into them. Something about Katie's soul had triggered this, not the other way around.

I watched Will carefully check over Katie. When he turned her head toward him to inspect the other side, she opened her eyes. "Hey there." He smiled as he greeted her quietly.

It took a moment before her eyes lit up with recognition. "Will!" she yelped, flinging herself into his arms. He wrapped his arms around her, patting her back, and she sobbed into his shoulder.

Ryder looked like he was about to burst into tears again over watching her cry.

"Can you stand?" Will asked Katie.

She nodded without pulling away from him. I heard a muffled, "I think so," as she kept her face buried against him.

He helped pull her into a standing position, then took a minute to inspect her head again.

Hunter stood up first, then helped me to my feet. I looked over to Ryder and reached my hand out to try to help him stand, but he shook his head and pushed himself up. "I'm good."

"Let's go upstairs; we need to get you looked at," Will said gently. He turned Katie toward the stairs.

"I feel okay," she murmured softly.

"I'm glad to hear that. That means they'll be quick about it," he reassured her.

Katie's mom looked up from the table where she had been waiting for us in the kitchen. "Katie!" She pushed to a standing position and reached for Katie, who recoiled from her touch.

"Mary, give her a minute," Will said, putting a hand up to ward Katie's mom off.

I blinked, realizing this was the first time I had heard her name. That's how little I respected her. All this time, and I hadn't even bothered to ask for it. Will said something quietly to Katie, who nodded in response. Then he motioned to Ryder, who rushed up and wrapped his arm around Katie, ushering her back into the hallway.

"Tell me what happened," Will said, turning back to Mary.

"John and I were just having a conversation," she said, wringing her hands as she spoke. It probably wasn't helping her anxiety to have Hunter, Vincent, Will, and me all watching her as she shared her story. To be fair, from where I was standing, I could see Vincent's face and could comfortably say at least the two of us were more than watching. We were glaring at her. "Katie came up the stairs as we were starting to argue. John accidentally bumped her. It was an accident."

I saw Will's eye twitch a little as he listened, but he didn't say anything.

I wasn't nearly as accepting of her answer. "Bumped her? Did you see the mark on her face?" I asked.

She turned those scared eyes at me, tears filling them. "It wasn't hard; he barely touched her." Was she trying to convince me or herself?

Without thinking, I took a step toward her. I was exhausted. I had put every bit of free energy I had into Katie, and the feeling of all of it battling for space inside her left my entire body feeling bruised. Yet, somehow, I felt a surge of anger inside me blistering enough that I was shaking with the control it took to contain it.

"She flew down a fucking flight of stairs, *Mary!*" I snapped. I felt Hunter grab my arm, but I shoved him off. I wasn't done, and I was not about to be shuffled out of the room and quieted. "And then you chased after your husband! You didn't even take care of Katie first. What the hell is the matter with you?" I was shouting.

"Sen…" Will's tone was quiet as he put a hand up to me.

She lifted her chin before she spoke. "It was an accident. I wasn't thinking."

The defiance in her voice was enough to tip me over the edge. "You stupid bitch!" It came out as a low growl. I started to lunge at her, drawing energy from somewhere I couldn't explain. By all rights, I should've been passed out on the floor, but I was fueled by my emotions. I had remained calm when Katie was lying on the floor in front of me, distracted by the task of healing her, but now all that fear and rage over what we had walked in on was washing over me. I wanted to tear her mother into pieces.

Arms wrapped around me, yanking me back. I tried wriggling free, but as I squirmed and kicked, I was dragged out of the room and backed up against a wall. I had expected it to be Hunter that interfered, but it was Vincent's face I glared into. He kept me pinned to the wall, his arms on either side of me, keeping me in place.

"Let me go," I said in a low voice, pushing at him with my hands that were caught between us.

He took my face in his hands as he leaned down to look at me. This close, my vision was filled with his dark eyes. "No," he said softly. "You need to calm down. Trust me. No one wants to hit something—or some-one—more than I do right now."

"That's debatable," Ryder said quietly from behind him. With a slight turn of my head, I could see he was holding Katie and scowling past us into the kitchen. Katie looked fragile in his arms and had her face hidden against his shoulder, avoiding the whole scene. Vincent had maneuvered me into the hallway where the two of them were waiting.

I took a deep breath and closed my eyes. It helped that I could feel Vincent's energy. It was angry too, but it was controlled, contained— not like the wild thing inside me that was still lashing out at my insides. I knew I couldn't attack the woman. That wasn't going to do anything useful. Anyway, Katie would probably be mad at me about it later. This was her mom, after all, and she wasn't the one who had done the damage.

I swallowed as I pushed my temper down, forcing it to imitate the stillness in Vincent.

"You're right," I said.

Vincent kept me there as I continued to take even breaths until it wasn't a forced effort. When he felt the tension leave my body, he pulled me away from the wall and into a hug. He kissed the side of my head. "Feel better?" he asked.

"Yeah," I said as I opened my eyes. "Thanks."

He nodded, then let me go. Hunter was standing in the doorway now, leaning against the frame as he watched us, his hands shoved in his pockets. He didn't look happy, but he hadn't interfered. I was thankful for that. I'm pretty sure if Hunter had joined in, I would have felt cornered and responded very poorly to the two of them overpowering me together.

The doorbell rang, making me jump.

Ryder reached over and opened it. A woman holding a medical case, in an official-looking uniform, stood in the doorway.

"Hello," she said. She had a smile on her face as she looked around curiously at all of us hovering in the hallway. Katie and Ryder were hidden from view behind the front door, or our smiling paramedic probably wouldn't be standing there, calmly waiting for instructions. One look at all the blood on the two of them, and I had no doubt she would have sprung into action.

"Hey, Julie," Will greeted her as he came out of the kitchen. He ushered the paramedic into the living room, holding out his hand.

She smiled and shook it. "Hi, Will. Where is she?"

Will nodded at Katie. She was clinging to Ryder, her shoulders hunched with anxiety. He coaxed her over to the living room sofa to sit. The room was destroyed. The coffee table had been knocked over, and magazines and empty cans spilled onto the floor. A small shelf that looked like it normally held various media was toppled onto the ground, its contents sprawled around it. From the look of it, Katie's parents had probably been arguing for a while before Katie got involved.

"Hi, Katie. Can I take a look at you?" Julie asked as she kneeled in front of her. Her voice was kind and soothing, with all the skill of someone experienced at handling trauma.

Katie bit her lip and looked up at Will. He gave her a quick nod. It was apparently enough reassurance. She turned back to Julie and said, "Okay."

Julie went to work, efficiently reviewing Katie's body and head. Ryder hovered nearby, refusing to leave her side. She also had a death grip on his hand, so even if he wanted to, he wasn't going anywhere. I wondered what was going on inside them both. Was Ryder able to shield from Katie right now? Was he keeping her calm? I felt his soul split, but just because it did, was he still able to filter what emotions he absorbed, or was he like me now? So many questions I couldn't ask in front of the friendly neighborhood medical professional.

I looked around, realizing Vincent and Will had both left the room again. I walked over to Hunter. He stood up straight and opened his arms for me. Suddenly, feeling as tired as I should have, I buried my face against his chest. He wrapped his arms around me. He felt warm and safe, and the smell of him made me want to curl up and sleep.

"Sorry," I muttered against him.

"For what?" he asked. I pulled back and looked up into his face. He was looking back at me, his eyebrows pulled up in confusion.

"Oh, I don't know. The mess of things I made with Ryder, and the horribly childish scene I made with Katie's mom?"

"Quit apologizing." He shook his head. "Ryder knew what he was doing. He'd do it again, no question. As far as Mary goes, you just said what the rest of us were thinking."

I groaned. "I am so glad Vincent stopped me from doing more than telling her off."

He pressed his lips together in response. "Mhmm." It wasn't exactly a rousing agreement.

"I thought it was you dragging me out of the room. I'm surprised you let Vincent do it." I eyed him.

He chuckled then. "I didn't like it. But you didn't exactly go willingly. Watching you attempt to fight him off was worth it."

I frowned at him.

"If it makes you feel better, I am guaranteed to have some bruises," Vincent said from behind me. I turned around to find him smiling sheepishly at me. He had a duffel bag slung over his back.

It did not make me feel better. Hurting Vincent wasn't something I would ever be proud of accomplishing. Feeling guilty, I said, "No, not at all." Then, nodding at the bag, I asked, "What's that?"

"Katie's clothes," he said, adding, "I don't care who she leaves with today, but she's leaving with one of us."

Hunter and I both nodded in agreement. I wondered which one of us was going to get the pleasure of breaking that news to her mom. As if reading my mind, Will's voice came from the entry to the kitchen. "I already told Mary I'm taking Katie to stay with me for a few days."

The three of us turned to look at him. I didn't mean for my face to hold so much surprise, but Will didn't strike me as the type who wanted a teenage girl in his personal space, or any female, for that matter. And I wasn't the only one looking at him that way. Seeing the expression on all our faces, he frowned. "I'm Katie's family. Her mom can't easily charge me with kidnapping if she changes her mind in the middle of the night."

Ah. That was the pragmatic Will I was learning to know and love. Or maybe not? I watched as he shifted his collar slightly, looking away from us all. He caught me scrutinizing. Giving a small smile before clearing his throat, he walked away to check on the progress Julie had made.

Julie concluded Katie was fine. She was a bit perplexed by the amount of blood everywhere until Will casually threw out that Katie's nose was bleeding badly when he showed up. When Katie left to take a shower and wash it off, Julie gathered her stuff and stood.

"You always have the interesting cases," she said, pulling her gloves off. Her tone implied she didn't fully believe him about what happened but wasn't going to press.

"Thanks again for coming." He reached out to shake her hand again.

She smiled up at him as she took it. "Anytime."

As she walked past me, she looked down at my hand. "All healed up, I hope?"

I stared at her for a moment, then realized she was the same person to clean me and Hunter up at the cabin. Would I have healed this well already if I was human? I flexed my hand, closing it into a fist, hiding the lack of a scar. "Yeah. You did a good job." I smiled back at her, hoping I looked more innocent than guilty.

She raised her eyebrows, then shook her head. Under her breath, she said, "Always interesting."

When she left, I looked down at my hands. I still had some of Katie's blood on me. Ryder had cleaned up in the kitchen, but since Katie was still occupying the bathroom, that was the only other place to do it. I wasn't about to go back in that room with her mother though. Will had skillfully kept us separated, and I wasn't going to tempt fate. I was in control of my temper for the moment, but it was a thin line.

"I'm going to go home and clean up," I said to Hunter.

"I'll come with you," he said.

"I can wash my hands myself."

The corner of his mouth tucked into a smirk. "Everything's more fun with company."

I shook my head, then looked at Vincent, who had taken up a spot on the sofa next to Ryder. Vincent was trying to distract him while they waited for Katie. He was showing Ryder videos on his phone as he described the mechanics of whatever game it was related to. Hearing me say I was leaving, he looked up. "I'll wait for Katie. We'll bring her over when she's done."

"I'm already done," Katie said quietly.

We all turned to see her standing in the entryway. She had on her favorite destroyed jeans and an oversized T-shirt. Her hair was still wet, but at least she was clean. Her skin looked paler than usual, making the freckles stand out. It made her seem younger. She ran one hand nervously over her upper arm and the shoulder we had healed.

"Does it hurt?" I asked.

She shook her head. "No, it feels good. I'm just tired."

I nodded and reached for her, putting my arm across her shoulders, careful not to touch her bare skin. I didn't know how she would react now. We needed to get out of here to find out. I sure as fuck wasn't willing to address anything with her mom within hearing distance. She had proven she couldn't be trusted. In so many ways.

"Let's get you out of here," I said.

Katie nodded.

We all piled out of the house, leaving Will to deal with Mary. I felt bad about that. But there really wasn't anything I could do about it. Having me reason with her certainly wasn't on the list of viable alternatives.

CHAPTER 8

O NCE everyone was inside my house, the living room seemed even smaller than normal. Ryder took Katie to the sofa and sat with her. They seemed perfectly fine keeping contact with each other. I would have thought it would be difficult, but Ryder seemed even more inclined to touch her arms and skin than he normally was—which was a lot.

Hunter sat on the sofa, resting his elbows on his knees as he watched them.

"I'm going to wash up, but we need to talk about you two when I get back," I said, heading toward the bathroom. I didn't have the full story of what had happened with Katie's stepdad either. But the specifics weren't that important in the grand scheme of things, and I didn't even know if Katie would really want to discuss the details yet. I grumbled while scrubbing the blood off my nails. Letting it dry had been a mistake, and it was taking longer than I wanted to remove it. By the time I finished, the skin on my hands was red and raw from all the scrubbing.

When I came back into the living room, the three of them were still sitting there. Katie was nodding as both Hunter and Ryder spoke in hushed tones, but Vincent was nowhere to be found.

"Vincent?" I called out.

He yelled back, "Do you want to select your unmentionables, or should I finish packing for you?"

"What?" I asked, following the sound of his voice into my bedroom.

Vincent had one of my duffel bags on the bed and had filled it almost to the brim with clothes. He stood by my dresser, with my underwear drawer pulled open. "You really need to be more organized than this. I can't tell what's a matching pair."

"Do not touch my underwear, Vincent," I said sternly as I stormed over to the drawer, swatting a black bra out of his hand.

Hunter's voice came from the doorway behind me. "I second that."

"Fine, as long as one of the two of you does it, but you should hurry," Vincent said. "Personally, I think you should trust me more than him at this. I dress better."

"Why are you packing my stuff?" I asked.

"You can't stay here. If that asshole comes back, he knows you're Katie's friend, and her mother will probably tell him you were there."

Hunter made a sound of hesitation, then he added, "He has a point, Sen."

I shook my head. "I have Benny for protection. I don't need to run away."

"What if he comes back during the day?" Vincent didn't wait for my answer, he just turned to head out of the room. "I'll get your laptop and tablet while you finish up here."

His paranoia was getting out of control. After Vincent left the room, I said, "He has lost his damned mind."

"I don't think so. He has a valid point," Hunter said.

"No, he doesn't. He's going through some kind of trauma. He showed me a news article yesterday of some guy blitzing out after waking up from a coma, and he's convinced it's Jonah."

Hunter's eyes widened. "Why would he think that?"

"The guy, apparently, bit a bunch of people during his escape."

Hunter stood pensively as he digested the information. I raised my eyebrows when he didn't immediately reject the idea.

"That's not possible, right?" I urged.

After another second, he said, "No. No, I don't think that's possible." He shook his head, casting the idea off.

"See? I'm worried about him, Hunter. This is not normal behavior for Vincent. He doesn't run."

"I am not running," Vincent said. As he stepped around Hunter, his cheeks flushed with anger. "I'm removing you from harm's way. That is not the same thing."

"Vincent…" I started.

He shook his head as he shoved my electronics into the front pocket of the bag and zipped it. "Either you leave with one of us tonight, or I'm sleeping here. But you're not staying here alone."

Hunter bristled at Vincent's suggestion of staying with me. He turned to me. "Why don't you just stay with me? You were going to come over tonight anyway."

I glared at them. "Do either of you remember that I'm a Nephilim, too? I could kill someone by taking their soul if I wanted. I do not need your protection. Besides, this isn't a big bad, it's a drunk human."

"Would you?" Vincent asked.

"Would I what?"

"Would you kill someone?" he asked me, pointedly.

I opened my mouth to answer, then paused. Would I? I didn't know. Maybe. In self-defense? Possibly. I had no problem frying Jonah when the opportunity arose. "Yes," I finally said.

Vincent shook his head. "You hesitated."

"Vincent, anyone would hesitate with that question. They *should* hesitate," I said.

He jabbed his thumb at Hunter. "He wouldn't hesitate."

I looked at Hunter. He simply stared back at me, not bothered at all by Vincent's statement. I knew it was true. It made me uncomfortable to hear it announced so blatantly, and even more so to see Hunter calmly accept it. Regardless of my feelings, I still knew it was true.

"Come on, love. We need to relocate Katie. Finish packing your bag," Vincent urged.

"What about Benny? I can't leave him here, especially with no information." Or worse, having him find out about Katie and be trapped here alone.

"I'll come back and talk to him tonight," Vincent offered.

"You can't understand what he's saying," I reminded him. "I have to be here to explain what's going on."

"*We'll* come back," Hunter threw out, then added, "and Vincent's right. We should move Katie now. Will can pick her up from our place later. We need to figure out how she and Ryder are doing, without having to worry about John showing up. I'll come back with you tonight, and we'll figure out what to do with Benny."

I stared back at the two of them. They were resolved, and my opinion wasn't going to count. I let out a frustrated growl, then I reached into the drawer, scooping up a handful of underwear and bras and tucking them into the bag.

Vincent's face looked horrified. "You just grabbed them... randomly."

"They're all black, Vincent. Everything matches," I said.

I watched Vincent shake his head in disbelief. "I'm sorry. I tried to teach her better than that," he said to Hunter as he walked out of the room.

Hunter let out a low laugh, his eyes twinkling as he walked toward me. I folded my arms over my chest and gave him as deadly of a look as I could muster. "If you make even one comment about my clothing, I'm staying here. Alone."

"Don't worry. I know Vincent's the only one who can get away with teasing you like that." He smiled. "I also know you hate feeling like you don't have choices. If you want to stay here tonight, we can."

"We?"

"I agree with Vincent. I'm not comfortable with you being here alone." Before I could protest, he continued, "I know you can protect yourself. I just don't want to put you in a situation where you have to. You're not like me; it would get to you."

I looked up into his eyes, that soft blue that felt warm and inviting, and realized he hadn't lost even an hour of sleep over Nathan. What he had done didn't affect him at all. Would I be like that when I had my memories back? Would I see humans as something other, lesser, than us? I thought about my dreams—the man Hunter and Jonah killed, and how I watched without remorse. Was that who I was?

"What are you thinking about?" he asked.

"You're right. It would bother me. Is that just because I don't remember myself?"

Hunter shook his head. "No. This is you." He pulled me into a hug and pressed his cheek to me, holding me close. Finally, he said, "Jonah and I weren't made of the same stuff as you, Sen. Please don't judge yourself based on what we are. You are not like us."

He kissed my cheek, then pulled back enough to look me in the eyes. "So, do you want to stay here, or should we just come back to get Benny? Your choice."

"What do you mean come back to get Benny?"

"If you can convince him to, he can come to our house. That is, if you decide you want to stay with me and Ryder."

"He can leave the house?" I asked, my voice raising in surprise.

Hunter laughed as he said, "He's not haunting the house. He's tied to you."

I stared at him. "I've just... never seen him anywhere else. You mean he's always been with me?"

Hunter nodded.

"Why didn't I see him before moving here?" I asked.

"Your guess is as good as mine," he said, shrugging.

I thought about his offer. I suppose, if I didn't have to leave Benny behind, I didn't really care where I slept. If Katie wasn't home and Benny was with me, there really wasn't any reason to stay here and tempt an altercation with her parents. I was less worried about her stepdad approaching me than I was controlling my own temper if I ran into him or Mary.

"Alright," I agreed, "let's come back for Benny."

Hunter gave me a brilliant smile—one that was full of dimples and reached his eyes. It made me smile back. He bent over and slung my bag over his shoulder. "I'll put it in the car."

"Wait," I said. I walked to the dresser and grabbed the gray stuffed bear Katie had given Benny, two of the large pillars, and my lighter. "Benny needs these." Hunter didn't question why, he just allowed me to pack Benny's things before following me through the door.

When we came out of the room, Vincent looked up from where he was sitting next to Katie. His face was full of relief as he watched Hunter leave with my things. "I let Will know we're taking Katie to Hunter's. He's on the way," he informed me.

I looked over at Katie. She seemed much better than she had an hour ago. The color was back to her face, and she was sitting up straighter, though, she still wasn't letting go of Ryder's hand. "You okay with this plan?" I asked her.

She nodded. "I'm sorry for making you go through all this trouble. I didn't mean to cause all this."

Vincent put his arm around her. "You didn't do anything to cause this, and it's not trouble."

I nodded in agreement. "Exactly. Besides, Katie, we'd do anything for you." I wanted to say that's what family is supposed to do, but I didn't want to remind her of the colossal failure her mother was at protecting her, not when she was finally starting to look like she wasn't terrified or heartbroken.

Ryder kissed her temple and squeezed her hand. She blushed and bit her bottom lip as she looked down at her lap. "Thanks," she said.

When the front door opened, Hunter walked back in, Will following close behind.

Hunter took up his usual position at my side, putting his arm around me comfortably like he belonged. His ease around me was still startling if I thought about it too much.

Will went straight to Katie, kneeling in front of her, his eyes appraising her before he gave a short nod. He looked pleased with the condition she was in. "I need to go back to work, but I will come to Hunter's tonight. Is that alright?"

Katie nodded, then lunged forward, wrapping her arms around his neck. "Thank you for coming," she said.

He held her, softly patting her on the back. "Sorry I wasn't here sooner."

I smiled. It would have been better under different circumstances, but this was going to be good for both of them. Their dad was gone, and Will never mentioned his mom. He wasn't a sharer type though, so for all any of us knew, she was alive and well—and amazing. Katie needed him though, and as shut down as he was, she would do wonders for his personality too.

"Are we ready to go?" Hunter asked the room.

We all nodded in response. He kissed the top of my head before turning to leave. I watched as Will helped Katie up and walked her out, with Ryder hovering nervously behind.

Vincent let out a breath and stood. On his way to the door, he paused, stopping in front of me. "I know I'm just the human, but if you need me, I'm here."

"Will you come to Hunter's? I don't want to leave Katie and Ryder alone when we come back for Benny later."

"Yeah. I can do that."

"Thanks." I smiled up at him. "What's with the 'just human' nonsense? As if you ever thought you were 'just' anything."

"Don't worry, I didn't mean it." He flicked at my hair, still in the messy knot on my head. "You may be supernatural, but I know how to match my clothes."

He laughed as I shoved him out the door, locking it behind us. We descended the steps to join where Katie was waving Will's car off. That's when I noticed the shiny, red, four-door sedan parked behind her. I faintly recalled it had been there when we all ran across the street, but I hadn't paid it any attention at the time. Neither of my neighbors was home, and I couldn't imagine either of them randomly parking their new car in front of my house.

I scrutinized the vehicle as we approached. Ryder spoke up cheerfully, pointing at it. "It's my new car!" He was nudging Katie excitedly, trying to cheer her up.

I turned to Hunter. "You bought him a car?"

He said, "No," adding, "I bought *me* a car. I'm letting him drive it."

"You sure you didn't mean to buy it for your grandma?" Vincent quipped from the other side of me, smirking at the very modern, safe vehicle.

Hunter narrowed his eyes at him.

"Whatever, man. I have a car!" Ryder said, beaming at Vincent.

Vincent smiled at him and gave his shoulder an encouraging pat. "My first car was my mom's. It was a grandma car, too. At least yours is new."

"I think it's a nice car," Katie said, her voice sweet as she squeezed Ryder's hand.

"When did you get it?" I asked.

"This morning," Hunter said.

He had been planning to sleep in with me this morning until I blew up at him and stormed home yesterday. "Did you just impulse-buy a car as retail therapy?" I asked him.

"Maybe I just got tired of your driving," he said, giving me a smirk.

I still refused to ride on the back of his motorcycle. Nothing was changing my mind on that. Rather than acknowledge his joke, I asked, "Are you actually giving up the bike?"

Hunter shrugged. "I'll still take it when Ryder has the car. Do I lose hot points if I give up my deathtrap?" he teased.

Without missing a beat, Vincent chimed in with, "Yes, but only to normal people. Luckily, you're dating the only woman I know who prefers walking everywhere."

I laughed. He wasn't wrong. Vincent had been the one to find this place when I was house hunting. I had chosen it due to the proximity to food and shopping. Being able to walk to caffeine had been a bigger selling point to me than the supposedly coveted garage space.

Vincent offered to Ryder, "You and Katie can go with me. My ride's cooler."

Ryder's smile widened. "Can I drive?"

Vincent laughed, then very seriously said, "No."

CHAPTER 9

HUNTER went straight to his room to drop off my bag. I'd been sleeping over a lot, but this felt different. After I thought about it in the car, I became more and more uncomfortable with the idea. Unfortunately, if I spoke up about my misgivings, Vincent was likely to snatch my bag and lock it in his car, forcing me to stay with him. Frankly, staying on Vincent's couch seemed like a better idea right now. Call me a skeptic, but I didn't think Hunter would take that decision well.

"What's the verdict?" Vincent asked, pulling me from my thoughts.

He was sitting on the sofa, one arm draped over the back, his other hand resting on his ankle that crossed over his thigh. His posture was relaxed as he looked over Katie and Ryder. They sat next to him, their sides nearly melting together. Ryder had his arm around her, while she rested her head against his shoulder, her forehead pressed into the nook of his neck.

My head quirked to the side. They were teenagers. To my knowledge, Ryder still hadn't kissed Katie on the mouth. This amount of touching should have had their pulses out of control, but from where I stood, they were completely comfortable. Then I had a horrifying thought. Maybe I was the only one who couldn't control myself that close to Hunter. A sixteen-year-old had better control of their hormones than me. Great.

I shook my head, then sat on the ottoman in front of Katie and Ryder. "Katie, do you mind if I check to see how your soul is holding up?"

I meant it literally but maybe a little emotionally too. This had been an intense day.

She nodded.

"How are you feeling?" I asked her softly.

"Really good, actually."

I looked over to Ryder. "What about you? Are you still able to control what you're feeding off?"

He laughed. "Hunter already put me through the parental act. Yeah, I'm good. I feel better when I'm near her, but I think it's just going to take practice."

I nodded. At least we had that going for us. I reached out and took Katie's hand in mine. My power brushed along her immediately on contact. To my surprise, her spirit didn't feel weaker or injured at all. What it did feel like? Hot.

"You're warm," I whispered.

She held the back of her hand to her head. "I feel fine."

"No, I mean your energy. It's not cold anymore." Her energy was calm as it ever was, but it sparked with heat that had never been there before.

I looked at Ryder. "Does she feel different to you?"

He nodded, then pressed his lips together, tucking his chin down as he looked up at me. He was looking at me like a puppy caught chewing a shoe.

"What's going on?" I asked.

Slowly, he reached over and touched the wrist of her hand that I held. He whispered in Katie's ear, "Show her."

Katie's eyebrows furrowed as she stared at me. I felt her pulse race now. Whatever she was about to do, she was afraid of my reaction. Then I felt the energy spill from Ryder to her. Not a lot, just a sliver. It curled up inside her as she absorbed it. Ryder's soul felt fine and eager to share. I realized they felt the same, and my eyes widened. What the hell was going on?

"What was that?" Vincent asked. He was sitting up straight now, staring at Katie, his eyes darting between Ryder's hand and the center of her chest. Ryder's face mirrored my shock as we exchanged a look before turning to Vincent.

"You saw that?" I asked. I recalled him grabbing Katie in the basement. He had reacted to Ryder's soul clinging to her then, too. It had been Vincent's touch that finally broke them apart.

"I…" He thought about his answer before continuing, then shook his head. "I don't know. I'm not sure what my eyes were seeing. What was it?"

My mouth parted in surprise as I stared at Vincent. How long had he been this sensitive? I tried racking my brain for any memories of him showing even an inkling of seeing any of this before. I had nothing. Was I that unobservant? When it came to Vincent, it was possible. I wouldn't have said that before, but we had been so out of step lately, it wasn't hard to question myself and my ability to read him.

"You've been healing him," Hunter's low voice carried from the hallway.

I looked over my shoulder to see him standing with his hands tucked in his pockets. His expression wasn't as submissive as Ryder's, but there was a similarity in their posture.

"What does that have to do with anything?" I asked.

"Healing him that many times, so close together; he has a lot of your spirit inside him right now."

I raised my eyebrows. "Is it permanent?"

"I don't think so." Hunter shook his head. "It should fade after a while, once you stop sharing." He seemed to say that last part more to Vincent than me.

"Thank God," Vincent said, letting out a breath as he leaned his head back against the sofa, looking up at the ceiling.

Hunter and Ryder both laughed at his response.

I looked between the three of them. It felt like they all understood something I didn't. "Vincent, are you having side effects that you haven't told me about?" I asked.

His head shot up, and his eyes darted to Hunter. Hunter was smirking back at him. He shrugged as if giving Vincent permission.

"Nothing worth worrying about now," Vincent said.

I heard Hunter chuckling quietly behind me. I was a little pissed he seemed to know what was happening to Vincent and I didn't, but I could yell at Vincent about it later. We had more pressing issues right now.

"So, what about Katie?" I asked, "Is this going to fade?"

Hunter shook his head as he walked toward us. He sat behind me, straddling my legs, then wrapped his arms around my waist, resting his chin on my shoulder. I frowned, recognizing his actions were a sign he was trying to calm me before giving me more answers. "Why are you and Ryder walking on eggshells about this? My temper isn't that bad."

"The bruises on my shin would imply otherwise," Vincent said.

I wrinkled my nose at him. "Nothing Ryder did could make me that angry."

Hunter kissed my cheek, then sighed. "Not even if we tell you *this* might be permanent?" he asked, nodding his head at Katie.

"What's permanent? I don't even understand what's going on." I was really getting sick of saying that to this group.

Katie leaned forward then and squeezed my hand, pushing some of her energy into me. It was familiar sharp electricity, but not the cold comfort of Katie. With a gasp, I realized why she and Ryder felt the same.

"She's a Nephilim?" I yelped. "How?"

Katie winced and pulled her hand back. She mistook my tone as being upset at her, but that wasn't it. This was hard. Being a teenager was difficult enough. Being a teenager as one of us? I wouldn't wish that on anyone—especially not someone like Katie. She was painfully empathetic just as a human. I reached out and took her hand again, squeezing it. She mustered up a small smile in response.

"Did you know this would happen?" I asked Ryder.

"Yes," he hesitated, then added, "I thought you did, too."

"Why would I?"

Hunter tensed behind me. Quietly, he said, "Benjamin."

I shut my eyes and swallowed as I realized how slow I was being. Benny. Ryder had said there was no such thing as ghosts. When humans died, they didn't stay here, but Benny did. "That's why he's here. He's not a human anymore," I rambled out loud as my mind connected the dots. That made sense. If he was my brother, he would have been like Katie. When I tried to heal him, I didn't just separate my soul, I turned him into one of us.

Hunter nodded. He wasn't exactly holding me down, but his body language definitely left me feeling as if he was bracing for my reaction. I must have really been a sight this morning if he was this worried about my response. That was going to be some heavy embarrassment for me to cope with later.

"Why wasn't he reborn when he died?" I asked.

"My guess? He died during the ritual. Something took or he wouldn't be stuck here, but it wasn't finished," he said.

Poor Benny. What rotten luck he had to be born with me as a sister. His entire life, and then death, was a disaster. All thanks to me. "We have to fix it."

"How do you suggest we do that?" Hunter asked.

"I don't know. Maybe I need to finish the ritual," I said.

"No," Hunter said.

"You didn't even take time to think about it." I frowned

Pulling away so he could look me in the face, he said, "I don't need to. The last time I performed it, Benny ended up dead, and I lost you for a century and a half. We're not doing that again."

"But I wasn't involved that time. You did it behind my back, which is why I was angry." At least, I thought it was… "And Benny's already dead, so that can't happen again." My voice was starting to rise. Maybe he did need to brace himself for my temper, but that was his own fault for being unreasonable.

"Or, something worse could happen," he countered.

"Or maybe you should stop underestimating her and exercise a little trust," Vincent said.

Hunter glared at him.

Vincent just raised his eyebrows, not intimidated in the least. "Or not. Just keep treating her like some delicate thing that couldn't kick your magical ass if she wanted to. That seems to have done well for you so far." While I appreciated the support, I couldn't help but eye Vincent over his comment. He was the one who had flipped out and wouldn't let me sleep alone in my own bed tonight. I didn't really want to undermine his argument, though, since it was in my favor, so I kept that to myself.

Katie cleared her throat. "She was the one to save us from Jonah. Just saying," she said quietly to Hunter.

When Hunter didn't respond, Vincent went on, "I just watched Sen rebuild Katie's skull on a basement floor, while you sat there for moral support. Katie and Ryder seem completely fine, so whatever is wrong with Sen and Benny is the result of your meddling. You need to sit down and let her do her thing."

Hunter looked back at me. "I hate him."

"And?" I asked. That was neither new nor helpful information.

"He's right," Hunter said softly.

"Usually am," Vincent said.

"Are we really going to bring Benny back?" Katie asked, and her face lit up like Christmas morning. This was the happiest she'd been in almost twenty-four hours. Ryder was looking at Hunter expectantly. If it made Katie happy, it got me his vote.

"This is a bad idea," Hunter said.

Katie let out a happy squeal as she kicked her feet excitedly.

I leaned back against Hunter, smiling as I kissed his cheek. "Thank you."

He gave me a quick kiss on the lips, a smile spreading across his face. "Don't thank me, yet. You still have Benny to convince. Good luck with that."

Well, fuck.

CHAPTER 10

I LEANED *on the balcony, trying to block out the screams coming from the room behind me. The sky was a beautiful, twinkling, black expanse, and a warm breeze carried the smell of the trees below.*

The room behind me fell silent. Moments later, I felt Jonah walk up beside me. He pressed his back to the balcony wall, resting on his elbows. "Why are you hiding out in the night?" he asked.

I turned to look at him, surveying the blood on his mouth and chin and the stains down his tunic. It looked black in the firelight that splashed across his face, but I knew the smell. His long blond hair fell in a lovely frame around his face. He smiled at me as I eyed him. No matter how handsome he was, even expressions of joy from Jonah lacked tenderness.

"The world is changing, Jonah. You will not always be able to satiate your thirst in such a way. You should get accustomed to less invasive methods, or it may come as a shock when they are all that is left," I said.

"Their laws don't matter to us," he scoffed.

"Maybe so. It's also repulsive," I said flatly.

"You only think that because you have abstained for so long." He leaned into me as if to kiss me with his blood-covered lips.

I wrinkled my nose and turned my face from him, putting a finger on his chest to keep him away. "Quit your teasing. You'll get it on me."

He laughed, then licked the blood off his lower lip, slowly. "You could be so much more fun."

"We are not in agreement on the definition of fun."

From the corner of my eye, I saw him watch me. He wiped his face on his sleeve. "I could be persuaded to your definition, with the right encouragement."

I made a soft snorting sound as I continued to stare out into the darkness. I knew better than to think anything would discourage Jonah from this behavior. It was easy for me to turn from it. It was a much more complicated ask of him. It didn't stop me from trying, but my belief that he could change was thinning.

He put a hand on my cheek, gently forcing me to turn back to him. His eyes held an unusual softness as they landed on my mouth.

"There is nothing on my lips for you to turn away from now," he said quietly as he moved to press them to mine.

"Hunter will see you into your next life if you continue," I warned.

"I shall take my chances."

I landed on the floor before I was even fully awake, the air knocked out of me. Benny leaned over me as I stared up at the ceiling. I looked over to see Hunter moving into a sitting position; he appeared as disoriented as me. We must have fallen asleep waiting for Benny to wake. I sprawled out on the floor, where I had been tossed from the sofa. I looked down at my body. Benny hovered near my feet. "What the fuck, Benny?"

He made a loud ringing sound as he threw Hunter's shoes at him. Hunter barely moved his arms up in time to block them from hitting his face, which also infuriated Benny.

"Benny! Stop!" I yelled.

Benny's form turned on me, and the image of him wavered in the light. The overhead lights sizzled, but at least he maintained enough control to not pop all my lightbulbs.

"Benny, I need you to listen. Something happened to Katie."

His core flashed with a bright light as he moved toward me, abandoning whatever attack on Hunter he had been planning next. They hadn't been in the same room since that first night, and this was going about as well as I had expected. I wish I hadn't fallen asleep. I meant to catch Benny before he got worked up about Hunter's presence, but it was too late for that now.

"She's okay, now, but her stepdad pushed her down the stairs."

Benny hit the ceiling. Literally.

"She's at Hunter's, waiting for Will to pick her up," I rushed to explain before he could react further. "We're going to go stay with Hunter for a while, okay?" I said as I looked up. He was spreading across the ceiling like something out of one of Katie's horror films. This wasn't going well. I could feel how torn he was between his rage and wanting to see Katie for himself. I was hoping the latter would win out.

"Will you come with me to see Katie?" I begged.

He lowered back down to the ground. He made another high-pitched keening noise at Hunter, who had moved into a standing position between me and the door, staying as quiet as possible as he watched me navigate the conversation.

"We had to relocate to his house, to keep Katie away from her parents," I said.

Benny grunted at me, appearing to cross his arms over his chest.

"I am not lying. Look, Katie was in pretty bad shape." I sucked in a breath, drawing the courage to finish what I had to tell him. "Ryder and I had to heal her."

Benny went very still. If I wasn't staring directly at him when he did it, I'm not sure I would have even noticed him in the room. I didn't realize how much the air around him typically filled with movement.

"I can't separate her from Ryder right now... His soul, kind of, did what mine did," I blurted out.

In one quick burst, Benny knocked Hunter flat on his back on the ground. I stared at him, my mouth open, as Benny very casually moved past Hunter's prone figure and toward the door. I crawled over to try to help Hunter back into a sitting position. He had one hand on his chest as he groaned, his face white from the oxygen being knocked from his body on impact.

When he could finally breathe, Hunter wheezed, "How is this my fault?"

Benny just trilled again as he waited impatiently for us at the door.

"Well, at least that part is settled," I said.

Hunter raised an eyebrow at me. "I formally request to not be anywhere nearby when you share your other plan with him."

"Your request is noted, but I make no promises," I said.

He grunted, then pushed into a standing position.

Luckily, under the cover of night, Benny wasn't easily visible. We hurried him to the car. I had no idea why, but I buckled him in. Safety first?

As soon as Hunter hit the gas pedal to reverse from the driveway, Benny slid to the floor.

"What's the matter?" I asked.

Benny made a growling chime noise as he puddled against the floorboards.

"He's a very good driver," I said, "I promise."

He chirped at me. It would seem my promises regarding Hunter did not hold any value to Benny. It was a short drive, but he hadn't been out of the house in years. Did ghosts get motion sickness?

Hunter tried rolling the window down to enjoy some air, but it immediately rolled back up. He gave the window a confused look, rolling it down again. It immediately rolled right back up, again. Realizing it was Benny, I laughed.

"I don't think he likes that," I said.

Giving up on the window, Hunter sighed and turned on the radio, settling on a quiet station playing soft pop songs. Benny wasn't having any of it and changed it to classical.

Hunter turned the radio off. "I got enough of this when it was new."

Benny turned it back on, then upped the volume.

I was pretty sure Benny didn't like instrumental music. He just enjoyed being a source of irritation for Hunter. I tried to smother my laughter, so I didn't encourage him, but since it seemed to be a good distraction from his terror about the ride, I didn't want to stop him.

"Hold on," Hunter said as he put his arm across me.

Before I could ask why, he slammed on the brakes, bringing a loud panicked sound out of Benny as he slammed against the back of my seat. Once we resumed speed, Hunter very calmly turned the radio off like nothing had just happened.

"That was a little unnecessary, don't you think?" I asked.

Hunter glanced at me, then turned his eyes back to the road.

Benny stayed put on the floor, vibrating in place.

He didn't touch the radio again.

When we finally arrived, Hunter parked in his garage. I think he was trying to make Benny more comfortable about exiting the vehicle. His neighbors' houses were far enough apart, there was no way they would have noticed Benny walking into the house through the front door. It was a thoughtful gesture, especially after Benny had regained his courage halfway through the ride and decided to tap Mozart's Symphony No. 40 on the back of Hunter's headrest.

"Benny!" Katie called out as we stepped through the garage door and into the kitchen.

Benny took no time rushing to her. He moved around her person, inspecting every visible inch. Ryder was smart enough to keep his distance. He gave Benny plenty of room to fawn over Katie.

"He's smarter than you," I said to Hunter as I nodded toward where Ryder stood in the doorway.

"He always is," he agreed.

I look over at Hunter. He looked exhausted, rubbing the back of his neck with his hand as he tossed his keys on the kitchen table. His hair was a mess, his dress shirt wrinkled. He must have gone into work first thing, which meant he likely had been up since the very early morning.

"Why don't you go to bed?" I asked.

He gave me a smirk. "You going to come with me?"

"Oh yeah, that's a great idea. Bring Benny over and immediately retreat to your bedroom together. Nothing bad could result from that."

"Mmm." The realization that he wasn't going to be able to touch me in front of Benny was sinking in, and his face did not look pleased about it.

Benny was chiding Ryder now, though his tone was more brotherly than angry—certainly not how he would have responded to Hunter in the same situation. Maybe it was the age difference? That still didn't make sense since Hunter had been roughly Ryder's age when Benny died. Guess it was just the whole responsible for his death thing.

Vincent came up behind Ryder and called to me, "I'm going to head out for the night."

"Are you sure?" I wiggled past Benny to follow Vincent to the front door.

Benny intentionally blocked Hunter from following me until Katie gave him a chastising look. "Benny, be nice," she said.

Shaking his head as he joined us, Hunter grumbled, "Want to take him with you?" to Vincent.

Vincent laughed. "I offered to stay at their place. This is your own fault."

Nodding, Hunter gestured to the sofa. "You are welcome to sleep on the pullout if you want to hang around?"

Vincent looked as shocked as I felt at the unexpected offer. Then he looked back and forth between the two of us. The corner of his mouth ticked up. "Thanks. I think I'll pass though." He turned to leave, then sucked air through his teeth as he balled his hand up into a fist. "I almost forgot. I may have promised Katie we would all go to the water-park tomorrow."

"What?" I gaped at him.

He gave me a shrug and bared his teeth. "Ryder was talking about how she needed to practice being around crowds before school starts. I didn't have the heart to tell her no when she brought it up. Not after all the shit she went through today."

"Is that wise? Will she really be up for that?" I asked.

He shrugged. "It's Katie. She seemed ecstatic."

I looked at Hunter, who gave an unconcerned shrug.

I contemplated his answer, then asked, "Do I have to go?"

"Yes," Vincent said.

"I don't even own a bathing suit."

"I'll text Jessie. She's bringing one for Katie tomorrow. I'm sure she can throw something in the bag for you," Vincent offered.

I narrowed my eyes at him.

He rolled his eyes in return. "I will make sure to request a one-piece."

Hunter nearly choked on his laughter.

Vincent leaned forward and kissed my cheek. "Thanks for listening to me." He looked Hunter up and down quickly, then added, "I'm sure it will be a difficult decision to cope with tonight."

"Good night, Vincent." I pretended to glare at him as I closed the door in his face. He just smiled over his shoulder at me as he walked down the steps toward his car.

When I turned around, Ryder and Katie were still giving Benny a very animated account of the day's events in the kitchen. He was poised in one of the chairs, hanging on to their every word.

"I'm going to shower and change," Hunter said, finally looking down at himself.

I nodded.

"Want to join me?" he smiled.

I pointed at Benny again. Hunter let out a sigh as he lowered his chin to his chest, then raised it back up again. "Right."

When he left, I sent Will a text.

I guess we're taking Katie to the water park tomorrow. Is that okay with you?

Isn't it a little soon for something like that? I'll be out of here in about thirty minutes. Sorry, this is taking so long.

It's fine. She's filling Benny in on all the details. And I don't know... Hunter and Ryder don't seem to think it's a bad idea.

I guess they would know better than me.

He didn't send anything after that. I curled up on the sofa and listened as the three of them conversed in the kitchen. Katie was getting good at interpreting Benny's responses—almost as good as me. Ryder looked between the two of them completely perplexed as Katie laughed at Benny's taunting. It made me smile.

Hunter tapped me on the shoulder. He had changed into a white T-shirt and joggers, his hair still wet from the shower, somehow managing to look even better in his pajamas than he had fully dressed. I enjoyed his dress shirts and the way he always wore the sleeves rolled up, but there was something more approachable about him this way. It made me think of chocolate milk and cuddles on the sofa. I shook my head to clear my thoughts. Cuddles? Really?

"Do I need to set up the pullout for Benny?" he asked.

I blinked. It had never occurred to me to put up a bed for Benny. Did he actually sleep during the day? "I don't know. It couldn't hurt?"

He nodded, then went over to start removing the pillows. "I'll get this set up. You go get comfortable."

I left him to prepare the bed for Benny. I didn't know if he'd use it, but it seemed like the sort of thing he might appreciate. Maybe Hunter could work to win him over with nice gestures... for the next hundred and fifty years.

My bag was sitting on Hunter's bed. The front pocket was unzipped, and my computer and tablet were missing. Looking around the room, I found he had rearranged his desk to plug them in. He also left the top two drawers of his dresser open. He didn't usually do things like that. When I walked over to close them, I realized they were empty. He had cleared out two drawers for my stuff. How long did he think we were staying? The panic from earlier started to bubble up. Sure, I'd been sleeping here half the nights out of the week anyway, but I never unpacked my things.

I hesitated, staring at my bag. Finally, I decided to put everything away. I had agreed to this. Plus, it would be very easy to pack back up if I needed to. I didn't want Hunter reading anything into my refusal to store T-shirts inside his dresser. It was just a piece of furniture, after all. No reason to make a big deal out of it. Yeah. No big deal.

As I unpacked, I discovered Vincent hadn't included any of my sleepwear. I decided to change into one of Hunter's T-shirts. I could slip out of my jeans for bed, but they'd have to stay for now.

When I came back into the living room, Hunter and Ryder were casually discussing the logistics of the binding ritual. Benny was hovering closely, interested in their conversation. Funny, neither of them seemed keen to tell him why they were focused on the topic.

The doorbell rang. I went to answer it and found Will on the doorstep. He looked exhausted. "Hey," I said, moving to let him in.

He nodded at me.

Once he was inside, Katie jumped up and ran to greet him with a hug. The tiredness that had been in his face a moment earlier washed away at the sight of her. Nothing like becoming responsible for the wellbeing of another person overnight.

He gave her shoulder a pat and pulled away. "How are you feeling?" he asked.

"I feel good!" she said.

Will inspected her quietly, then looked to Hunter. "It hasn't faded."

"No." Hunter shook his head, running a hand through his hair.

"What hasn't?" Katie asked.

"Ryder's spirit," Will answered.

I asked him, "Can it fade?" Hunter had implied it was permanent earlier. Was there a way to reverse it?

Will pressed his lips together, then said, "Who knows. You and Benny are the only precedent we have, and he died immediately after."

Benny made a shrill sound behind me.

"I already apologized for that. Multiple times!" Hunter snapped.

"Can she stay here?" Will asked. "They need to stay close together until we figure things out."

Hunter nodded. "She can take the couch."

Benny's response was much happier this time. I decided to not translate it for Will. Katie had slept on my sofa next to Benny many times, but Will's nerves seemed a little frayed already.

"I can stay the night?" she squealed. "That's perfect. We're going to the water park tomorrow!"

Will hesitated, and he turned to Hunter. "Do you think it's safe?"

Hunter nodded. "We'll be there. We have to test it some time, and it's as good a place as any."

Will nodded.

Katie wiggled and scrunched her face in delight.

Ryder reached out and pulled her to the sofa bed, grabbing the remote to turn on the television. Will grunted at him—maybe the first sign of him not being pleased with Ryder's interaction with Katie? Or maybe he was just tired.

"I'll check in tomorrow," Will said.

I gave his arm a squeeze as he walked past me to leave. "Benny will keep an eye on her, and Ryder will sleep in his room."

Will nodded at me before taking his leave.

Benny was happy about the bed. I should have thought to do something like that sooner. Of course, it could have just been having Katie there and not the mattress itself. Once she fell asleep, Benny set to shooing us all away so our chatter wouldn't wake her.

As the three of us shuffled down the hall toward the bedrooms, Hunter had to get one last jab in. "Do you need a bowl of water and kibble before you go down for the day?" he asked Benny.

I didn't even argue with the names Benny gargled at him.

CHAPTER 11

T HE *sky was a clear blue, and all the flowers were in bloom around us,*
making the rows of hills a lush and colorful backdrop. Couples were
dancing and singing. Their brightly covered robes were accented with bril-
liant jewelry, and all the women had taken the time to tie back their hair
so that it glittered from the copper coils twining through their twists and
braids. I stood back from the ceremony.

My frame was hidden behind the stone column as I relaxed against it.
The cool, reddish-colored stone was grainy and harsh against my shoulder,
but at least it offered support as I spied on the festivities.

I watched the priest lead a bleating animal through the crowd and up
to the altar. A sheepskin covered one of his shoulders, and the top of his head
was covered with a pointed cap. Once he was done coaxing the animal into
place, he handed a small, curved staff to a young boy standing near him.
The boy took it without lifting his eyes from the ground, his hands shaking
from the responsibility offered to him.

The priest then pulled a blade from his belt, the amber handle gleaming in the sun as he traced the circle around the altar, marking the name into the ground to announce the recipient of the offering. I turned away as he carved the animal, allowing the ritual blood to pour down the stone and into the ground.

I felt the familiar electricity in the air as he called out the sacrifice.

Movement on the mattress woke me. Hunter had rolled on top of me, holding himself up on his elbows, and he was kissing along my shoulder as he pulled the neck of the shirt I was wearing out of the way.

"Good morning, beautiful," he whispered.

His whiskers tickled my skin, and a laugh bubbled out of my throat, causing me to scrunch my shoulder and neck together out of reflex. "What are you doing?" I asked.

He smiled and shifted his body higher, so his face was hovering over mine. "I thought sleeping next to you after kissing you all night was agonizing. Having to sit so close to you, and not touch you at all, was worse. Much worse," he said.

He kissed me softly, running his hands along my bare legs. When he traced his hand up my thigh and realized I didn't have shorts on under the T-shirt, he let out a moan against my mouth. He was half asleep before I even pulled back the covers to crawl in last night, so he hadn't had a chance to notice it was all I wore to bed. He shifted me under him, so his lower half was pressed against me between my legs, his hand continuing to move up my hip under the shirt.

I slid my hands down and tugged at his T-shirt as I kissed him back. "Off," I said.

He lifted, reaching over his shoulder and pulling his shirt over his head in one swift movement. Then he immediately found my mouth again. I ran my hands over his shoulders and along his neck. I was careful to avoid his birthmark. He was still shielding successfully, and I didn't want to bring his barriers crashing down.

He broke away from the kiss, looking me in the eyes. "I want you."

My heart was thundering in my ears. I wasn't feeding off him. He had somehow kept all his emotions in check. Everything I was feeling right now was me, and I didn't want him to stop.

I nodded, cupping his face as I pressed my lips against him. He kissed me deeply, barely giving either of us a chance to breathe. He moved his hand slowly along my hip, teasing my skin.

The doorbell rang.

I froze under him.

"Ignore it. It's probably a package for R," he mumbled.

He continued kissing me, his fingers curling under the strap of my underwear. I had randomly grabbed the pretty ones with a thin lace band when I changed last night. I had almost put them back for something else but was too tired to walk back to the dresser. I was very thankful for that right now.

The doorbell rang again.

Hunter continued to disregard the sound as he moved down to push my shirt up around my waist with his teeth. He kept his hands on my hips, under the lace band, as he kissed and ran his tongue along my stomach, making his way in a line down my body. My breath caught as his lips hovered just below my navel, and he looked up to watch me.

My phone vibrated across the nightstand, and the doorbell started having fits like someone was hitting it repeatedly.

"I don't think that's a delivery," I whispered as I reached for the phone.

Hunter growled, "Uh-uh," as he tried pinning me under his mouth, his body pressing my hips into the bed. I laughed as I stretched to grab the phone. He moved, kissing a line up my bared side.

I answered, trying to control my breathing as Hunter slowly peeled the shirt higher. "What do you want, Vincent?"

"You're fucking kidding me?" Hunter blurted out, his hands clenching the fistfuls of T-shirt mid-motion.

I shushed him.

"I want you to answer the door," Vincent said.

"What?" "I'm outside. Katie said to meet everyone here."

I pushed Hunter's hands away from the shirt and moved to sit up. "Give me a minute, I'll let you in."

Once I hung up the phone, Hunter immediately closed his lips over mine, kissing and exploring my mouth. I pulled away as he moved to kiss my neck.

"Okay, okay, stop." I half-breathed and half-laughed as I ran my fingers through his hair, gently pulling him away from me. Hunter's face was a combination of heat. He was still looking at me like he may not let me out of the bed, and under that, his anger was starting to flare up.

"You need to let me up. We'll finish this later, but I can't leave Vincent standing on the porch. He'll just keep interrupting."

Hunter let out a groan before he buried his face against my chest, wrapping his arms around my waist. "I'm sorry, but I hate him a little." His words were muffled against the shirt.

"Just a little?" I laughed.

"No, but I was hoping since I said it that way, you would forgive me easier." He grinned up at me. I kissed him quickly and had to push him away as he tried pulling me back into an embrace.

Rushing to the front door, I pulled it open. Vincent stood there, staring down at his phone. He was in silver swim trunks and a white T-shirt. He had skipped the socks but was still wearing sneakers. I don't think Vincent owned anything that resembled sandals.

"About time. I was…" He trailed off, leaving his mouth open as his eyes traveled up my body. I looked down. I was still only wearing Hunter's T-shirt. Finally closing his mouth, Vincent asked, "Why have you never answered the door like that at your house?"

I laughed. It was the most Vincent-like comment I'd heard in weeks.

Hunter walked up behind me, putting his arm around my waist. He had been smart enough to pull on a T-shirt and sweats before coming to the door. He kissed my cheek as he pulled me back from the door and against his body. He was staring at Vincent as he held me possessively, greeting him in a low voice, "Vincent."

Vincent raised his eyebrow and shook his head as he entered the house. "No need to mark your territory," he said to Hunter, then added, "Hi, love," as he leaned forward and kissed me on the cheek. It was his typical greeting, but he was smiling mischievously at Hunter as he did it. I felt Hunter's hand flex against my stomach as he watched.

"Behave yourself," I whispered to Vincent.

"So, you're saying I shouldn't tease him that you look better in my shirts?" He pretended to smile innocently at me as he wandered to sit on the sofa. For Hunter's benefit, he added, "We used to have sleepovers all the time too. Bestie privileges."

Hunter made a growling noise under his breath. Just then, Ryder came out of his room. He had large headphones on his head as he tapped away at his phone. He looked up and stopped in his tracks as his eyes nervously darted over me and then to Hunter before he landed on Vincent. He pulled his headphones down around his neck and gave Vincent a quick nod.

"Does she walk around like that all the time when she's here?" Vincent asked him, his voice full of amused laughter at Ryder's obvious discomfort.

Ryder looked at me quickly, then back down at his phone. "Uh, no." His tone was short as he shook his head. "Jessie just texted. She and Ian are pulling up."

"Where's Katie?" I asked.

"My room. She sent me to get a bag from Jessie."

"Alright, I'm going to take a quick shower," I said. I kissed Hunter on the cheek before heading down the hall.

"I'll send Katie in with the swimsuit," he said.

My shoulders hunched as I remembered I had to don swimming apparel for the day's activities too. Ugh.

I should have showered last night, but I didn't want to leave Benny alone with Hunter and Ryder while he was up. He had minded himself at Katie's request, but I wasn't taking any chances. Once Benny was tucked in, I couldn't bring myself to do anything but sleep.

I wondered if he was having a good rest since Hunter had put a bed out. Where exactly did Benny go during the day? Since Hunter had rolled the sleeper back into the sofa, would Benny reappear on the floor today? He used my closet at home, which as I thought about it was really strange. When I moved in, I had imagined maybe he was murdered in the house and the closet is where they stuffed the body. It made sense in my head. Now I had no idea what the hell he had been doing.

I was trying to take as quick a shower as possible when I heard Katie call through the curtain, "Morning, Sen!"

"Morning, sunshine!" I answered.

Katie laughed. "Hunter told me to leave the swimsuit on the sink," she said.

I popped my head around the curtain. Katie was standing in a purple one-piece, with an open, sleeveless hoodie over it as a cover. Her hair was up in two buns on top of her head. She looked adorable, and like absolutely nothing strange had happened yesterday.

"Thanks. Are you feeling okay today?" I asked.

"Still amazing! I'll let you finish up. Jessie and Ian are waiting outside. We'll see you when you're done?" she called.

I nodded and went back to washing off. Either Katie was forcibly repressing her feelings about recent events, or being a Nephilim was interfering with her emotional response. Both of those options were concerning.

The swimsuit was a black strapless one-piece. It was very flattering. It was also completely nonfunctional. How was anyone supposed to swim in something without straps? I guess it would work for my purposes as I had no plans of submerging myself in the water today. I fully intended to stand on the sidelines as awkwardly as possible while they all had fun.

I stepped out of the bathroom uncomfortably. I hadn't worn a swimsuit in public since I hit puberty. Plus, as I pulled my hair up into a wet bun to avoid drying it, I realized that not only did that leave my neck and shoulders completely bare, but it also left my birthmark on display. I felt naked.

Vincent and Hunter were standing in the living room chatting as they waited for me. Hunter's swim trunks were a gray background with a black pattern that made me think of the mountains. With his black T-shirt, he didn't look like he was going swimming. He and Vincent both looked like they were just heading out for a normal summer's day. Why do guys get to wear what are essentially waterproof versions of their regular clothes to the pool? Meanwhile, I owned underwear that covered more than most women's swimsuits.

"I want a cover-up," I announced as I looked at the two of them.

They both turned to face me. Hunter's eyes were trailing down me slowly, a small smile on his face. I could tell from across the room he approved. It almost made wearing the thing worth it.

Vincent's eyebrows raised as he took in my attire. "Why have you been hiding that under T-shirts the last half-decade?" he teased.

Hunter side-eyed at him, causing Vincent to clear his throat. "I'll be waiting outside." As he walked past me to leave, Vincent looked me up and down one more time. Then he smiled and shook his head.

"Don't mind him, he's just trying to embarrass me," I said as I walked up to Hunter.

He reached down to wrap his arms around me. "Can we let them go and stay here?" he asked.

I laughed. "That option has my vote. I hate swimming."

"You'll love the slides."

I wrinkled my nose. "I will not be going on any slides."

"We'll see about that." He gave me a big, full smile, dimples and all, then released me. "I'll be right back."

I watched him disappear into his bedroom, slipping my shoes on while I waited. He came out with a white button-down shirt made of thin, casual fabric.

"What's that for?" I ask.

"You wanted something over your swimsuit," he said. He draped it around me, holding it in place as I slipped my arms in. Once it was on, he rolled up the sleeves a quarter of the way until they hit me just above my wrists. The collar was high enough that it even obscured the view of my birthmark.

After adjusting it, he stepped back. "Better?"

I smiled. "Yes, thank you."

We walked outside to join the group. Katie, Jessie, and Ian were huddled around Jessie's car, waiting for us. Vincent was showing Ryder something under the hood of Hunter's car. I heard him say, "If you're going to drive, you have to take care of it. Luckily, your car doesn't have a carburetor like mine, but there's still plenty of things you need to check up on."

I immediately tuned him out. He gave this same speech to me at sixteen, too. I still don't change my own oil. Contrary to Vincent's opinion, having someone else do it does not affect my ability to drive.

Jessie was wearing a swimsuit with more cutouts than fabric, under a pair of tattered shorts, and her long, blond hair was pulled into a messy side braid. I was suddenly thankful for the amount of coverage my suit offered. I wouldn't have been comfortable in her outfit, but she pulled it off like she had walked right out of a magazine.

"Will they let her in the park dressed like that?" I asked Hunter.

Hunter just laughed.

"Sin!" Jessie called and waved at us.

I walked up to her and Ian, who was leaning against her car. He had shaved all the red out of his hair, leaving a tight fade. Without the playful color, his features looked more serious. He didn't even bother with a T-shirt. Instead, he just wore bright red trunks, proudly showing off as he stood there with his arms folded over his chest. He and Jessie made a very attractive couple. He greeted me with a big smile. "Hey, Sin!"

I smiled back. I didn't even care that he picked up Jessie's ridiculous nickname. Ian reminded me of a large Labrador. He was always sincerely happy to see everyone. It's hard to be angry at that kind of person. I was surprised to see him still hanging around Jessie though. Or maybe a more accurate statement would be, I was surprised she was still hanging around him. Add that to the list of things I needed a chance to ask Katie about—albeit maybe a bit low in priority right now.

"How are you doing, Ian?" I ask.

"Alright. You know how it is. School's starting soon, so I gotta get my hustle back on." He did a little dance move, shifting his hips and shoulders, and I laughed.

Jessie walked up to me, pulling me into a hug. Startled, I stood unmoving as she squeezed me tight and whispered, "Thank you," in my ear. I realized she was talking about Katie, and I smiled, relaxing and hugging her back. She couldn't say much more than that in front of Ian, but it was enough.

"Nothing to thank me for," I whispered back.

"Let me take a look at you," she said, letting me go. She pulled her sunglasses down to get a better visual. Then she tugged at the white dress shirt, eyeing how the swimsuit fit. I looked past her, over to Katie, and gave an exasperated sigh. Katie stifled her giggles into her hand.

"Perfect," Jessie decried. "The shirt is a nice touch."

I shrugged. "It's Hunter's."

"Even better." She smiled. "Also, we *need* to go wardrobe shopping before school. You're coming with us."

Before I could argue, she gave Ian a nudge to get inside the car. He slid into the driver's seat as Jessie went around to hop into the passenger side.

I looked over at Katie. "Going to a water park when I can't swim is practically endangering my life for you. Are you really dragging me back to the mall too?"

Katie just grinned at me. The knowledge that I wouldn't tell her no was on full display in her expression.

"You can't swim?" Ryder interrupted from behind me. He and Vincent had finally joined us.

I shook my head. "No."

"Why not?"

"We live in a landlocked state. Why would I need to learn to swim?" I asked.

Wouldn't it be funny if you were an Olympic swimmer in a past life?" Vincent joked.

Hunter let out a roll of laughter. "I can confirm that was not the case. She's always hated water."

Widening my eyes at him, I asked, "Then why are we doing this?"

"It's what Katie wanted to do," he said, his eyes glittering at me.

I gave Katie a fake glare. She shrugged at me, a small smile dimpling her cheeks.

Hunter leaned forward and whispered in my ear, "And, you may hate to swim, but I always like you in a swimsuit."

I felt my face flush. Clearing my throat, I headed toward his car. "Whatever. Let's get this over with."

CHAPTER 12

THE waterpark was part of the local amusement park nestled down-town. This was one of the last weekends it would be open, and it was packed. Cars filled the lot, and there were large groups of people still standing in line. Loud music pumped through the air, and the sound of rollercoaster screams was loud enough to reach the edge of the parking lot.

I grimaced as I stepped out of the car. "Hunter, are you sure this is a good idea?" I asked. I was going to struggle with this many people. It was a bit much to test Katie's abilities out in such a crowd. Not to mention, I didn't know what Ryder was experiencing. He could be looking at a simi-lar struggle in trying to block everyone out.

"It will be fine. We're all here. Better for something to happen here than when one of them is alone at school," Hunter offered.

I watched Vincent get out of his car, his hand reaching up to rub his side, just over the scar. I wondered if he was touching it because it hurt or because he was self-conscious about it. My worried thoughts making me forget about our surroundings, I walked over to him as he shut the car door.

"What's up, love?"

"Do you want me to..." I trail off as I reach toward his side.

He snatched my hand up and backed away, falling back against his car. "No. Don't."

I raised my eyebrows at his overly dramatic response. "Are you sure?" I asked.

"I said no, Sen. I'm good," he snapped, then abruptly dropped my hand, practically throwing it back at me.

"What the hell is wrong with you?" I asked.

"Nothing is wrong with me. I just don't need your hands on me right now." His eyes had managed to shift a shade darker, making them almost black. They always did that when he was angry. "Can we talk about this later?"

"No, we can't." Everyone was staring at us, and I really didn't give a damn. I was over Vincent's mood swings, and I was tired of being the only one who didn't know what the hell was up with him.

Vincent lowered his head. Without looking up, he asked, "Can we have some privacy, please?"

I looked over my shoulder at everyone hovering in a circle. Everyone but Jessie and Hunter looked away, trying not to impose on our argument. Jessie was smirking like she was seconds away from butting in and answering for Vincent.

Hunter's eyebrows were laced together as he watched Vincent. He looked like he was warring inside over whether or not to leave. Finally, he shook his head and ushered everyone toward the entrance. "We'll see you inside," he called over his shoulder to me.

I turned back to Vincent who was leaning against his car door, his arms crossed over his chest. "You look like a petulant child," I said.

He just stared at his feet, unmoving.

"Well," I asked, "what's with the hot and cold temps, huh? You're giving me whiplash with your moods."

"I just don't need you healing me," he said quietly, looking up at me through his lashes. Vincent was never this coy, and I wasn't having it.

"Bull. You said it isn't painful. What's the harm if it doesn't even hurt?" I asked.

He let out a rough breath and rubbed his hands over his face. "Fuck, Sen. Do we really have to go into this? Can't you just respect my space?"

"Your *space*? Yeah, sure. Next time you're bleeding out in my lap, I'll make sure to respect your space, Vincent. No problem," I said.

He winced at my words. "That's not what I meant."

My voice was starting to rise as I continued, all my anger and fear from the last month bubbling up at once. "I know I should have told you sooner. I get that I kept stuff from you—that maybe you would have been more careful if I had just told you what the hell was going on—but I can't change that. Stop punishing me for it." After that last bit, I turned away from him. I was dangerously close to crying, and I didn't want him to see. Not when I was so angry with him.

"Sen." He reached out and grabbed my arm, stopping me from taking off. "I'm not mad at you for that."

I sighed and hunched my shoulders, refusing to turn to face him. "Then what is it? What did I do?"

"I'm not mad," he said softly.

I scoffed as I turned to glare at him. "Really? You're being an asshole for no reason at all then? Peachy."

He growled and tugged me toward him. "Would you calm down and listen? You talk about my mood swings. Your temper is out of control lately."

"I've had a lot of good reasons to be angry, Vincent."

Through his teeth, he said, "Maybe so, but that doesn't give you the right to do whatever you want to me—especially if I'm asking you to stop."

"I just don't get what the big deal is? I don't want you to have permanent organ damage. Why is that an issue?"

He glared back at me. "So, because you can, you should get to walk around putting your hands on whoever you want? Doing whatever you want, regardless of how other people feel? Is that it? It's all about what you want. Why heal me? Why not someone else? Why not my mom?" As soon as the words were out of his mouth, he pressed his lips together. He let go of my arm.

It felt like he had slapped me. "Your mom?"

"Shit," he said as he turned to open the car door.

Without hesitating, I leaned into him, wrapping my arms around his waist. I squeezed him as I pressed my cheek against his back. "Vincent."

"Don't. I'm sorry. I shouldn't have said that. I don't even know why I said it."

"But, I did," I said quietly, my face buried in his back.

"What did you say?" He turned in my arms to face me.

I felt the tears falling down my cheeks. "I tried, Vincent, and it worked at first. She went into remission. I tried. But it came back, and then nothing helped. It was like I made it worse." I buried my face into his chest as I babbled through my tears. I felt him wrap his arms around me as he pressed his cheek against my hair. "I made it worse," I whispered.

"Hey, shhhh." He rocked me and kissed my head. "You didn't make it worse. I'm sorry, Sen. I shouldn't have put that on you. I'm sorry."

"I tried. I loved your mom—maybe not as much as you, but pretty damn close." My voice cracked as I sniffled around my words. "Do you really think I would sit back and watch her die if I had a choice? That I would have watched my grandfather die if I could have stopped it?"

"No. I know." He squeezed me tighter. "Please, let's pretend I didn't say something that stupid to you, okay?"

I pulled away, wiping the tears off my cheeks. "Is that why you didn't want me healing you?"

He laughed, nervously. "No. I mean, yes, it was bothering me. I wasn't angry with you, not really. You know I already felt guilty about my mom and then turning around and surviving something like that because of a literal fucking miracle..." He shook his head as he paused.

More of my traitor tears escaped me. I did know Vincent was still dealing with his mom's death. In his mind, she struggled to raise him alone, went without things, and put her needs away for his. Before he was able to be an adult and pay her back for it, she was gone. It made sense that he would somehow twist his being alive right now into guilt because she wasn't here too.

"I'm sorry," I said.

"Don't be. I don't know what made me blurt that out. It really isn't the reason why I don't want you healing me," he said. He may be trying to convince himself more than me, but based on his tone, there truly was more to it. What other horrible thing had I done besides adding fuel to his trauma—as if that weren't enough?

"You're killing me, keeping stuff from me, Vincent. I know I have no right to say that, but I am. Would you just tell me?"

He ran his thumb along my cheek, wiping the moisture off my face. "It doesn't hurt."

"What doesn't hurt?"

"When you do your little magic trick. It doesn't hurt. It's the exact opposite. It feels good... really good."

Startled, I asked, "Wait. What?"

He raised his eyebrow at me, waiting for my mind to catch up with what he was getting at.

"Oh, God." I snatched my arms back from him, even faster than he had moved away from me earlier.

A smile spread across his lips as he said, "The excruciating embarrassment of this moment is worth that look on your face."

"Why didn't you say something?" I asked.

"I did! I said don't," he teased.

"Oh yeah, really helpful."

"Do you think me describing what you were doing to me was the better option? How much detail would you have liked me to include?" he asked. When my face flushed at his question, he laughed, adding, "I never expected you to ignore my bodily autonomy and demand a reason for saying 'no'. Some feminist you are."

I covered my mouth with my hands. "Oh, God, Vincent. I'm sorry. You're right. I didn't mean to. I would never force you to...I don't want... I mean..." *Fuck.* I was rambling.

Vincent continued to laugh and pulled me back in a hug. "Sen, I love you. I know you aren't doing it on purpose." He smiled and kissed my temple, then added, "But, and I cannot believe I'm having to ask this of you, can you please keep your damn hands to yourself?"

I groaned and pulled away from him. "I promise I will not touch you like that again."

"Good." He chuckled. "Now, let's get inside so you can get back to throwing yourself at Hunter."

"I am not throwing myself at him," I grumbled as I rubbed my face on the sleeve of the dress shirt, wiping away what was left of my tears.

"Did you not see yourself this morning?" he asked.

I glared at him, making his laugh deepen.

"Come on," he said, putting his arm around my shoulder and slipping his sunglasses on. "He's probably panicking right now, wondering if I stole you."

"Hunter knew what it was doing to you?" I asked.

"Love, everyone but you knew it."

Well, that's just great. Really fucking great. I sighed.

He squeezed my shoulders again. "You should have told me about everything when we were younger, though."

"I know. I was afraid it would change things," I said.

"It would have. Just maybe not in the way you think," he said softly as he smiled down at me.

CHAPTER 13

I CLUNG to Vincent's side as we converged with all the people into the entrance. Being this close to so many strangers, I was having to focus heavily on my shields. It was also fueling my concern over how Katie was doing inside. I was not excited that I had to let go of Vincent long enough to go through the metal detector.

"I'm right behind you," he said, squeezing my shoulder.

I held my breath as the bored teenager at the turnstile scanned my wristband. It felt much longer than the handful of seconds that passed, but eventually, Vincent and I spilled into the main walkway of the theme park. A song made of whistles and piano keys drifted loudly from a large carousel full of laughing children, and the smell of popcorn and chlorine overwhelmed the air as Vincent hustled me through the people and past the shops with turn of the century façades. I'm sure it was all very cute. The energy was happy, and the people were joyous. The children were all delighted in their sugar highs, and I was going to have a panic attack in the middle of it all if we didn't get to a less crowded space soon.

When we turned a corner, I could hear yells, laughter, and the sound of water splashing. There was a large zero-entry pool, with pipes and slides painted bright colors towering over it. Chairs were lined in rows in front of the water, and most of them were full of towels and people. Vincent ushered me toward the front where Hunter waited.

Hunter ran a hand through his hair, digging it into the curls on the back of his head as he looked through the crowd. When he spotted us approaching, he dropped his arm, crossing both of them over his chest. He was frowning at Vincent.

I looked up at Vincent, who was smirking.

"Did I miss something?" I asked.

"Nope," he said.

I wrinkled my eyebrows as I turned back to Hunter. His jaw was tight, and his nostrils were flaring. Why was he angry now?

"How was your talk?" he asked us.

I stared at him, confused by his sharp tone. Then it occurred to me that Vincent had his arm around me, and I was clinging to him as we walked. Knowing the topic of our conversation, this probably looked bad. I didn't think Vincent did it on purpose, but…I pulled away and sped up to reach Hunter. Wrapping my arms around his neck, I hugged him.

Hunter froze, hesitating, then unfolded his arms and tentatively hugged me back. "Is everything okay?" he asked. The sound of his voice implied he wasn't sure what he was getting the hug for.

"If by 'is everything okay?' you mean 'is she still going home with you after this?', then, yes. Everything's fine," Vincent said, his voice flat.

Hunter's body didn't relax in my arms. Instead, his frown deepened.

I turned to give Vincent a stern look. "Don't act like you made a play for me just to mess with him."

Vincent's face broke out in a wide grin. "She's all yours, man. She even promised to keep her hands off me. *Finally.*"

I narrowed my eyes at him in a playful threat.

Hunter let out a breath as he shook his head at Vincent, then tightened his arms around me. "I'm glad you two are better."

I smiled up at him. "Me too."

Vincent caught sight of Jessie waving from the pool, beckoning him to join them, and I watched all the females circling us turn to stare as he pulled his shirt off. Always well aware of his effect on people, Vincent didn't acknowledge any of them. He wasn't oblivious, he was outright ignoring. I was pretty sure by their whispering that at least a few of them recognized him from his streams.

He looked around and asked, "We're not sitting all the way up here, are we?"

Hunter nodded at the row of chairs in front of us that had towels. Jessie's shoes were tucked under one of them. "Yeah, we're right here."

"Never pick the front row. Your stuff gets wet," Vincent complained.

"Next time be here to pick your own chair. You're going to get soaked in the pool anyway," Hunter said.

"Which is why I like my stuff dry when I get done," Vincent replied.

"Glad to see the two of you are back to normal, too," I said.

"Sen! Hurry, we're heading down the funnel slide!" Katie yelled from the middle of the pool as Ryder splashed her. Squealing, she hid behind Jessie who gave Ryder a threatening look, warning him not to get her hair wet. He smiled mischievously, making a move toward her. Ian charged at him with an overly dramatic tackle, taking them both back into the water as they laughed. The wave ended up splashing Jessie anyway. She let out a screech as it hit her. I would not want to be Ian right now.

"Katie seems perfect," I said.

Hunter nodded. "She's as good as Ryder at shielding. I don't know if it's because it's his soul or what, but she's just fine."

Huh. Maybe she could give me lessons.

"Let's go," he said.

"Absolutely not. I am not going in there."

He gave and impish smile as he tugged my hands, dragging me toward the water. "Hunter!" I yelled. "At least let me get my shoes off."

"Take off the shirt, too," he instructed as he let me go.

My breath caught in my throat at the request, and I pulled my head back.

He chuckled at my startled response. "It will catch on the slide; you're safer without it."

"Oh." Of course. He wasn't actually asking me to undress in public. I slid it off my shoulders, lamenting the loss of my extra coverage but mentally promising the shirt that I would be back soon. Once my shoes were tucked under a towel, Hunter swooped me up in his arms and started to carry me.

"Put me down!" I yelled.

"You sure you want me to do that?" He laughed, tilting me forward to make a point that it would mean dropping me into the shallow end of the pool. I squeaked and clung to his neck.

"Don't you dare," I threatened.

He brushed his face against my cheek. "I'm never letting go of you."

It would have been sweet if he wasn't moving us closer to the line for the slide. This must be what cats being carried toward a bath feel like. I listened to the screams swirling overhead of someone riding down. The large blue tube circled several times in the sky before spilling its victims into the deep end of the pool. Kids were swimming near the exit so they could scream from the splashes and waves of water as riders shot out.

"I'm going to drown."

"You will not. It's not deep enough for that," Hunter chastised.

Katie and the group were already in line, several individuals ahead of us. Hunter finally put me down near the steps when Vincent came up behind us. He had left his sunglasses back with the rest of his belongings.

"I'll go first," Vincent offered.

I didn't stop him.

In line, Hunter stood behind me, his arms wrapped around my waist and his cheek pressed against my head. I'm sure it was partially to keep in contact with my skin, so he could help control my fear with his own emotions. I had a sneaking suspicion it was also to keep me from running.

About halfway up the steps, I looked over the railing. From here I could see a good view of the park. My eyes roamed over the rides in the distance. The Ferris wheel had stopped to load people. Even from here, I could hear the screams coming from several roller coasters rocketing through the sky. It was vibrant and colorful with all the attractions at work together. At this distance, with no one but Hunter touching me, the energy of the park gave me a pleasant buzz. I could see how the environment was such a draw for people. You just had to survive getting inside first.

"Excuse me," a soft voice said. I turned to see someone rushing down the steps in a flurry. She had beautiful dark hair that cascaded in damp curls down her back and large hazel eyes set in soft features. When she tried to squeeze past Vincent, he turned, accidentally bumping against her. She made the mistake of turning her eyes up from her feet to look at his face, losing her footing and stumbling back into me. Hunter and I both put our hands up to stop her from falling.

"Shit. Sorry." She shook her head as she turned to me, then put her hand on my arm to steady herself. As soon as she reached out, her spirit pooled over, sending familiar, cold electricity up my arm.

"Oh, thank goodness!" she gushed, then let out a loud breath. After spilling all the excess into me, her spirit settled calmly around her. Relaxing her shoulders, she smiled, showing the most perfect teeth and dimples I'd ever seen. "Girl, you were in just the right place! I freaked out when I got to the top. I thought I was going to have an anxiety attack. I think having to make my way back down the steps, through everyone in line, is almost worse than going down the stupid slide." She released my arm and straightened up.

"Glad I could help," I said, recognizing the cold feel of her spirit. She was like Katie—part Nephilim.

She looked over my shoulder. "Hunter?"

"Hey, Aelina," he said.

"You know each other?" I asked.

Hunter nodded. "She's good friends with Chris."

She gave me another full-dimpled smile. "I always know the people who drop the good parties. Chris has been inviting me since the start of freshman year. Best way to unload test anxiety."

"Makes sense," I said. The university was less than two miles from the amusement park. Between Hunter and Vincent, there was no way we were getting out of here without someone recognizing one of them. We were lucky enough to get away from the girls that were eyeing Vincent poolside. I needed more introverts in my life.

"Who might you be?" Still smiling, Aelina batted her eyelashes at me.

"Sen," I said, giving her an awkward hello wave.

"Oh, my, gosh. You're Sen? Hunter's Sen?" she gushed at me and then smiled past me at him.

Hunter wrapped his arms back around me. I felt him nod as he kissed the side of my head. I smiled at the realization that this random person knew about me. "I guess so," I said.

She nodded. "Of course. You're exactly how I pictured! It's nice to meet you." Her face and body language, all bubbly animation, made me wonder if Will was the only half-Nephilim that was so reserved.

Vincent cleared his throat, raised his eyebrows at me, and nodded his head at the girl as he took in her appearance. She was in a cute vintage-style swimsuit, all colors and cheerfulness bouncing in front of him. I was surprised he waited this long to insert himself in the introductions.

Noticing me watch him, Aelina asked, "Who's this?" She looked him up and down with one eyebrow raised and a smirk on her face.

Grinning at Vincent, I said, "That? That's just Vincent. Don't pay him any attention."

He gave me a mock pained look, holding his heart. "Excuse me. She meant to say, 'That's my amazing best friend, Vincent.' Don't downplay how important I am to you."

"Fine. That's my best friend, Vincent." I continued to grin, leaving off the amazing part just to get at him. Hunter laughed behind me as Vincent reached out to shake her hand.

"Nice," Aelina said as she appraised Vincent. I could feel the smile on my face stretching to my ears as I watched Vincent struggle to think of something to say. He stared at her, not letting go of her hand. What had gotten into him?

"You going to keep a souvenir?" I asked him.

Vincent looked down and immediately dropped her hand before scowling at me.

I turned to Aelina. "I'm sorry, he doesn't usually fumble this hard asking someone out."

She gave me a big smile and raised her eyebrows. "He would need to be a lot more than pretty for me to agree to that."

Vincent's mouth dropped open, shocked she was dismissing him so quickly. That didn't happen to him often—or maybe ever. I could feel Hunter suppressing his laughter.

"Look at that face." She nodded to Vincent. "It just baffles you when someone doesn't fall all over you, doesn't it?" she asked.

Collecting himself, Vincent smirked. "Yeah. You're the eighth wonder of the world."

She tilted her head to the side. "I can't tell if you're complimenting me or yourself," she said.

I laughed. I already liked her and couldn't wait to introduce her to Katie.

Before I could tease Vincent further, Hunter asked, "You up for a party this weekend?"

Startled, I turned to look at him. Hunter was watching Aelina and Vincent with an amused look. I wasn't the only one entertained to see Vincent mentally tripping over a girl. Seeing me watch him, Hunter added, "Chris and I were thinking of throwing something for the start of school."

I smiled at him for handing me the perfect opportunity to set her up with Vincent—or at least to get another chance to watch him squirm as she avoided him. "You definitely should come," I told her.

"Girl, I'm so down, just tell me when and where."

"I'll make sure to text you when we finalize the plan," Hunter offered.

"Cool, cool," she nodded, then looked at me. "You goin' down this thing?"

I eyed Hunter. "Apparently."

She nodded, resolute. "Okay, then. I can't leave you to do it alone."

Vincent made a motion to her to step in front of him. "Ladies first?"

She smirked and glided past him up the steps. He watched her intently until she was far enough away, then turned to me and Hunter. "Why did you invite her to a party?" he hissed.

My eyes widened. "Why are you mad at us for that?"

"Because *he* invited her," he said, jabbing a finger at Hunter. "You should have given me a chance to ask her out myself."

No good deed… "What difference does it make? You'll both be there," I asked.

"Yes, but now we're not there together, and I'm going to have to spend half the night figuring out whether she's interested or not. You just over-complicated things."

"You're welcome," Hunter said, smirking.

Vincent shook his head at him, then turned to follow Aelina up the steps.

I looked over my shoulder at Hunter. "So, did you invite her to help him, or were you blocking to get back at him?"

"Can't it be both?" he asked.

I laughed and shook my head.

Once we were at the top, the butterflies in my stomach were threatening to burst from my body. "Do you want to go first? Or do you want me to, so I can wait for you at the bottom?" Hunter asked as I stared at the blue cylinder in front of me. Water rushed through it, waiting to carry us down. My heart was pounding. I had heard Aelina scream on the way down, and it didn't sound excited.

"You go first. At least I can tell myself you will keep me from drowning when I get there," I said.

Hunter leaned down and kissed me, causing the guy manning the entrance to let out a frustrated sound. Pulling away, Hunter shot him a threatening look before sitting at the opening, crossing his arms over his chest. He smiled back at me, then pushed himself forward, flattening against the bottom as he swooshed out of sight.

The annoyed attendant held a hand up to me, making sure I didn't immediately follow Hunter—like I needed someone to keep me from rushing to throw myself to my death. He waited for a signal from someone at the bottom, then made a beckoning motion to me. I took a deep breath before sitting, imitating Hunter's posture as I crossed my ankles and arms. I closed my eyes tight as I pushed off.

At first, it was just like jumping into water, but as I curved around and picked up speed, it felt like I was falling.

"Benjamin, hurry!" I yelled as I trudged back up the hill.

He laughed and tugged the wooden contraption behind him. "I would think you would be tired by now," he said.

"Just once more, please?" I begged as he joined me at the top.

"You're such a spoilt thing."

When I pouted up at him, he sighed, smiling.

"Once more." He nodded. We settled on the sled. Me in front, Benjamin behind, his arms wrapped around me so he could steer. "Ready?" he asked.

"Take it away!" I exclaimed.

He laughed as he pushed us off, and we plummeted down the ramp he had carved in the snow. We both yelled out on the descent. I threw my hands in the air, feeling the cold breeze rush through my fingers.

We smashed into the bank of snow at the bottom, both of us laughing. We were covered, the patches of ice clinging to us, soaking the underside of my dress. It was going to be heavy and impossible to walk home in, but it was worth it.

I heard a low voice say, "That looks fun."

I looked up to see eyes the color of the sky smiling down at me.

"Hunter."

"Oh, not that boy again," Benjamin teased. *"Well, since you're here, you can make yourself useful and help her carry her skirts home."*

Reaching to help me up, Hunter gave me a sly smile.

I gasped for air as Hunter pulled me out of the water. "Grab my shoulders."

I wrapped my arm around him, using my other hand to wipe the water out of my eyes. Blinking, I looked up at the slide.

"What did you think?" he asked.

"I'm never doing that again."

He laughed. "I'm sorry. I really thought you'd like it," he apologized as he carried me toward the chairs.

"I think I would have if it didn't dump me into a hundred gallons of water at the end," I said.

Hunter sat me down on the cement, then pushed some stray strands of hair out of my face. "I'll think of something better next time."

"We should go sledding when it snows."

"Sledding? Why sledding?" he asked.

As I started to explain the memory I just had, Ryder yelled, "Hunter! We're doing the Tsunami!" He waved excitedly at a large red and yellow monstrosity of pipes.

Hunter hesitated.

"Go. I'm not going down that, but there's no reason you shouldn't have fun," I offered.

"Are you sure you'll be okay here?" he asked.

"I'm a big girl."

He pulled me close and kissed me softly. "I know. I just don't like leaving you alone in a crowd like this."

I breathed in his smell. The water mixed with his cologne smelled even better than normal. It smelled like summer. "I'm actually doing pretty good. Aelina helped." All the energy that had been stressing her had fortified my shields when she passed it off. I was going to have to thank her for it.

"Hunter!" Ryder yelled again.

"Go. I'll be enjoying myself lying in the sun—like a wet cat," I said.

Hunter laughed. He kissed me quickly, then took off after Ryder.

I turned to find our chairs. After scanning the first row, I didn't see my shoes or Jessie's. I looked again, thinking maybe I just passed them over. Nothing. Frowning I scanned the rest of the chairs, walking through the rows. Did someone take our stuff? The phones and bags were all safe in a locker, so why would anyone steal just our shoes? I finally spotted Vincent's sneakers, on a chair in the back row. He must have decided to move everything while Hunter wasn't looking.

A stinging feeling spread over my back as I reached to grab a towel. I looked over my shoulder to see a rough scrape approximately the size of my palm. I must have caught something on the slide. I wrinkled up my nose as I tried to get a decent look at it, stretching my neck to see how much it was bleeding.

"Damn it," I said.

"Why don't you let me help you with that?" a voice asked. Shifting, I turned to see a man standing behind me. He was only a few inches taller than me and appeared roughly the same age, but there was something oddly imposing about him. He had high cheekbones and an imperfect nose like it had been broken and not perfectly set as it healed. His blue eyes fixed on me.

"No, thanks. I can take care of it." I turned, trying to end the conversation while I grabbed my towel.

Arms circled my waist, pulling me against someone's chest as I jumped with surprise. He held me tightly, preventing my ability to turn in his arms. Then I felt a cheek press against mine, and a feeling of dread filled me. Dread because a complete stranger was touching me, followed by the realization that it wasn't a stranger. His power crawled along my skin, almost painful on my face.

I gasped. "Jonah."

"Did you like your roses?" he asked, his voice growling in my ear. It wasn't Jonah's voice, but somehow, it held the same inflection. He had left the flowers on my porch. Vincent was right. How was Jonah standing here?

"How?" I asked.

"Let's get out of here, and I will give you all the explanation your heart desires," he offered.

"Fat chance."

He laughed.

"So, what, you've been sneaking around for days, poking at the emotions of everyone around me? Petty, don't you think?" I had no doubt he had triggered Vincent's outburst in the parking lot, and he was probably what set off the entire event with Katie the other day. Not to mention my rage at her mom. That kind of emotional disruption had Jonah written all over it.

"Ah, just a little foreplay," he whispered.

I stood there, frozen, as he dragged one hand across my waist, sliding it slowly up my side and over my shoulder blade. His thumb ran over the scrape, causing me to suck in a pained breath. "How did you manage to do this in a body of water?" he asked.

"Caught it on the slide," I said. I was looking around for Hunter or Vincent. I didn't see any of our group—they were all probably still stuck in line for the attraction. I didn't want to scream for help. We were surrounded by kids and teenagers. What if he hurt one of them because I drew attention to us?

Jonah lifted his hand to his mouth, sucking the blood off his thumb before letting out a deep breath. "This is lovely," he finally said, running his finger along the top of the swimsuit, over my cleavage. I had to fight the urge to recoil into myself.

Two teenage girls walked by, looking at Jonah and his hands on me. They giggled and covered their mouths. "Ladies," he called after them, a smile in his voice.

Once they were out of hearing range, I asked, "What do you want, Jonah? You can't be here just to play with me and Vincent."

"I'm surprised you still need to ask that." He pressed his mouth to the top of my shoulder, kissing along it. Everywhere his mouth touched felt like needling heat. It was painful and taking all of my concentration not to wince. When he got to the back of my shoulder, I felt him lick a line up the tender, torn skin. This time, I did wince and tried to pull away. It fucking hurt.

"Can't you find yourself a nice little Nephilim girl—one that doesn't hate your guts—to settle down with?"

He laughed against my skin. "But I have. You don't hate me, Senlis. You just don't remember that you don't."

I thought about my memories of Jonah. He was usually doing something horrific in them—something I was reprimanding him for—but he wasn't hurting me. Not in most of them. "Maybe I don't hate you, Jonah. But that doesn't mean I like you."

He moved his head back up to rest his chin on my shoulder, whispering in my ear, "I don't need you to like me."

"Yeah, I get it. You just want a walking, talking battery pack," I said.

Jonah turned me abruptly to face him. He pressed me harshly against the front of his body. Actual clothing would have been real nice right about now. I didn't even have Hunter's dress shirt to help shield me from the feel of Jonah against me.

"That's a very nice bonus, to be sure," he said. His gaze traveled along my face, over my eyes, and down to my mouth. "But there are at least a few other reasons that come to mind."

As he leaned down to kiss me, I blurted out, "I hate roses."

The random outburst made him pause, and he smirked at me. "Then I will have to find a better gift."

"How about you leave? That would be a fantastic gift."

He cocked his head to the side at my remark. "You taste different." He paused, licking his lips. I would have said it was a nervous gesture if it wasn't Jonah doing it. "You're not as afraid."

"Maybe I figured out you're not that scary. Want to play another round of light up the Jonah?" I was bluffing. He scared me—a lot—but I was also pissed that he thought he could intimidate me, and that anger was getting the best of me. It's never really a good idea to taunt an angry sociopath though.

He let out a full belly laugh that vibrated through us both. When he composed himself, he smiled, and it may not have been his face, but that wicked smile was all Jonah. "Maybe that's so. Or maybe you're starting to remember."

I just stared back at him. His accusation made my heart pound faster than the fear of him standing before me. He was right. My memories of him were full of banter. Semi-friendly banter at that. It was changing my tone toward him, whether I wanted it to or not.

I watched his eyes widen as he took in my silence. "And just what has your mind decided to share?" he asked. When I just gave him a blank look, he let out another, quieter, laugh. "I was planning to push your reset button, but this could turn out to be much more fun."

I wanted to say something sarcastic and witty—anything to keep him busy while I thought of a way to get out of his arms without putting every innocent person around me at risk. My thoughts were cut off when he pressed his lips to mine. His movement was a harsh forcefulness, and his energy snaked into me, making me want to gag against his mouth.

"That was amazing!" Katie's happy voice cut through the sound of my own blood rushing through me at a hysterical pace.

Jonah let go of me in a jerking motion, leaving me to stumble as I regained my balance.

When I turned to see Katie and Ryder approaching, her face fell. "Sen?"

I must have looked as horrified as I felt. Hunter was coming up behind them, laughing with Ian and Jessie. He turned to face me, and his eyebrows immediately furrowed.

"What happened?" he asked, hurrying past Ryder. Within seconds he was on me, taking my face in his hands. I let out a breath as his warmth slowly replaced the feeling in my core. I think I was in shock.

Jonah laughed beside me. Hunter's eyes darted over my shoulder, seeing him for the first time. He appraised Jonah, recognition flickering in his eyes but not quite placing why this stranger was familiar.

I looked over toward where Vincent and Aelina were laughing, slowly making their way to us. Aelina's hand movements were animated as she laughed and reenacted what looked like her reaction on the way down the pipe. Vincent was holding his stomach as he laughed. He looked over at us all standing there, watching them. His face immediately sobered at my expression. I saw his eyes move to where Jonah stood behind me. Vincent's hands dropped to his sides and balled into fists. He stormed over to us, pushing me behind him and into Hunter.

"Get the fuck away from her," he growled at Jonah.

"I would have thought that was your line, my friend," Jonah taunted Hunter.

I felt more than saw Hunter's reaction as he realized who was standing in front of him. His entire body radiated with anger. I gasped and pulled his hands from my face before it found its way inside me.

I turned to touch Vincent's shoulder. I wanted to calm him, but Jonah had my anxiety on overdrive. The best I could do was shield so I wouldn't push Vincent further. "Don't provoke him, Vincent."

Vincent curled his lip back as he looked over his shoulder at me. "I am not afraid of him."

"Then you aren't very smart," Jonah said. His expression was amused as he watched Vincent.

"Vincent"—Hunter's voice was low as he stepped up beside me—"she's right, we can't do this here. There are kids around."

"Afraid seeing you bleeding on the ground will scar the little parasites, are you?" Jonah laughed.

I squeezed Vincent's shoulder to stop him from taking a step forward. He took a deep breath, lowering his head as he compressed all his anger down. "If you're still here when I open my eyes, I won't care how much therapy these people will need," he said.

Jonah's eyes roamed over us, settling on me. He was calculating his options. I think if he still planned to kill me today, there wouldn't have been a decision to make. He would have attacked Vincent. Since he'd decided I was more fun alive, at least for the moment, he just smiled at me.

"See you soon," he sang before turning and walking away. As I watched him leave, I began to shake, both from being wet and the feel of his sick, awful spirit under my skin. Before he turned to exit, he looked over his shoulder, blowing me a kiss.

Vincent whirled on me, grabbing my shoulders. "Are you okay?"

I winced as his fingers dug into the scrape, causing him to turn me, inspecting it. "Did he do this?" he asked, his voice rising.

I looked over my shoulder at where his eyes had fallen. I was still bleeding. Damn. "No, I did that on the slide."

Aelina had her hands on her hips as she watched us all. "Clingy ex, huh? They can be real assholes."

Hunter made a snorting noise. "You have no idea."

I had expected him to snap that Jonah was not my ex. Maybe I was overthinking his response. It could be that he didn't want to explain what was going on in front of Ian. Stalkerish ex was as good a cover as any.

"How is he here, Hunter?" I asked. If Hunter wasn't worried about it, then Aelina overhearing us was the least of my concerns right now. Ian didn't seem like he was even tracking the conversation. Jessie had caught on pretty quick and was distracting him a few feet away.

"I don't know," Hunter said.

"He started the ritual again, right?" Katie asked from behind him.

Vincent, Hunter, and I all turned to look at her, and she shifted delicately on her feet. "He died during a ritual. Isn't that like Benny? Is he tied here to you because of that?"

I looked at Hunter. He was that usual perfect stillness that meant he didn't like what he was hearing. When he didn't immediately shut her idea down, I realized it could very well be true. "Fuck," I whispered.

Hunter reached out and pulled me away from Vincent, wrapping his arms around me. I stood, my face pressed against his chest, listening to his heart speeding under my cheek. We all stayed there as Hunter contemplated our options. After a few moments, he kissed the top of my head, breathing in the smell of my hair. "I need my phone."

"What are you going to do?"

"Ask someone for help," he said.

"Who?" I asked.

He pulled away from me, then looked down into my eyes. His shoulders slumped as he responded, "You are not going to like that answer."

"Who can possibly help us that I would be mad about?" I asked.

I heard someone say 'Mm-mmm' and turned to see Ryder had his lips pressed tightly together as he shook his head at Hunter.

"For fuck's sake, all, this is getting old!" I snapped.

"I'm not talking about this here," Hunter said. When I glared at him, refusing to budge, he let out a sigh. "You are most likely going to yell at me. Forgive me if I don't want a pool full of witnesses."

"What are we waiting for, then?" Aelina's voice broke our standoff. "The sooner we're out of here, the sooner he spills the tea. Let's go."

I couldn't help myself. Laughter trickled out of my mouth at her eagerness. Hunter was right, she had no idea. When I stopped laughing, it hit me. Jonah's alive.

Vincent was going to hold this over my head forever.

CHAPTER 14

I WAS comfortably back in a pair of jeans and a T-shirt after we changed
out of our swimwear. It took a lot of coaxing to get Hunter to let us go
into the public restroom to change. Jessie was the one to finally convince
him we would stick together, emphasizing the mathematical improba-
bility of Jonah hiding in wait in the women's restroom.

"Thanks for letting me borrow this," I said, handing Jessie the swimsuit as she was getting into her car. Ian was already in the passenger's seat,
waiting for her.

She nodded. "Either you or Katie better call me later, got it?"

"As soon as we have any information," I promised.

She looked over my shoulder to where Aelina was sitting next to
Vincent on the hood of his car. Katie and Ryder were leaning against the
driver's side door chatting with her. "I can't believe you all kept me in

the dark for weeks, and she gets to stay and hear the plan, while I have to chauffer Ian home."

I laughed. "I promise I won't let you miss out on anything important."

"You better not."

When she pulled away, I walked over to stand near Hunter.

"I missed actual clothing," I said as I let him wrap his arm around me.

"Didn't like the swimsuit?" Aelina asked.

I shrugged.

She looked me up and down, squinting her eyes at me. "Please don't tell me you're one of those pretty girls who thinks she's ugly?"

"I know what I look like. I just don't like attention."

Accepting my answer, she nodded. "You don't like the creepers. I get it."

I laughed.

"Speaking of creepers, what are we doing about Jonah?" Vincent asked.

"We're waiting to hear back from Will," Hunter said. "He's getting in touch with someone for me."

"Who?" I asked.

"Another Nephilim."

Ryder snorted, causing Katie to raise her eyebrows.

"Okay," I said. Katie and I both eyed Ryder. "Why do we need another Nephilim?"

"You want to redo the ritual for Benny, yes?" Hunter asked.

"Yes."

"Theoretically, the only way to break your tie with Jonah is to cancel it out. If you finish binding to Benny, it should work. I just don't know exactly how to do it."

"Weren't you the one who started the first one?" Vincent scoffed.

I could feel Hunter's irritation at that question as he started to answer. "Yes, but Jonah helped. I remember some of it, but the real issue is that the ritual requires—"

I cut Hunter off. "Blood." My mind had flashed back on the memory with the strange-looking priest. The circle on the ground and symbols were the same as what Jonah had drawn on the ground. I remembered now that they were names. The blood was an offering. "It requires blood and a sacrifice," I added.

"A sacrifice? Like a goat?" Vincent asked.

"Think bigger," Hunter added.

"Why bigger?" I asked. I was with Vincent's suggestion. The ceremony I had watched in my dream used something similar to a goat.

"It takes a lot of energy—more than I understood the last time," Hunter explained softly. He was watching me as he said it, maybe trying to remind me he hadn't killed Benjamin willingly or intentionally.

"So, what, a cow?" Vincent asked.

Katie shook her head. "That doesn't make any sense. Nothing was sacrificed when Jonah tried to bind me and Ryder."

Hunter let out a quiet groan as he buried his face in my hair. "That's not true."

"What do you mean?"

He sighed and lifted his head. "Like the idiot I am, I helped him along with that. Again."

"Nathan?" I asked, immediately realizing what he did.

He nodded. "I should have been more careful, but I wasn't thinking. I heard Katie screaming and just reacted. When I ran out and found them there, the first thing I did was reach down to touch the circle. I'm the one who invoked it."

"Oh, this is getting good." Aelina leaned forward, bracing her forearm across Vincent's lap. She didn't seem to notice she was pressing on his thighs. He wasn't nearly as oblivious, based on the way he was staring at her arm.

I had a moment to panic that Hunter had loosely admitted to murdering someone in front of Aelina. Will had said it was clear self-defense. Nathan was in Hunter's house. He and Jonah had arrived together, and Katie and Ryder were witnesses that they had been attacked. It still seemed like the kind of thing you only openly shared with close friends—the help-you-hide-the-body kind of close friends. There was no fear on Aelina's face, though. She was reacting to the entire thing with interest and excitement.

"To add to the complication, besides an outside donor," Hunter carefully worded that last part, "you have to exchange blood."

My shoulders slumped as I said, "That could prove difficult."

"Why?" Aelina asked.

"Because Benny's a ghost!" Katie exclaimed as she leaned around Ryder toward Aelina. She was clearly delighted to share all about one of her favorite people with our new friend. Katie had taken to the other girl instantly. When I whispered in her ear that Vincent was a little hormone struck, Katie immediately vowed to enlist Jessie to find out about Aelina's relationship status.

He might want to murder me when he finds that out.

"For real?" Aelina asked.

I nodded. "He's my brother. We had an unfortunate incident, and he got trapped in between this and… wherever he was supposed to go after he died."

"I picked the right day to let my cousin drag me downtown." she laughed, sitting up straight.

CHAPTER 14

"Right. So we have no power source, and Benny can't bleed. Any other issues?" Vincent asked, finally snapping out of his distraction.

"That's not enough for you?" Ryder chuckled.

Hunter was quiet. I knew that pause meant there was more, but he didn't want to say it. I touched his arm that was resting across my waist. "Want to share with the class?" I asked softly.

"Not really," he said. I felt his phone vibrate in his pocket, and he pulled it out and answered with, "Did you find him?"

I heard Will's voice on the other end saying, "Yeah. He'll meet us at Tim's in an hour. You sure about this?"

Hunter looked into my eyes. "No," he said into the phone, then hung up.

"Who are we meeting?" I asked.

"Fulton."

"Is that name supposed to mean anything to me?" I asked.

"Not yet," he said, quietly.

Not giving me the chance to complain about that not being an answer, Vincent asked, "The cryptic thing is just an obnoxious personality trait of yours, then?"

Ryder laughed and said, "Yes. It really is."

"Let's go," Hunter said, pulling his keys out of his pocket.

"Wait, that's it? You're seriously not going to explain who Fulton is?" I asked.

He shook his head. "We need to see him. If I tell you now, you may not want to. You can yell at me afterward, but we need him."

"That's ridiculous," I said, pulling away from him.

He let out a breath as he ran his hand through his hair. "I'm asking you to wait an hour. Can you give me that, please?"

127

I folded my arms over my chest. We didn't have all day to fight about this. "Alright. Lead the way."

"How do you feel about cinnamon rolls?" Vincent asked Aelina.

"No." Hunter's tone was stern as he shook his head. "Sorry, Aelina, but neither of you can come along to this."

"Why not?" Vincent asked. His shoulders were already tense and ruffled at Hunter shutting him out.

"Fulton's...old school. Sharing this much about us with humans is considered taboo, and he might walk out if he spots you."

Aelina hopped off Vincent's car. "It's cool. I need to be getting home anyway. Just don't forget to invite me to the party," she said.

Hunter nodded to her.

Vincent made a hesitant sound. "Wait, is she safe? Or is Jonah going to target her now that he saw her with us?"

She scoffed at him, "Babe, don't worry. My dog will eat him if he tries anything."

"Your dog?" Vincent asked.

Aelina beamed at him as she pulled out her phone, sharing her backdrop like a proud parent. "That's Nala." Big brown eyes stared up from a furry black and white face on her screen.

"You have a pitty named Nala?" Vincent asked, snatching her phone from her.

She laughed. "She's a lover, but she'll eat your face off if I tell her to."

"Aren't those illegal?" Ryder asked.

Aelina and Vincent both turned to glower at him, causing Ryder to lift his hands up defensively.

"Not anymore. Besides, they would have to pry her out of my cold dead hands," Aelina asserted, taking her phone back from Vincent.

"I think she's going to be just fine," I said to Vincent.

"Did you drive here alone?" he asked.

"No, I came with my cousin." She made a quiet tsk noise. "She and her boyfriend ditched me when I chickened out on the slide, though. They're somewhere in the park."

"Want me to give you a ride home?" he asked.

She gave him a quick up-and-down look. "I guess that wouldn't hurt. You can meet Nala."

"Perfect," he said, walking over to open the passenger side door for her.

"We'll see you Saturday," Hunter said.

Aelina nodded. "Sounds good! Girl, it was good to meet you!" she exclaimed at me before turning to walk around to the passenger side.

After she settled into his car and he closed the door, Vincent looked over the roof at me. He folded his hands together and silently mouthed, "Oh my god!"

"I don't understand," Hunter said, a smirk on his face, "is he that excited about the girl or the dog?"

"Who even knows?" I laughed.

CHAPTER 15

THE bell on the door jingled as we all shuffled inside. I was ecstatic to get to the diner. We had granola bars on the way to the waterpark, and I was looking forward to cinnamon rolls. Granola bars are not a meal.

"Hey, Tim!" I called.

He poked his head around the door to the kitchen. "Hey, kids! You know where to find Will. I'll bring you some menus."

"Don't bother. We'll have four breakfast specials with cinnamon rolls on the side." I smiled as we made our way to the back room where Will always sat.

"And orange juice!" Katie called.

Chuckling, Tim nodded and disappeared back into the kitchen.

The diner looked like time had stood still in the fifties—and not in the shiny, themed way. More in the I-was-pretty-sure-this-is-exactly-what-it-had-looked-like-then kind of way. It was a trucker favorite, and no one made better eggs or cinnamon rolls than Tim. The place was packed early in the morning, but by mid-afternoon, they were ready to start closing. There was one man at the counter who nodded at us as we walked by. The rest of the seats were empty.

Once we were in the back and Katie caught sight of Will, she called out, "Will!" and rushed toward the table, causing him to break into a smile. Katie was still the only thing I have ever seen make Will actually smile. Not his curt, small reaction when he felt he had to. An honest, sincere smile.

Hunter went to put his arm around me as we approached the table. I was still mad about whatever surprise was in store, so I shrugged him off, raising my eyebrow at him in a challenge when he looked at me. He shook his head, but he kept his hands to himself.

The man opposite Will had black hair, truly black, long enough to fall in waves around his head. As we came around the table, he looked up at me, a smirk on his face. His eyes were a gray that was nearly silver, and his skin looked like he spent a lot of time outdoors. Although his features weren't soft, the lines of his face were very appealing, especially with the striking color combination. He had his hands folded under his chin as he appraised us all.

"Fulton," Hunter said.

"Hunter," Fulton greeted him coolly.

Will cleared his throat. "Should we move over to the table?"

Fulton made a motion at the booth. "Don't want to snuggle next to me?"

Rather than respond, Hunter just turned me around to sit at the table. He pulled my chair out for me, and I ignored the childish urge to sit in another chair just to spite him. I guess I didn't need Fulton to know how mad I was at Hunter—not until I understood why I wasn't going to like him.

Fulton and Will took the chairs across from us. Surprising me, Ryder flopped into the seat on my right, putting Katie on his other side. Angsty teenager that he was, he usually kept a comfortable distance between us. Now he sat beside me, his face fixed in a serious expression as he stared across the table at Fulton. Maybe stranger still, Ryder was giving off a protective vibe. Who the hell was this guy to invoke that emotion in Ryder?

Fulton stared back at him, his expression relaxed and maybe a little amused. His eyes flicked back and forth over Ryder and Katie as he rose an eyebrow. "Did someone get you wet?" Fulton asked. When we all just stared at him, he waved his finger between Ryder and Katie. "You multiplied."

After a second, Katie burst into laughter. "I love that movie!"

"At least one of you has a personality," he said, then he turned to Hunter as he slouched in his chair, resting his arm on the back. "Why am I here, Hunter?"

"We need to complete a binding."

Fulton let out a deep, raspy laugh. "Haven't you learned your lesson, kid?"

"Don't call me a kid, Fulton," Hunter said, his voice low with warning.

"Yeah, yeah." Fulton leaned forward then, putting his elbows on the table. He ran a hand over his knuckles as he settled those silver eyes on me. "Is this for you?"

I nodded.

"You sure getting stuck with him is what you really want?" he asked. His voice was soft as he watched me for a response.

I was startled by the question. I hadn't planned to bind myself to Hunter, and I was taken aback by his tone. Why did he care what I wanted?

"It's not for him. I want it to help my brother."

Both his eyebrows raised. "Benjamin?"

I sat back in my seat. "Yes. How do you know about him?"

He studied me silently, then asked, "You didn't tell her?" without taking his eyes off me.

"Tell me what?" I asked.

When no one answered, Will finally started with, "Sen…" He hesitated as if he were looking for the right words. He exchanged a look with Hunter, who stayed silent.

Ryder finally let out an impatient breath, then he blurted out, "He's your dad."

Hunter and I both turned to Ryder. Katie's mouth fell open as she stared from the other side of him.

"What are you talking about?" I asked.

In a condescending tone, Fulton started to say, "Well, you see, when a man and a woman really…"

"Shut the hell up. No one was asking you!" I snapped at him. My nostrils were flaring as I fought to control my temper.

He let out an abrupt laugh. "That's about what I expected."

I turned to Will. "Is this true?"

He just nodded, his face showing an unusual amount of emotion as he pressed his lips together. I looked away. I could not take the empathy suddenly pouring out of Will. Fine time for him to decide to be a person.

"Where the hell have you been?" I asked Fulton.

He stared back at me, then asked, "Oh, am I allowed to speak now, sugar? Or would you like to cuss me out some more first?"

My nostrils flared again. "I'm sorry. Was I supposed to yell 'Papa!' and run into your arms? Fuck you." My mother had died of an overdose, likely because being a half-breed descendent like Katie meant she had an overabundance of energy. Similar to a chemical imbalance. Without a

Nephilim around to help counter it, she binged and self-medicated. Growing up, I had assumed my father met the same fate or was strung out in a box somewhere. They had left me alone to be raised by my grandfather. Yet, here was this perfectly sober man, smirking at me. A full-fledged Nephilim at that. That meant he could have helped my mom. Maybe she would still be alive. Hell, even if she had been a lost cause, he could have helped me. Maybe not having to raise a teenager going through a soul transformation would have meant my grandfather had lived longer. I had a whole list of what-ifs that my mind was quickly pinning on Fulton's disappearing act.

He chuckled and shook his head. "Even without your memories, you're the same feisty thing you've always been. Look, if I had any idea your mother was Everly's daughter, I wouldn't have touched her. We don't parent each other. It gets too complicated."

"What does my grandmother have to do with this?" I asked.

"Everly is a Nephilim," Hunter said. "You always choose her bloodline."

"Why?" I asked.

"You trust her," was all he said. Our souls didn't move onto the afterlife—whatever that was. We were reborn, again and again, but we had to be conceived by another Nephilim or half-breed—someone with enough Nephilim DNA to pass down to us. My grandmother died before I was born, so we didn't meet in this lifetime. If Everly's bloodline, her DNA, is something I look for, we must have a strong connection.

Hunter reached out to put his arm across the back of my chair. He was trying to comfort me but not risking touching me if I was still angry at him.

I was still angry. Very angry.

"Alright, put a pin in that for later." I turned back to Fulton. "So, what? It's complicated, so you just skipped out on my entire life?"

"Believe me, when you get your head back, you will thank me for not sticking around to change your diapers and bathe you," he quipped.

"I highly doubt I will thank you for leaving me parentless my entire life, Fulton."

He was interrupted from whatever sarcastic retort he was gearing up for when Beth brought a large tray and set it down next to us. "Here you go, Will, honey," she said as she started unloading the plates. When she sat the last one in front of Fulton, she stopped. She batted her eyelashes at him and lifted her hands subconsciously to smooth her hair on the sides. "Anything else I can get you, honey?"

Fulton smiled up at her, his face full of handsome smile lines. "Not right now, sweetheart."

Beth giggled as she walked away. Could this get any weirder? Fulton turned back to me, his expression immediately wiped clean. "Here's the deal. I'm sorry about your mom. I tried to check in on you when you were fourteen—even I wouldn't leave a Nephilim to transform on their own—but the old man wouldn't let me. Thought I'd be a bad influence." He seemed to think for a moment, then went on. "He was probably right about that. You seemed to be getting along alright though. You had that little Victor boy following you around, keeping you out of trouble. He was doing as good a job as anyone helping you sort yourself out."

"Vincent," I snapped.

"Excuse me?"

"His name is Vincent."

"Whatever," he said, and he picked up his fork and shoved a large bite of egg in his mouth. "Point is, you two had it under control," he mumbled around a mouthful of food.

"Unbelievable," I closed my eyes and took a breath. "Explain to me why we need this asshole, again?"

Hunter spoke up, "We need to do the ritual without a sacrifice, and since Benny is a ghost, he can't share his own blood."

"That's a real bitch," Fulton said.

"Any suggestions?" Hunter pressed.

Fulton took another bite. He sat there chewing his food as we all watched in silence. After he took a swig of coffee to wash it down, he looked at me. "You can't bind yourself to Benjamin unless you're willing to tie both of you to Hunter. You need his blood if Benjamin can't participate. So, I'll ask again, is that what you want?"

I looked at Hunter. I could see the pulse in his neck speed up, but he didn't look at me. He kept his eyes on Fulton. "I don't know. I'm pretty pissed at him right now for springing you on me"—I dropped my eyes to my food as I took a bite of my cinnamon roll—"but how about you let me worry about that and just tell us what we need to know?"

I swallowed my bite. When I raised my eyes, Fulton was grinning at me. "Alright, sugar. You're going to need a lot of energy if you don't want a blood sacrifice. The sacrifice isn't necessary, it's just easier."

"Would a party work?" I asked, thinking about how much energy I'd picked up not even trying at Hunter's last rager. "A large gathering of people would mean an excess of energy, right?"

He turned his mouth down and back up, tilting his head. "Sure. It's as close to a ceremony as you'll get these days. You work well enough as a familiar; you should be able to funnel it into your target. Do you know how to do that?"

Yeah. That I did know how to do. I nodded.

Fulton gave me a curt head bob. "Well, there you go. Gather up all the souls your greedy little hearts can manage, set the circle, and feed. Then you can knock yourself out pouring all that energy into Benjamin."

"You're saying this like you're not going to be there to help us," I said.

He grunted. "Jonah is an annoying little prick. I wish you the best in shaking him, but I don't want to get any more involved than I have to. Sorry, sugar, but I'm sure you've got it under control."

I let out a huff as I watched him shovel food in his mouth. "I guess we got what we came for then," I said as I poked at my own food. This seemed like something we could have sorted out without me needing to know this asshole was alive and kicking. I refused to be disappointed.

"For what it's worth, you'll understand afterward. This is just how we do things," Fulton said as he continued to focus on his food. At the moment, the way he stabbed his fork around on the plate, he almost seemed to be feeling regret.

"That's a crap excuse," Ryder mumbled.

Fulton shot him a dry look over the plate. "You know the rules as well as I do, Ryder. Your choosing to ignore them doesn't negate their purpose. This mischief you're causing may very well come back to bite you."

"It's worked out fine so far," Ryder said, smugly.

Fulton looked over at Katie. "Guess we'll see about that, won't we?"

Seriously. What an asshole. My grandfather must have been so disappointed in my mother when she brought this loser home. Fulton was right about one thing, though. I was already thankful this was the first—and hopefully last—time I had to talk to him.

CHAPTER 16

I REFUSED to leave without finishing my food. Tim's craftmanship should not go to waste just because the guy sitting across from me made me want to shove my plate in his face and walk out. Ryder and I were waiting by the car as Hunter spoke quietly to Fulton, presumably drilling him for more useful information. I held a box of cinnamon rolls to my chest as I watched them. Tim had caught my sour mood and slid them to me on the way out—at least someone was worth this little visit.

When Hunter finally turned to walk toward us, I pivoted and hopped into the passenger's side of the car as Ryder quietly got into the backseat. Katie and Ryder had both been my shadows, following my lead in the restaurant and out to the car until Will came to take her home. Fulton had convinced him Katie was safe to be away from Ryder for short periods, and he wanted to see how it went for the night. I put Katie in charge of bringing Jessie up to speed on the conversation. I wasn't up to dealing with her reaction, even though part of me wished she had been present for the whole thing. I managed to not throw my food at Fulton. I had a solid feeling Jessie would have done it for me. Vincent would have hauled off and decked him. Hunter had probably made the right choice to minimize the group for this.

That left Ryder and me to wait silently for Hunter. Hunter crawled into the driver's seat without saying anything and started the car. I waited until we were on the highway before speaking.

"Was this necessary?" I asked.

"Yes," Hunter said.

"How? He didn't tell us anything we didn't already know."

"I didn't know the party would work or that I could stand in for Benjamin. You didn't either. You're just starting to regain things as conversations trigger your memory," he said softly. "He's the only other one of us nearby that I knew could help."

"Couldn't have texted someone farther away?" I asked.

Hunter let out a slow breath as his hands squeezed the steering wheel. "I didn't think he'd just give us a recipe and send us on our way, Sen. I thought he'd help more."

"I would have thought his ditching me as a newborn would have been sufficient proof that wasn't going to happen." I looked out the window, watching the cars weave in and out around us. It was rush hour by now, and they were all eager to get home. "Why don't you or Ryder know how to do the ritual, but Fulton and I do?" I asked, then added, "I mean, I'm assuming I do. When I'm me."

Hunter's eyes dashed to me quick, then back to the road. He decided to risk putting his hand on my knee. "You are you."

"Way to focus on the least important thing I just said." I snorted before continuing, "And what is the ritual for? Jonah used it like a weapon, but what's the real purpose?" I asked.

"You never liked the rules," Ryder said quietly in the back seat.

I turned to face him. As the only person in the car I wasn't angry with, I'd rather hear about this from him anyway. "What does that mean?"

"You know the ritual because it's yours. You gifted it so we wouldn't have to be alone if we didn't want to be. The rules say we aren't supposed to be this close. You never liked it, and you were strong enough that no one forced you to obey. The rest of us were expected to scatter," he said.

"Why?" I asked. And what spell had fallen on Ryder to get him to speak this freely? It was a complete breath of fresh air to have someone just tell me what the hell was going on.

Ryder pursed his lips. "Fulton's right. Things can get problematic if we're around each other. And there's always a consolidation of power concern. Separating us makes that less of a risk."

"Jonah is a pretty solid example of why," Hunter interrupted.

Ryder nodded in agreement. "A few of us stay within a bloodline or two, like you and Everly, because we have to, but it's always a few generations in between—grandchildren, great-nephews, things like that. Otherwise, it can get very complicated."

"Being born as Hunter's brother, that's not normal for you?" I asked.

Hunter added a curt, "No," to our conversation.

Ryder shook his head. "I've violated several rules this lifetime."

"Katie," I added.

He nodded.

"I know why you did that one, but why violate the proximity rule?" I asked.

Ryder smiled at me, full dimples and teeth. "Because Hunter just can't seem to take care of Jonah by himself. I thought some reinforcements might help."

I laughed as Hunter tightened his fists on the steering wheel.

Still smiling, Ryder added, "Really, I just wanted to help you. You always broke the rules when you thought it was best for everyone else. It didn't seem fair that we all sat back and watched."

"You keep saying rules. Whose rules?" I asked.

"Ah," Ryder ran his hand through his hair. "The Keepers. They maintain the balance for humans and for us. It's their responsibility to make sure we don't… you know, destroy human-kind and all that."

"We're Nephilim. So, what, the Keepers are Angels?" I asked.

"Angels or demons. Or just cosmic ooze that occasionally decides to walk around us and tell us what to do," he joked.

I thought about what Ryder said. "What did you mean by 'I gifted the ritual'?"

"If our souls are bound, there's nothing to be done about us being separated. You knew that, so you found a way to do it," he said.

"How?" I asked.

"Your priests. Humans have a talent for messing with their souls, trying to wield things beyond their capabilities. You used their ritual— what they created to worship and bind themselves, in exchange for our blessings and power," Ryder spoke like there was nothing at all unusual about what he was explaining.

"My priests?" I asked. This was feeling like a round of twenty-one questions.

Hunter, suddenly deciding he wanted to be part of the conversation, replied, "Priests and temples like the good little goddess you were worshiped as." He stole a look at my face as he said it, the corner of his mouth tucked into a smile.

I blinked at him. "I'm sorry, but what?"

"What part are you confused about?" Hunter asked, trying to hide his smile as he stared out at the highway. I wasn't sure he had any right being this amused at my response.

"I'm not a deity," I said, stating the obvious.

Hunter shrugged, then reasoned, "You can persuade emotions, you have visions, and you're immortal—if not in the traditional sense of the word."

"No one claimed you had to make rain and grow crops. That was another god, anyway." Ryder laughed from the backseat.

"This is insane. All of it," I said, sitting back in my seat and staring forward. I remembered Hunter saying Jonah had once thought of himself as a god. I thought he was meaning it in a self-imposed narcissistic way, not that there was an actual premise there.

Ryder sat forward in his seat, leaning over the armrest between us, clearly enjoying my shock and confusion. "Thirty percent of humans believe sprinkling water on their head dictates where they go in the afterlife, yet you're struggling to believe a civilization would worship you for your ability to assist emotional endeavors?"

"If we were worshipped as gods, why would anyone accept being called Nephilim?" I asked.

"When it was decided we were no longer allowed to be worshiped, you were one of the few not forced to comply." Ryder shrugged. "Once monotheism decided to label all of the old gods Nephilim so they could be forgotten, most of us embraced it. Kind of out of irony, really."

"And not all of us were worshiped as such, to begin with," Hunter added.

"Why was I allowed to continue?" I asked.

"You didn't start wars," Hunter said.

"That's why Jonah's so eager—the consolidation of power thing," I said, not really asking a question this time. It made sense. Jonah obviously wasn't concerned with hiding in the background and completely ignoring laws and restrictions. Being more powerful would mean more freedom to do just that.

Hunter shrugged a shoulder next to me. "Yeah. That's part of it. The other part is he just wants you, Sen. It's not all nefarious world domination. He legitimately thinks if he's bound to you, you'll want him back."

I watched him as he looked out the window, his eyes carefully watching drivers around us. He had said all of that calmly like it was something he'd come to accept a long time ago. He didn't even seem annoyed or jealous, just stating facts.

"So, this is all my fault?" I said quietly. I had accused Hunter of setting Jonah on me by trying to invoke the ritual, but it was my own damn fault the thing existed, to begin with. And if my memories were any indication, I hadn't done a stellar job of discouraging Jonah's behavior. Maybe he wasn't a full-blown obsessed sociopath all along, but the signs were there, and I just let him be jealous and angry with Hunter while I played with him.

Ryder shook his head, scooting back in his seat. "You can't control what people do with your good intentions."

We sat silently for the rest of the ride home. Hunter kept his hand on my knee. I was becoming angrier with myself than him at this point, so I didn't push him away. I was glad we would be back at Hunter's soon. The sun was setting earlier, and it would be dark shortly. Benny waking up alone in Hunter's house felt like something we should avoid. Plus, the car ride was giving me a headache. Or maybe it was the conversation. Not that I was heading into a better one. Once we got back, I was going to have to convince Benny to participate in another ritual, and not just with me. He was going to have to bind himself to Hunter. This week just kept getting better and better.

CHAPTER 17

We still had some time before sunset when we pulled up to the house. Hunter went to the kitchen, and I went straight to the room. I flopped face down on his bed and buried my head in his pillow. It was really hard to stay angry at someone who smelled so good that even his pillows made me want to wrap him around me. The entire car ride was a conversation we should have had a month ago when Jonah tried to bind us. Not that it would have made a hell of a lot more sense even then, but at least I would have had more time to digest it. You would think someone like Hunter would be a better communicator. With as much time to perfect it as he had, it was baffling that he was this bad at it.

There was a rapping at the door. I turned my head to see Hunter walking in, his knuckles tapping on the door to let me know he was there. There was steam coming off the cup he was carrying toward me. I rolled over and sat up against the headboard as he crawled onto the bed to sit next to me. When he handed the cup over, the smell of vanilla and lavender instantly made the tension between my shoulders ease. I wrapped my fingers around the cup and brought it up to my nose to breathe in, smiling because it was perfect.

Hunter smiled as he watched me. "I'm not sure if I should be jealous of that cup or thankful you don't look at me that way so I can maintain some self-control."

"I'm still mad at you," I said. One cup of tea and a flirty comment was not getting him off the hook for the last few hours.

"I know."

"You know you deserve it, too, right?" I asked, taking a sip.

He let out a soft laugh as he ran his hands through his hair, then leaned back against the headboard. "Yeah, I know."

I side-eyed him over the mug. He closed his eyes as he rested his head back against the edge of the wood, his fingers laced together over his stomach. I was being hard on him. I knew why he gave me information the way he did. It was hard to break years' worth of habits, sure, but I had also asked him not to dump information on me once my memories started surfacing. It wasn't his fault he couldn't discern between what information was overload and what I would want regardless.

"Sorry I'm so fickle," I said.

He blinked his eyes open and turned his head slightly to face me. "What do you mean?"

"I know I'm the reason you haven't shared all of this with me. I told you not to, and now I'm mad that you did exactly what I asked. It's not really a winning situation for you, either way, is it?"

The corner of his mouth tugged into a smile. "That's not being fickle. It's hard to be consistent when you don't have all the information."

I took another sip of the drink, enjoying its warmth before I sat the cup on the nightstand. Then, I scooted over the mattress and put my head on Hunter's shoulder, wrapping my arm across his waist. Startled by my movements, he went still under me.

"While that's true, it doesn't change that you've had to deal with the repercussions of my decisions," I said.

He reached down, running his fingers along the back of my hand and arm. "You said in the car this is all your fault. That's not true, Sen. You didn't cause this. I did."

I hesitated. Hunter wasn't the only person who had been keeping information to themselves. I hadn't been entirely honest about my memories of Jonah, either. "I've had a lot of memories come back."

"I know," he said.

I shook my head. "No, you really don't. I don't understand all of it, but Jonah is there. A lot."

I felt him shift as he leaned his head down to rest his cheek against me. "That's not surprising. We spent a lot of time together, all of us."

"Why?" I asked. Hunter didn't seem to like Jonah in my memories. It didn't make sense that he put up with him.

He made a 'hmm' noise as he contemplated my question. "I wouldn't say Jonah and I ever liked each other, not really, but we were friends of a sort. He was unhinged from the start, but he made things more interesting."

"And me?" I asked.

"And then you came along." I could hear the smile in his voice as he said it. "Jonah wasn't all bad. At least, not until you chose me, and he wouldn't leave you to your decision."

I thought about my memories of Jonah. *I shall take my chances.*

"That was my fault," I said.

"How did you come to that conclusion?" Hunter asked.

"I let him feed off me. I didn't discourage his comments or thoughts. I don't have all my memories, but I have enough to know I didn't stop him or shut him down when he was getting out of hand."

"Hey." Hunter took my chin and turned me up to him. "That is just who you are. Jonah knew that, and he knew what it meant. It's his problem that he took advantage of it."

I stared up at him, not quite sure what he was saying. Just who I am? Was I someone who wouldn't push Jonah away? Was that it?

"We should take Benny up to the cabin tonight. The sooner we get him settled in for Saturday, the better he will be," Hunter said, watching me. "That's if you're still set on this."

I took a deep breath. I knew what he was really asking. He knew I was set on helping Benny, it was the binding-us-to-him part he wasn't sure about. "Yeah, I am."

I felt some tension leave his shoulders with my answer. He gave me a small smile. "Benjamin's about to wake up," he said softly. "Can I kiss you before I have to spend another twelve hours not able to touch you, or are you still too angry with me?"

A grin spread across my face. "I should tell you no and make you suffer."

"You should"—he smiled back, then leaned his head down—"but you won't."

He pressed his lips against mine. He was warm and soft, everything he was supposed to be. The feel of him made me exhale as I relaxed against his body. He ran his fingers along my jaw until he cupped my neck, and his fingers played along my birthmark as he pulled me deeper into his kiss. I felt his tongue brush softly against mine right before the room swam.

"Hunter..." I moaned as I leaned my head back against the wall.

"Shhh."

"I cannot promise to keep quiet if you continue," I whispered.

He laughed quietly. "If you don't try, Benjamin is sure to find us out," *he whispered as he kissed along my neck, causing me to bite my lip. His* *hand moved up the inside of my thigh as his mouth closed over mine, kiss-* *ing me to smother the sounds escaping. I felt hot everywhere our skin met* *and could barely control my breathing. In the moment, I didn't care if we* *were caught. I wanted his hands on me more than reasonable thought could* *detour it. When I reached down, guiding him toward me, he forgot himself* *and moaned into my mouth.*

"Shhh," I teased.

I blinked up at Hunter as I pushed away from him. His breathing had sped up, and I could feel his heart beating under my hand.

"Was that your memory or mine?" I asked.

"I don't know," he said, not opening his eyes as he reached to pull me back against his lips. He kissed me softly before asking, "What are the chances you would let me do any of that right now?"

I laughed. "I don't remember how that ended, but I feel like there's an even bigger chance of Benny catching you this time if you try."

He groaned, then gave me a quick kiss as he pulled away. "Enjoy your talk."

I reached for him, stopping him from standing. "Wait, where are you going?"

"I am going to take a shower."

"You're leaving me to convince him alone?" I asked.

He smiled, then lowered himself back down, placing a kiss on my neck. "Yes, because I do remember how it ended. Benny would like me even less if he caught us in the middle of that," he whispered as he kissed along my collarbone.

Feeling the heat rush to my face, I cleared my throat. "Enjoy that cold shower."

He flashed a smile full of dimples, then stood and walked out of the room.

I stayed there while my pulse slowed. I wanted a cold shower too. The lights flickered as I stared up at the ceiling. "Hey, Benny," I called out, not moving. My view took on a distorted wave as Benny leaned over my face, trilling inquisitively.

"I'm just tired," I lied. I sat up, then added, "It was a long day." At least that part was true. I almost laughed at what his response would have been, had I told him the real reason he found me sprawled out on the bed. It might have been worth his reaction if I wasn't already planning to tell him something that he was guaranteed to be angry about.

As I ran my hands over my face and took a deep breath to start my pitch to Benny, my phone vibrated across the nightstand. I crawled over the bed to reach for it.

"Hey, Will. Everything okay?" I answered.

"No," he said.

"What happened? Is Katie alright?" I had already pulled myself into a standing position next to the bed before the question had left my mouth. At the sound of Katie's name, Benny was practically on top of me trying to hear the conversation on the phone. I swatted at him to give me space.

"Katie's fine. I'm at your house. I need you to meet me here."

"My house, why?" I asked.

"I'm here with some patrol vehicles. They found a body in your house."

"What?" I yelped. "Whose body?"

"John's," Will answered quietly into the phone as if he didn't want someone to overhear.

"John who?" I asked.

"Katie's stepdad."

"What the hell was he doing in my house?" I asked.

"That's what they're trying to figure out. I need you to get here ASAP," he said.

"Okay. I'm on my way. Where's Katie? Is she safe?" I asked as I slipped my shoes on.

Will hesitated, then said, "She's here; she's sitting in my car."

"What the fuck, Will. Why did you bring her there?"

"We were on our way back when I got the call. Besides, she's safer locked in my car surrounded by police vehicles than she would be alone in my apartment." His tone was tired.

"Right. Alright, sorry," I said. "I need to call Vincent. I'll be there as soon as I can."

"Make it quick," he said before hanging up.

I turned to find Hunter standing behind me in his towel. I didn't even have time to enjoy the fact he was dripping wet in front of me. "We need to go," I said.

"Why? What happened?" he asked.

"They found Katie's stepdad in my house," I said as I walked toward the bedroom door.

"What was he doing in your house?" Hunter asked.

"Dying, apparently," I replied. "Get dressed. I'm calling Vincent."

I left Hunter in his room, and Benny followed me to the living room. He was being uncharacteristically calm as he paced behind me through the house. I brought Vincent's number up on my phone.

"How'd your meeting go?" he asked.

Fuck. I hadn't told him about Fulton. I wasn't in the mood to talk about it on the drive, and now was not a good time to get him riled up over it. "Delightful, but I have something more important to ask you right now."

"What's up?"

"Can you come get Benny and take him to the cabin?" I asked. I ignored Benny as he made a loud sound of protest from behind me.

"Uh, sure? Why can't you do it?"

I took a deep breath. "I'll meet you there. I need to meet Will at my house. They found John's body there."

"What?" he questioned, his voice raised.

"I will tell you absolutely everything, if you will please help me relocate Benny while I deal with it," I begged.

"Yeah. Yeah, I'll take care of Benny," he said. I heard the sound of him grabbing his keys off the table in the background. "I'm on my way."

"Thank you, Vincent. I'll see you later tonight." When I hung up, I turned to face Benny. He was wound up and ready for a fight.

"Look, I don't have time to argue with you about this. I need you to go with Vincent when he gets here. A lot has happened today, and none of it was something you're going to like. So, you're going to do what I say because right now we have limited options, and you'd hate all of them anyway." I turned and walked down the hall. Benny stayed in the living room. Either he wasn't going to fight, or he was so mad he hadn't figured out how to react yet. I decided to pack my suitcase while he figured that out.

I knocked on Hunter's bedroom door. "Are you dressed?"

He called through the door, "Come on in."

When I opened it, he was in a fresh T-shirt and jeans, rubbing the towel over his head to dry his hair. "Vincent's going to come and get Benny," I said.

He nodded. "I'll get Ryder."

"I got myself," Ryder called from the hallway. He had a backpack slung over his shoulder. When he saw me looking at him, he held up his phone. "Katie sent me a text. Will has her locked in his car at your house. What's going on?"

I turned to Hunter. "Want to fill him in while I throw my stuff in the bag?"

He nodded as he reached down for his own backpack and then stopped to kiss my forehead as he passed me on his way out. I let out a sigh as I looked at my bag on the floor. I missed my own room. I really hoped John wasn't bleeding all over my bedroom floor. That was going to make it really hard to sleep in there after this was all over.

CHAPTER 18

W<small>E</small> could see the red and blue lights from the police cars from halfway down the block. Several of the neighbors were standing outside, watching. Well, at least we established the tolerance level of the neighbors. They stopped ignoring stuff when the police showed up.

Will was standing by his car, his arm leaning on the roof as he spoke to Katie through the window. Hunter had barely turned off the engine when Ryder hopped out of the car and ran over to them. I watched Will shake his hand and pat him on the back before handing Ryder his keys so he and Katie could sit in the back seat together. Will then waved at me as he headed toward Hunter's car.

"Hey," he said as he approached us.

Hunter nodded at him in greeting.

"How's Katie?" I asked.

"She's fine. Her mom was demanding to see her, so I locked her in my car to keep Mary away from her," he said.

"Oh, fuck. How's Mary?" I asked, realizing it was her husband lying a few feet from us inside my house.

Will's eyebrows rose as he pressed his lips together. "You may want to hold off on feeling too bad about how she's dealing with this," he said.

"Oh?" I asked.

"She told the first officer on the scene that you threatened her and John yesterday."

Hunter and I both yelled, "What?"

Will just nodded. "I let him know I was there when it happened, but his boss still wants to talk to you."

"Wait, they aren't arresting her, are they?" Hunter asked, waving his hand toward my house. "She wasn't even home."

"No one is arresting anyone. They just want to talk to her," Will assured us. He looked at me before continuing, "You have several alibis confirming you haven't been home in the last twelve hours, including mine."

"You could have told me that on the phone, Will," I said. Hunter made a sound in agreement.

Will eyed Hunter then. "Would you have brought her if I did?"

Hunter crossed his arms over his chest. "Maybe."

"Point taken," I said. "Alright"—I wiped my palms off on my jeans—"lead the way."

Will nodded and motioned with his hand for me to head inside. When Hunter started to follow, Will put his hand up. "Just her."

"Why?" Hunter asked.

"It's an active crime scene. She gets to go in because it's her house. And"—Will paused, flicking his eyes at me—"technically, she's a suspect. You are a civilian with no reason to be inside. Wait out here."

Hunter stared back at him with his jaw clenched.

"Hunter, I'm fine. I didn't do anything," I said softly.

"She's not going in there alone," Will said, patting Hunter on the shoulder.

I walked up to my front door. The screen was propped open, and I could hear people inside. I hesitated at the door. I didn't want to go in. Will hadn't warned me what I was going to find, and suddenly, I had sweat on the back of my neck thinking about it.

"I'm right behind you," Will said quietly from the steps.

I nodded, not turning around to look at him. I took a deep breath and stepped inside. As I came around the corner, I saw several individuals in matching black jackets kneeling around my living room floor. I had a thought that, hopefully, all of them huddling here meant it hadn't happened near my bed.

"Hi," I said awkwardly as several heads turned to look at me.

A loud voice boomed from across the room, "What are you doing in here? Michael, I thought you were watching the door?"

"I was, sir." I jumped at the voice next to me. I hadn't noticed the person standing to my right until he spoke. He didn't look much older than me. His blond hair was cut short, and he was shaved completely clean, his uniform perfectly pressed. He looked like he was playing dress-up for career day, not like someone old enough to be carrying the gun he had strapped to his hip.

"Then what the hell am I seeing?" the other man asked. He was easily in his fifties, his hair graying at his temples. He looked tired and frustrated with his young helper.

"You said to watch the door until Will came back. He's back, sir."

Will stepped up behind me. "Tyler, this is Senlis. It's her house," he explained.

The older man looked me up and down, finally settling back on my face. "Well, you sure don't look like you took on a two-hundred-pound man today. Come with me." He nodded toward my kitchen. I walked around the group of individuals, trying to not bump the tech taking photos. I made the mistake of looking down at the center of my floor. John's body was stomach down on the carpet, his head turned to the side, facing me. His mouth was open, jaw slack against the floor. Cold eyes stared off at nothing, the color muddy and unclear. There was blood pooled under his face. As my eyes moved around his body, I realized he was in a circle. Someone had drawn a circle of blood around him.

I had stopped walking, and I let out a startled yelp when Will touched my arm. I turned to look at him, and I could only imagine what my face looked like. I took a deep breath, which was a mistake. The room smelled horrible. That must be why they had the front door open. I felt a wave of nausea as I tried to take shallow breaths through my mouth. "I think I might be sick," I said.

Will just nodded.

We shuffled into the kitchen, and I walked over to the sink, leaning over it while I caught my breath. I really hoped I didn't throw up in front of the big scary officer standing next to me. I closed my eyes, trying to calm down. *Shit.* There was a dead body on my floor. How was I going to get that out of the carpet? I leaned my head back and opened my eyes. I stared out the window over the sink, then reached up and opened it. The fresh air helped. I took a moment to appreciate that the mess was in the living room and not my bedroom. Even better, it wasn't in the studio. If Jonah had splattered blood on any of my grandfather's keepsakes that I kept in there, I would have been crushed. Focusing on how pissed that would have made me helped me regain my composure.

Tyler was watching me as I turned to lean back against the counter, letting the cold air dry the sweat on my neck.

"You going to be alright?" he asked. His voice was still deep but softer than when he was addressing us in the other room.

I nodded. "I'll be fine." I looked at Will then. "Why was he in my house, Will? What happened?"

Will looked over at Tyler, who gave him a nod. "Someone broke the glass panel on your front porch. Looked like they forced their way inside. We took fingerprints, but we won't know until those come back if it was John or someone else who entered first."

"Is it possible someone was acting in self-defense if John was breaking in?" Tyler asked.

I shook my head. "No one else was here. I live alone." Technically. Even then, Benny was with us. "Hunter and I left last night to stay at his place," I added. Not to mention, who paints a circle in blood if they're defending themselves? You don't play with your attacker if you're the victim. I didn't say that out loud though.

"Any idea who might have done this?" he asked then, watching my face. I stared back at Tyler. He knew it wasn't self-defense. He was seeing if I would take the bait and admit it was me.

I looked over at Will. I knew exactly who had done this. Was I supposed to admit that or keep it to myself? "Will?" I asked.

He nodded. "Tyler, I need to get you a case file."

"Why's that?" he asked.

"The hospital patient—the one that attacked the staff?" Will prompted.

"What's he got to do with this?" Tyler asked.

"They have a history," Will said. "There was an altercation earlier today. It's highly likely he broke into her place and was waiting for her."

Tyler looked at me then. "This true?"

I nodded. "He was at the water park earlier today," I said, taking Will's lead. I pointed to the roses. "He left flowers on my porch the other day. When he showed up today at the park, I told him I didn't like them." I swallowed, the realization of what Jonah had done was hitting me, then I whispered, "He said he was going to leave me a better gift."

Tyler's eyebrows rose. "This the kind of thing he'd think was romantic?"

I looked out the entrance to my living room, at all the people efficiently working. "Fuck, I don't know." I honestly didn't know if Jonah was trying to scare me, or if he really thought this was a gift. Did he think killing Katie's stepdad would make me happy?

"If you didn't want the flowers, why'd you put them in a vase on your counter?" he asked, nodding at them.

I turned to see the bouquet. The pink rose was missing from the center. I really hoped Jonah hadn't read something into the fact I'd put them in water, too. "I thought they were from my boyfriend at first," I said, my eyes tearing up. I should have been smarter than this.

Tyler scrutinized me for a few more minutes, then nodded. "You got somewhere to stay tonight?" he asked.

Will piped in, "We're relocating her to a friend's place in the mountains."

Tyler grunted. "You'll need to come downtown in a few days, sign an official statement." He pulled a slim wallet out of the inside pocket of his jacket, handing me a card. "If you have any more run-ins with this guy, call me," he said.

I nodded as I took it. The emblem was different, but it was the same starch-white business card as Will's. Hey, look at that. I was starting a collection.

CHAPTER 19

I STARED out the window, taking in the inside of the garage. When we pulled up at the cabin, Vincent's car was parked out front, and all the lights were on inside. Katie and Ryder had rushed in together immediately—Katie couldn't wait to see Benny. She was taking this better than I was. Will had agreed to let her come stay with us since he had work in the morning. He didn't want to leave her alone with Jonah on the loose. That was all it took to put her in a good mood.

"Hey, beautiful," Hunter said softly as he reached up to tuck a stray piece of hair behind my ear. "You okay?"

I turned to him. "Sure." I didn't know how to articulate what I was feeling. Not without gushing a stream of consciousness at him. Was there anything I could have said to Jonah today that would have changed what he did? I wasn't all that upset that it was John's body on my floor, just that there was one. Did he intentionally target John, or was Jonah waiting for me when that asshole got home, and it was just convenient?

"Mhmm." Hunter just smiled at me in the dark.

"Why didn't I see it?" I asked.

"See what?"

"When he murdered those girls and attacked Vincent, I saw it. Why didn't I see this happening?"

"I don't know. Jonah shouldn't be able to do anything he's doing right now."

I may have gotten there in time to stop him if I had seen it. I would have believed Vincent sooner, too. He didn't care that I saw what he was doing before. Was he deliberately stopping me this time or had something changed? I rubbed the space between my eyebrows, trying to find my own answer, then let out a slow breath.

"Let's go inside," I said, reaching for the door handle.

"Wait." Hunter unbuckled himself and leaned over, putting his hand on my side to stop me from moving. He kissed me gently, then pressed his forehead against mine. "You didn't cause this."

"I didn't say I did," I said.

"I know that look. You're trying to find all the reasons this is your fault." He pulled back and took my face in his hands. "That man was going to end up dead from drinking and driving or just drinking. If he touched Katie again, it's possible I would be bailing Ryder out for his murder. The worst part of this is you having to deal with it, but don't overthink it. It may have been the only good thing Jonah did in his existence."

"Hunter, that's a horrible thing to say," I said.

"Why?"

"John was a person. An asshole of one, sure, but it is not a good thing to kill people."

Hunter smiled at me. I couldn't help but feel like it was a little conde-scending. "Fine. Killing people: bad. Got it. Still not your fault."

I narrowed my eyes at him. He just continued to smile back, then kissed me again, not bothering to shield his spirit from me. It curled up, warm and comforting inside my chest as his lips and hands pressed softly against my face. When he pulled away, he asked, "Are you ready to go in? We can sit here as long as you need."

"Let's go. This day has been the longest day of my life. Might as well end it with a bang."

He chuckled before releasing me. "Maybe Benny will think it's a brilliant idea."

"Yeah, sure," I said as I crawled out of the car.

I could hear Katie's muffled laughter as we stepped inside. "Where are they?" I asked Hunter.

"Basement," he said, nodding at the stairway.

I headed down the stairs. When I stepped into the basement, I found the four of them, including Benny, sitting on a large, fluffy blue sofa. There were several large bean bags piled up on either side of it. Movie posters covered the walls, making a collage of cars and monsters through the room, and one corner had plastic containers stacked clear to the window. They looked like they were full of bright-colored bricks. Kid's toys. Next to them was an air hockey table that had seen lots of play and had stickers slapped on the side with band names and cartoon characters.

Katie and Ryder were holding controllers as they played a racing game on the television. Vincent was patiently explaining the rules to Benny who was vibrating in place, on the edge of his seat. When Ryder crashed, Katie yelled out in joy, causing Benny to bounce into the air, cheering for her.

"What is this?" I asked.

Hunter put his arm around my shoulders. "It's our room."

Ryder grinned up at me as he continued jabbing furiously at the controller in his hand. "We were too 'rowdy' to be allowed upstairs when we played."

Hunter laughed and pulled me to the side where he opened one of the doors along the wall. I looked in to see a small room, painted a soft blue color. A bright red bunk bed took up the center of the far wall. The sidewall had been painted with thick yellow stripes, and there were stuffed animals hanging from nets in the ceiling and more movie posters. The closet door was open and was spilling over with stacks of board games.

"I get the top bunk this time!" Katie yelled.

"No way. Top bunk is mine. It's been mine since Hunter moved to his own room." Ryder laughed at her.

Benny made an alarmed sound.

"I'm going to have to side with Benny on this one. You two are not sleeping alone in the same room," I said.

"Why not?" Katie asked. "That's where we slept last time."

I turned to Hunter. He gave me a guilty shrug. "Jessie was down here with them."

"Oh sure, she's a solid chaperone in that area," I quipped.

He laughed, then motioned to Ryder. "He hasn't even kissed her yet. It's not going to escalate that quickly."

Ryder glared up at Hunter, losing track of his game. A crashing noise came out of the speakers, and Katie let out another happy whoop.

"Little man is respectful. Nice." Vincent put a hand up at Ryder.

Ryder eyed him, then gave Vincent a hesitant high five. I raised my eyebrows. I remembered Vincent at sixteen. He was only encouraging Ryder because it was Katie. "If this was us in high school, no one in their right mind would have left you alone in a basement with your girlfriend," I said.

"They left me alone with you plenty." He smiled at me.

Hunter made an agitated noise beside me, which for some reason made Benny laugh.

Katie was expertly ignoring the conversation. I knew from our chats she was not as excited about Ryder's 'respectful' behavior as the rest of us, but she wasn't going to share that with the room.

"Will isn't going to like it," I hedged.

"I'll sleep down here on the sofa, mom," Vincent offered, shaking his head at me. Benny trilled in agreement.

"There's another bed down here. You can sleep there," Hunter offered to Vincent, pointing to the other door.

"Ooh, was this your room?" I asked.

He smiled. "Yes."

I scuttered over and opened the door, flipping on the light to the room. The walls were gray, with a more muted yellow stripe pattern on the accent wall, and there was a black bedspread folded at the end of the mattress. The walls were covered in dark band posters, and the windows had been blacked out with dark curtains. A stack of books on the nightstand all sported covers that looked like science-fiction stories.

"My, someone was angsty," I chirped.

"What exactly did you expect for a teenager that fed off jealousy?" he asked.

Ryder called from the other room, "And one that was already obsessed and pining over you."

"Thanks, R," Hunter said.

Laughter erupted in the other room as Ryder and Vincent continued to make quiet jabs at Hunter. The lights flickered as Benny joined in.

"I'm disappointed there aren't more pink teddy bears," I teased.

"There's a brown one in the closet," Hunter said, dismissively, as he glared out at the other three guys in the living room.

"No way!" I ran over to the closet, opening it to find several baseball-style caps on a shelf and, sure enough, a tattered brown teddy bear. I pulled it down. The arms and legs had moveable joints, and the little tag in its ear had been rubbed until the logo was no longer visible. His little nose was missing some of the felt. I spun around to face Hunter, who was now leaning against the wall, his arms across his chest as he smirked at me.

"Was this your teddy?" I asked.

"Yes."

"That is adorable." I squeezed the little bear to my chest.

"Glad you think so," he said.

I started to walk out of the room with it when he straightened up. "Uh, what are you doing?" he asked.

"Taking it with us," I said.

"Why would you bring that out there for Vincent to mock me with?" he asked.

"Because he shouldn't have to sleep in the basement. Shame on you for leaving him alone in a closet."

He chuckled at me. "It isn't alive."

I covered the bear's ears. "Shhh. He'll hear you." Then I smiled at him. "Benny's teddy is upstairs in my bag. If Vincent makes fun of you, he has to tease Benny too, which he won't do."

He shook his head, then a smile spread across his face. "What was your comfort object?"

I raised an eyebrow at his question, then said, "A mug." The middle-of-the-night-chocolate-milk mug my grandfather always had prepared for my nightmares was better than any stuffed toy.

"That is so you."

I walked past him and into the game area, leaving him to chuckle behind me as he shut off the light.

I cuddled the stuffed bear to me as Hunter pulled one of the bean bags over in front of the sofa. He flopped down into it and reached up, pulling me onto his lap. Vincent looked over, his eyes settling on the bear, then he looked at my face. I stared back, challenging him to say anything. His eyes shot to Hunter, then back to me. He smiled before turning back to their game, then muttered, "Aw, cute," under his breath.

Benny made a few gurgling snort noises. I was glad Hunter couldn't understand what he was saying. None of his comments were about the bear. They were all questions about how I could stand sitting so close to Hunter.

"Benny, we need to have a chat," I started. Katie and Ryder both looked at me, and Katie nodded. She put her controller down and reached over to pat Benny. I watched him spark where she touched him, and the outline of his figure brightened.

"Benny, we have a little problem to solve," she said, encouragingly. I appreciated her prep work. Having Katie present was going to be a big help with this conversation. At least, I hoped so.

It was time to rip the bandage off, though. "Jonah wasn't exactly unsuccessful with his last attempt at the binding ritual. Now he's stuck to me, like you, and the only way to sever that tie is to finish the original spell," I blurted out.

The entire room went quiet, and Katie gave me wide eyes. I think she expected me to feed it a little slower, but we were running out of time. I was anticipating Benny would react negatively and need some time to sulk, and Saturday night was less than forty-eight hours away. Benny was humming with energy as he tried to comprehend what I was saying. He wavered and growled at me.

"Yes. You and me"—I paused for a second as I winced—"and Hunter."

Benny scoffed loudly and flickered.

"Ouch!" Vincent yanked his arm back from where Benny shocked him and shifted himself further away on the sofa. "It wasn't my idea," he said.

Benny chimed apologetically at Vincent, who nodded. "I think it's stupid too. But if I were you, I'd rather be stuck with him than Jonah," Vincent offered.

Benny begrudgingly concurred.

"Wait, did you understand him?" I asked Vincent.

"No. I just know what I'd be thinking right now," he said, shooting Hunter an appraising look. Actually, both Vincent and Benny's silhouette had similar body language as they stared down at us from the sofa. Hunter shifted underneath me as they both scrutinized him.

"Bright side," Katie interjected, "when it's over, you'll be alive, and we'll get to actually hang out!"

"Who's bright side?" Hunter muttered behind me.

Benny was torn between being annoyed with Hunter and excited with Katie. He flickered with concern as he warred with the two extremes.

"Please, Benny?" I asked softly.

Katie took his hand and stared, her eyes pleading with him as we waited for his response.

Finally, Benny reached over and snatched her controller up, gurgling as he plowed the race car through the debris in the game and across the finish line. Katie raised her arms and cheered while Ryder yelled, "That was cheating! I wasn't playing!"

I let out a breath. Hunter wrapped his arms around me and gave me a big squeeze. Benny wasn't going to fight it. One obstacle down.

"I'll call Chris tomorrow," Hunter whispered in my ear.

I nodded. There was still a lot of prep work to do, but I was feeling pretty optimistic right now. I relaxed against Hunter, Teddy safe in my arms, and I watched as everyone I loved cheerfully played video games through the night.

CHAPTER 20

THE horses trotted past us as we watched from the alley.

"There!" Everly pointed as she spotted two men conspiring at the edge of the crowd, their backs to us. The taller of the two had brown curling hair and stood calmly despite the mood around us. The other was blond and much more invested in the mob in front of him.

"They seem quite harmless," I said, appraising them. From what I could see, they were both lovely creatures. The taller one laughed as his friend leaned over and said something quietly to him. It seemed they were both full of youthful fun, nothing more.

"Tell that to the man about to be hanged," she said.

I looked back at her. "This was their doing?"

She nodded.

"And you're quite certain they've been sent for?"

Again, she nodded. "I conversed with the messenger just this morning. I think they already know, as well."

I turned back to the men. The blond leaned forward, clapping a man in front of them on the shoulder with encouragement. I felt the ripple of his energy flow through his victim and out to the crowd, making the lot of them more agitated and restless. The blond laughed as his friend shook his head at him. It was a blatant show of power, and they had to be aware it was drawing unwanted attention. I couldn't comprehend why they would be so reckless.

As we observed, the man with curls looked over his shoulder as if he were searching for something. Finally, his blue eyes settled on me. They were bright and sparkling, and I had a sudden thought that it would seem such a waste if he were to be taken. He stared back at me, his gaze drawing down my figure and back up. When his eyes met mine again, one side of his mouth pulled up into a smile.

I took a step forward, and he turned fully to face me, waiting for my approach.

"Whatever are you doing?" Everly asked as she grabbed my arm.

I smiled back at her. "Distracting them."

I could see her wheels turning as she caught my intention. "You think you can stop it?"

The man grew impatient with our chatter and started toward us.

"You doubt me?" I asked.

"Never, dear one,"—she laughed—"but that one looks enough to lose yourself in."

"Some faith then, please," I chided. "If anyone is lost, it shall be him."

She drew her hand to her mouth to cover the tinkling of her laughter.

"Will you locate the messenger and help to buy me some time?" I asked quietly.

"I will. I just hope you understand what you are about to get your-self into."

I watched as the man approached, a full smile now on his face.

I hoped so, too.

I rolled over, my arm pooling into cool sheets. I squinted at the clock on the nightstand. It was already noon. I stayed there thinking about my dream, listening to the quietness around me. Then it occurred to me—I was alone. I sat up in Hunter's bed, pulling the white sheets and comforter up around my chest as I surveyed the room. Unlike his child-hood bedroom, the room upstairs that we slept in was empty of posters or any signs a teenager had ever been in here. Like his room at home, the only signs of Hunter were the hoodie on the back of the white chair that sat in the corner and his backpack on the floor next to the bed. Where the room at his house was all shades of blue, this room was bright white.

I crawled out of bed and picked my jeans off the floor where I'd dropped them last night. I slid them on under Hunter's T-shirt that I'd slept in and went to brush my teeth and hair.

When I wandered out to the kitchen, I found Vincent on a barstool at the center island, clicking away on his laptop.

"Morning, love," he called when he saw me walk into the room.

"Morning," I said.

Hunter had a dishtowel over his shoulder and was cracking eggs over a pan. I walked up behind him and wrapped my arms around his waist. "Hi," I said. By the time Benny let everyone go to sleep, I was exhausted. I was asleep before Hunter had even finished changing in the bathroom. I woke up just enough to feel him curl up around me and nestle his face into the back of my neck. It was my favorite way to sleep. I never thought I'd say that about sleeping near another person.

He smiled down at me. "Sleep okay?"

"Yeah, all things considered." I reached down and snatched a piece of bacon from the plate in front of him.

"He's nice and domesticated, isn't he?" Vincent teased from behind us.

"I take it you don't want to eat?" Hunter asked.

"I retract my question," Vincent said, grinning.

I smiled at him and shook my head as I snacked on the stolen bacon.

"I started the oven if you want to heat up your cinnamon rolls." Hunter nodded toward the box on the counter. He'd brought Tim's cinnamon rolls with us. I'd completely forgotten them in the kitchen when we were leaving. That's how upset I had been. I never forgot about food.

"Ooh!" I said as I walked over to put them on the cookie sheet waiting on the counter. As I prepped the rolls and put them in the oven, Ryder wandered up the stairs, yawning.

"Hey, little man," Vincent greeted him.

Ryder just nodded in response.

"Katie still asleep?" I asked.

"Yeah," Ryder said, as his mouth spread into a dopey, dimpled smile. "She sleeps with the blanket pulled completely over her head. It's cute."

Vincent laughed. "Probably won't be as cute when you're sharing it."

Ryder and I both scowled at him, making him laugh harder.

"The trick with a blanket thief is to sleep really close to them," Hunter added, smiling at me.

"I am not a blanket thief," I said, taking the stool on the end of the counter.

"You sleep exactly like Katie if I'm not wrapped around you," he replied.

"That is actually very true," Vincent added. Hunter gave him a look that implied he was not pleased with Vincent's support. Seeing his expression, Vincent clarified, "I meant it's true she sleeps with the blanket wrapped over her head…not with me wrapped around her." Vincent gave me wide eyes before he looked back down at his laptop.

Ryder was leaning on the counter next to us, drinking juice he'd grabbed from the fridge. As I watched him, I noticed he had the start of dark lines under his eyes. He said he was doing fine after healing Katie, but he was looking a little worse for wear this morning.

"Are you feeling okay?" I asked. I reached out for his arm, but he yanked it out from under me.

Ryder's face flushed as he gave me an almost horrified look. Then he mumbled, "I'm good, thanks. I'm going to grab my games."

I watched as he shuffled away from us and back down the stairs. "I know he's naturally shy, but I really thought he was warming up to me after yesterday."

Both Vincent and Hunter laughed. I turned to face them. "What's so funny?" I asked.

After a few more chuckles, Vincent cleared his throat. "He doesn't feel comfortable with you touching him," he said.

"Yeah, I got that." I had picked up on that earlier this summer. "What's his issue?"

Grinning, Vincent looked at Hunter. "Oh, can I tell her, please?"

Hunter smirked and shook his head. "Better you than me."

"What?" I looked back and forth between the two of them. "What is it?"

Hunter ignored me as he divided the eggs up on five plates. Then he went to work adding bacon. He silently moved around the kitchen, avoiding my eyes as he pulled the cinnamon rolls out of the oven and slid one on each of the plates.

"Vincent?" I prodded.

"You know what your healing did to me," he said.

"Yeah, so?" I asked. What the hell did that have to do with Ryder?

"So, you know your spirit wasn't always, let's call it 'a jack of all trades', right?" he asked.

"Yes…what does that have to do with anything?"

"Do you know what you used to feed off?" Vincent sang, his face barely containing his laughter.

Glaring, I said, "Spill it already, Vincent."

Vincent leaned into me, cupping his hand near his mouth, and whispered, "Lust."

"Oh, shut up." I rolled my eyes at him. He was still grinning proudly, and I scowled back at him. "You're not funny."

"I'm not joking." He laughed.

I gave an annoyed look at Hunter, who just watched me as he carried the plates to the island. Something about the expression on his face made me pause. "He's not serious?" I asked.

Hunter sat a plate in front of Vincent, then two more in front of each of us before sitting on the stool next to me. His lack of response was enough to tell me it was true. Vincent wasn't just screwing with me. "Oh my god!" I covered my mouth with my hands, "You don't mean?"

Vincent was practically giggling beside us. "You make our little Ryder very uncomfortable."

I groaned and buried my face in Hunter's chest as I yelped, "Shut up, Vincent!" Looking back up at Hunter, confirming it by his expression, I winced. "I didn't mean to."

It was Hunter's turn to laugh at me. "You haven't done anything to R, don't worry. He's just being cautious."

Then, I had a horrifying thought. "This doesn't happen to everyone I heal, does it?'

Shaking his head, Hunter smiled. "No. You just weren't being very careful with Vincent. I think you just shared energy with him too often and too close together. You were effectively lacing him with your own spirit."

"You make it sound like I was drugging him."

Hunter shrugged.

My eyes widened. "Is this why I struggle so much to keep my shields up when you're kissing me?"

He nodded.

Making a whimpering noise, I lowered my face back down to his chest. "This is horrible." I didn't even like talking to people. How in the hell was this what I fed off of?

"I can't tell if you having this information is better or worse for me. Does knowing this mean you're never letting me near you?" He laughed.

Vincent turned to Hunter. "Yeah, about that. I have to know: how could you go cold turkey and then sleep next to her every night?"

I pulled away from Hunter and gaped at Vincent. "Vincent, stop," I warned.

The corner of Hunter's mouth twitched in a frown, but he didn't turn to look at Vincent.

Vincent shook his head. "I just don't get it. I mean, I get you"—he waved at me—"because you had that whole touch aversion thing, so you don't understand what you're missing. But how is he able to stand it? I'm not even sexually attracted to you, and I think I'd go mad."

"I believe I told you to stop," I said.

Vincent took a playful bite of his food.

"It's been long enough he probably doesn't remember," Ryder piped in. He stood in the hallway, snickering over his gamepad.

Hunter shot him an angry look. "No one needs your help."

Vincent coughed as he nearly choked on his food. "Wait, you don't mean… you've been celibate longer than just the last couple of months?"

"What makes you think I would have this conversation with you?" Hunter asked in a flat tone.

Ryder snickered as he went to grab one of the plates off the counter.

I looked at Hunter. "Are you saying you didn't date in high school or college? Not at all until we met?" I asked.

His nostrils flared as he continued to shoot daggers at Vincent. Then he closed his eyes and let out a breath before answering me. "I'm saying I haven't dated, period. Not this lifetime, not any other."

"Why?" I asked, my mouth falling open at the information. Vincent was right, I had no interest in partners before Hunter because of my fear of damaging humans. Hunter didn't have the same control issues with his spirit that I had though.

"I didn't want anyone else," he said, flatly. He stood up, leaving his plate of food on the counter while grabbing his phone. "I'm going to call Chris about tomorrow." Then he walked out of the room and down the hall, closing the bedroom door behind him. I exchanged glances with Vincent.

"Nice going, Vincent," Ryder said.

Vincent replied, "Hey now, you're the one who outed his lack of experience to the room."

Ryder just shook his head and raised his eyebrows at me. "Just to be clear, I'm not going after him to make sure he's okay. That's officially your job now."

I pushed myself up from my seat. "Alright. I'll be back. Maybe." I wasn't really sure what had just happened. Vincent was just teasing Hunter, and I certainly wasn't going to give him a hard time about his lack of relationship history. He seemed awfully angry over a conversation that had started out at my expense.

"I'm actually going to head out," Vincent said, standing with me. "I'll be back tonight. I need to pick some stuff up from my place."

"You going to bring the headsets?" Ryder asked.

"You got it, little man."

Ryder made a fist pump motion before high-fiving Vincent, then he grabbed his plate and Katie's and headed back down the stairs.

Vincent smiled at me, then closed his laptop. "Have fun," he said, kissing my cheek before he turned to leave.

I rolled my eyes at him as I headed down the hall.

CHAPTER 21

I TAPPED on Hunter's door. He didn't acknowledge the knocking, so I took a chance and opened it anyway. He was sitting on the foot of the bed talking quietly into his phone.

He looked up at me as I closed the door and leaned back against it.

Not taking his eyes off me, he continued to speak into the phone. "Oui, elle est là." He listened, then smiled. Pulling it away from his mouth, he said to me, "Chris says hello, and they're excited to see you tomorrow."

"Hi, Chris! Can't wait to see you!" I called.

"Tu l'as entendue?" he asked into the phone. Hunter laughed and shook his head at whatever Chris said in response. "À demain." He tossed his phone to the side and leaned back on his arms as he watched me.

"You know, I have memories of you saying a lot of really pretty things in French," I said.

"Oh, yeah? What am I saying?" he asked.

I shrugged. "I have absolutely no idea, but they sound pretty."

He laughed as I padded over to him, standing with his knees on either side of my legs. "Why did you storm off?" I asked.

"I didn't. I needed to call Chris."

"Right. You made food so you could let it get cold, while you hid in your room on the phone. Logical," I said.

He gave me a stern look. "Are you done?"

"Depends on if you're going to start being honest or not. I can sling sarcasm at you all day. Your call."

He took a deep breath, then sat forward, wrapping his arms around my hips as he stared up at me. "I gave you enough reasons to be angry with me. I didn't want to add sleeping around to the list."

"While it was completely unnecessary, I think that's just great. Why is that admission something that sent you running from the room, though?" I asked.

"It's not that." He pressed his forehead against my stomach, burying his face against the shirt. After breathing in, he pulled back. "I almost gave up. I didn't even look for you this time. I thought you had made up your mind that you didn't want to be with me. I decided to get out of the way. I even tried asking Ashley out, but it just didn't go anywhere because I didn't really want it to."

I ran my fingers through his hair as he stared up at me, all his emotions swirling in those bright eyes that held me. He closed them and leaned his head into my hand, then continued quietly, "Then you walked into the coffee shop. I turned around, and you were standing there. You looked perfect, and I almost fell apart right there. For a split second, I thought you had come looking for me." He laughed at his admission. "I caught on quick that you had no clue who I was, but you didn't completely hate me, either."

"I didn't hate you at all," I said softly.

"God, Senlis." He reached up to grab my wrist, pulling my hand from his hair and kissing my palm. "Please don't be angry with me."

"Why would I be angry with you?" I asked. My pulse was starting to race from him holding my skin. He was trying to shield, but his emotions were so raw he was failing to block most of it from me.

"Vincent's right. I can't stand it. I was furious at him for interrupting us yesterday morning," he admitted.

I laughed. "Yeah, you didn't exactly hide that."

His mouth quirked in a smile. "Yeah. But it was good he did. Sen, if we do the ritual tomorrow, you are going to wake up."

"So?" I asked.

"So"—he let go of my wrist and leaned back on his arms again, putting distance between us—"everything we are doing together. You don't have all of your memories. I've been treating this entire time like a second chance, but you may wake up tomorrow night and absolutely hate me. I knew that. I knew there was a chance I would sleep with you, and you would wake up and hate me for it."

He lay back on his bed and stared up at the ceiling. He looked utterly crushed over his confession. A laugh bubbled up out of my throat. I tried covering my mouth to stop it, with no such luck. I was suddenly laughing hard enough tears were stinging my eyes.

"Why are you laughing?" he asked. He was watching me from the mattress like I had lost my mind. Maybe I had.

"Apparently, I feed off lust. And you're worried I'm going to be angry with you... for what, exactly? Taking advantage of me when I'm a willing party? You have got to see the irony in that, Hunter." I tried swallowing the last few giggles as I shook my head at him. He stayed flat on his back, watching me. He didn't seem to find the humor in the situation that I did. When I had finally suppressed my laughter, I looked down at him. "You're ridiculous."

"Glad you think so," he said.

I kneeled on the bed, crawling toward him until my legs straddled his lap. I watched his face as I pushed his shirt up. Leaning down, I kissed a line up his stomach.

He sucked in a breath. "What are you doing?" he asked.

I continued to push at his shirt as I kissed my way up his body. I placed a kiss over his heart before straightening back up, tugging him into a sitting position. I pulled his shirt off, throwing it on the floor behind me, then took his face in my hands and kissed him. He sat there at first, letting me taste his lips, completely pliant under me. He was cautiously guarding his spirit as I pressed against him. When I ran my tongue along his bottom lip, he let out a sigh, giving me access to his mouth. I curled my tongue around his and kissed him deeply, feeding all my desire into him.

When I pulled away, he was gasping for air, his pulse racing against his neck. I kissed down his chin and along his jaw until my mouth hovered over his pulse, then I sucked the skin gently between my teeth. Hunter let out a low, guttural sound as his arms wrapped around my waist, pulling me tight against him. I kissed his neck gently before I moved back to his mouth.

He kissed me back this time like he wanted to crawl inside where all his energy normally curled up and pooled in my soul. When I broke away from his lips, it was my turn to gasp for air. I leaned my forehead against his as he closed his eyes, his hands kneading against my lower back, just above the band of my jeans.

"I am not going to be angry with you," I whispered.

"You can't know that," he said.

"Yes, I can," I said. "You said I'm me. I'll still be this version of me tomorrow, Hunter. And this me loves you."

He opened his eyes and blinked into mine. "It's going to destroy me if you don't tomorrow."

"Guess you'll just have to trust that I'm right," I said.

He laughed softly as he kissed me, then he lowered his hands under my thighs, lifting me in the air. He rolled me under him on the mattress, then slid his hands to the button of my jeans, undoing them. He managed to peel them off with one smooth motion as he moved down my legs, finally tugging them off my ankles. Jeans really were not made to be removed quickly, but he managed it. I watched as he kissed my ankle, up my leg, and over the top of my thigh as he crawled up me. He looked up to meet my eyes as his mouth hovered over my leg.

"You look amazing in my T-shirts," he said. When he licked a line up to my hip, my breath caught.

"I really want to say something witty and sexy back, but I'm drawing a blank right now," I whispered.

He smiled as he pushed the shirt up higher, baring my stomach. I curled my fingers in his hair as he made his way back up my body, his mouth wandering over me. When he bit down gently, just above my hip, I felt the heat of his energy spread under my skin. The feel of it brought a moan from me as I lay my head back. The familiar sensation of my memories forcing their way to the surface started, and I swallowed, taking a deep breath as I tried to push it back.

"Hunter, stop."

He froze on top of me. I felt his hesitation, then his body shifted as he started to move off me. I grabbed his shoulders to keep him from leaving.

"I just need a second," I said.

He hovered there, waiting for me to tell him what to do. When I was sure I had control and wouldn't get lost in a memory again, I opened my eyes to find him watching me, his expression cautious. I cupped his face in my hands as I leaned forward to kiss him, pulling him toward me as I fell back to the bed. Taking it as the invitation I meant it to be, he crawled forward so he could keep his lips pressed to mine. He slid his hands under the shirt, gliding them up my sides and over my ribs, pushing the fabric up with his movements. He kissed down my chin to my neck before pulling away to get the shirt over my head. Then he forced my arms up, tracing his hands along them as he pulled the shirt off.

A flush burned through my chest and face as his eyes trailed down my body, and I realized I was lying under Hunter in nothing but tiny black underwear. When he looked back up at my face, he smiled.

"You are so beautiful," he said, then brushed his hand over my cheek before kissing me again. He lowered himself against me, pressing our bare skin together, and I gasped into his mouth. His skin felt so good. He was still shielding as much as he could, but his spirit was needy and excited, and I wanted to drown in it. I wrapped my arms around his shoulders and clung to him as we kissed, his hands caressing my body.

He licked along the inside of my upper lip playfully before moving down my throat, kissing along my collarbone and down my chest until his mouth hovered over my heart, mirroring where I had kissed him. I sucked in a breath, digging my fingers into his shoulders. I felt more than heard his moan as it vibrated against my skin. He kept his lips pressed against me as he lifted up enough to push his sweats and boxers down, kicking them off and onto the floor. My heart was pounding as he rolled his eyes up to watch me while he slid my underwear off. I just stared at him as I tried to swallow my pulse. He finally crawled back up the length of me, holding himself up on his elbows as he stared down into my eyes.

I could have stayed right there, enjoying the look on his face, but he kissed me and whispered, "Don't move."

He leaned over to the side of the bed to grab something. While he stretched out above me, I ran my hands over his shoulders and down his side as I looked at him, enjoying the lines of his body. When he pulled back over me, he caught me admiring him, and a smile spread across his face.

"Enjoying the view?" he asked.

I raised my eyebrow at him. "You want me to look away?"

His expression softened as he dropped the teasing tone from his voice. "No. I don't want you to ever take your eyes off me again."

He wrapped his hand around the back of my neck, pulling me to his lips, and kissed me softly. Alright, maybe I didn't just want to lie here staring at him. Just his kisses were enough to make my breath speed up. It took all of my control to patiently wait as I felt his other hand moving between us, then he shifted his hips. His tongue curled against mine at the same time as I felt him slide inside me. He was being so tender and careful, and I couldn't take it.

I sighed softly into his kiss, losing that last bit of patience, and I raised my body up to meet him, forcing him the rest of the way. He shuddered as he pulled away from my mouth, biting his lip and swallowing a sound deep in his throat. When I dug my fingers into his hair, he buried his face against my neck. I felt as his hand wrapped around my thigh, his fingers digging gently into the flesh as he held me and started to move above me. He went slow at first as he kissed softly at my neck between heavy breaths. Then, he started to move in a comfortable, urgent rhythm, like he knew every part of my body and exactly what to do.

His movements were soft and gentle but intense as he pulled me against him. Like his kisses, everything was sweet and controlled, meant to drive me completely crazy. And it was working. Even his breath on my skin felt deliberate. He pressed his lips against the pulse in my neck, and I felt a sharp, tingling heat start deep inside me, expanding until it burst over me, causing me to arch my lower back and press against Hunter as I cried out. He moaned into my skin, and his hand tightened on my leg as he thrust into me, bringing hot waves through me until I was shaking from it.

When I finally felt his body release, his shields came crashing down with it. His energy poured into me, hot and melting into mine as he rocked against me. All the emotions he lost control of swirled and curled up, mixing with my own. Then he collapsed on me, wrapping his arms around me.

When he finally pulled away, he lifted himself on his elbows and ran his hand over my hair, brushing it back from my face.

He whispered, "I love you," as he kissed me softly.

I smiled and closed my eyes as I said, "Yeah, I gathered that."

He laughed and pressed his lips to my forehead, then shifted to move away.

"Please, don't leave yet," I mumbled, wrapping my arms around him. I felt warm and safe and more whole than I could remember ever feeling as I fell asleep with him wrapped around me.

The ballroom was brimming with energy. The assembly of dancers covered in layers of red and gold complemented the flourishes and molding of the room. Masks obscured their faces, providing anonymity and permitting them to fulfill their intended purpose of acting as life-sized ornaments. Hunter stalked through them, gracefully avoiding their turns and invitations as he drew closer to where we stood. He caught me watching him as he weaved through the gowns and coats. Pushing his mask atop his head, his lips curved into a smile as he trapped my eyes with his. They were the most extraordinary blue and glittered in such a way as he approached us that it took my breath away. It was undeniably intentional that he chose a jacket of such deep ocean hues for the occasion. He knew how well it would complement the color of his eyes.

"Salut, beauté," he said quietly. He took my hand, placing his lips upon the back, lingering longer than was civil in company.

"Calm your salaciousness, my friend. It will startle the prey." Jonah chuckled at Hunter, patting his shoulder with affection. Hunter released me with a smile and a wink. Bolstered by his closeness, I gave a short nod and directed my eyes to the man in the corner. He lounged upon an ornate chair, gulping without discretion from his cup, his mask of black and gold perched precariously across his vision. Snapping his fingers crudely, he made demands of the attendant to bring him more to drink. He would be an easy target, if not a pleasant one. I smoothed the front of my gown with my palms.

"Remain steadfast," Jonah whispered near my ear.

I woke to the sensation of something moving along my hip. I blinked the sleep from my eyes, not sure if I was still dreaming or not. When I looked down, I was on my side, and Hunter's wrist was resting on the side of my hip as his fingers traced a line down the front of it. I turned my head to find his blue eyes sparkling back at me.

"This is my favorite part of your body," he said as he continued to play along my skin.

"Is that so?" I asked.

"Mhmm." He moved forward and kissed me. "Followed by a very close second of this spot," he whispered, then pulled his hand back and brushed his fingers along my lower back as he kissed me again. "Oh, and this one," he added, sliding his hand down and over my thigh. "Actually, I think all of you is my favorite."

I smiled. "Good, then can you feed all of me? Because you interrupted my breakfast earlier."

He laughed as he wrapped his arms around me and pulled me tight. "Yes, I will make you anything you want."

"Even tea?"

"Yes." He brushed his lips against mine. "Even tea."

I reached up and ran my fingers across his cheek and into his hair, pulling him in closer as I kissed him. I could feel him smiling against my lips.

"If you keep doing that, I'm not going to leave the bed."

I laughed and pushed him gently away.

"Just don't cover up while I'm gone," he countered. I felt the heat rush to my face as I blushed. I was still naked. He gave me a full-dimpled smile in response before pulling away, tugging his sweats back on as he stood. "Stay there. I'll be back," he said.

He didn't honestly expect me to wait here, naked, on his bed? I shook my head and looked down at my jeans crumpled on the floor. I had some jean shorts in my bag, but nothing that was really comfortable enough to lounge in. I reached over for my phone to send Vincent a text.

Is there any way you could bring me some pajamas from my house? You didn't pack any.

His response was immediate. *I know. I've seen what you sleep in. You don't need them.*

Vincent.

If I can get in the house, I'll bring them. You should consider buying something more flattering though. And some fancier panties.

I had almost forgotten my house was a crime scene at the moment. How long would it take for them to clear everything out so I could get it cleaned up? I had snuck out the back door to avoid the view of John again. I wondered if it was just the carpet or if my sofa was ruined, too. I responded with: *Don't call my underwear panties. Just bring me some shorts, please.*

Buy new panties.

I shook my head as I sent back, *Buy yourself panties.*

I grabbed clean clothes from my bag and headed to the bathroom. It had a large tub and a separate shower. Everything in here was white, too. I had to question whether it was a good choice for a bathroom or not. Hunter didn't use makeup or anything that would smudge all this sparkly brightness, so I guess it was fine. White wouldn't have been my choice, but it wasn't my bathroom.

When I was under the water, enjoying the scalding heat, I realized I left my shampoo and body wash at the other house. I had grabbed my toothbrush but completely forgot everything in the shower. Of course. Hunter's shampoo was a tube with a big green leaf and the word organic on the front. It seemed harmless enough as I worked it through my hair.

Hopefully, I wouldn't end up with a bunch of tangles. Conditioner is a necessity for some of us. When I rinsed it out, I reached down and grabbed another white bottle. It was another self-proclaimed all-natural, organic product. When I popped the top open it smelled warm and woodsy and strongly of vanilla. That's why he smelled so damn good.

"Don't use that," Hunter's voice came from behind me, and I jumped, nearly dropping the bottle.

"What the hell is wrong with you?" I yelped, spinning to face him. "Can't you warn me when you walk in a room and not wait to be inches from me?"

He laughed as he stepped into the water with me, taking the bottle from my hand. "I wasn't being quiet when I came in. It's not my fault you didn't hear me."

He grabbed an identical bottle to the one he had taken from me.

"What was wrong with the other one?" I asked, trying to focus on his face and not the fact he was standing naked in front of me in a shower.

"I don't want you to smell like me." He smiled as he poured out the clear liquid in his hand. He lathered his hands together, and the shower filled with an oddly familiar scent of flowers and something sweet I couldn't place. Something edible for sure.

"That smells amazing," I said. I started to reach for the bottle when he gently grabbed my arm. He shook his head and leaned forward to kiss me as he reached out and ran his hands up my sides, smoothing the soap over me. I sucked in a breath.

"It smells like you." He breathed in and kissed me again, running his hands up over my shoulders, then down my arms. "You always wear stuff with pears and roses," he said softly.

That was the smell. Pears. "Do I want to know why you have soap that smells like me in your shower?" I asked, swallowing as he moved his hands down to my legs.

He laughed and kissed me again, pressing my back against the shower wall.

"What's the plan today?" I asked, trying to focus on anything other than where his hands were moving.

"This." He smiled back.

"What's this?" I asked.

"Ryder and Katie are watching some eighties horror movie marathon. They'll order food later. We're staying here."

"In the shower?" I asked as he leaned down to kiss me.

Hunter smiled. "Shower, bed, maybe somewhere more creative." He brushed his lips against mine softly. "You need a day off."

That actually sounded pretty good. "Okay, but did you make me tea?"

"Yes. It's on the nightstand. It will be cool enough to drink when I'm done here."

"Oh?"

"Mhmm," he breathed, then moved down to kiss my neck.

I leaned my head back and closed my eyes. "As long as you're still feeding me."

"Stop trying to distract me."

It was my turn to laugh. Yeah. Okay. I could use a day without any new self-realizations or dead bodies. I didn't say that out loud. It seemed a little insulting to imply having him kiss me in a shower was only exciting because it was better than finding a corpse in my living room.

CHAPTER 22

"WHERE are we putting these?" Vincent asked.

Hunter looked over his shoulder at the stack of chairs Vincent was holding up. "Just scatter them around the clearing. It's going to get colder tonight, so not far from the fires."

Vincent nodded and carried off the stack.

"When is Chris getting here?" I asked.

Hunter pulled out his phone and looked at the time. "Another hour. They'll help set up the drinks, but I want to get all the tables and chairs out."

Ryder had spent most of Friday afternoon and Saturday periodically spraying down the area around the clearing with water until Hunter had determined everything was safe enough to light bonfires that night. Will had texted that he would be here after making a stop. He was getting more clothing and things for Katie from her house. I was getting anxious and

189

glad he was going to be here to make sure things didn't get out of control. Katie was excitedly waiting for him on the porch steps.

"I'm done. I need to shower before anyone gets here," Vincent called out as he jogged back from the clearing.

"You mean before Aelina gets here?" I sang back.

"That's exactly what I mean, and you're not embarrassing me by pointing it out." He shrugged as he started toward the front door of the cabin.

I grinned after him.

Hunter pointed to the open garage door. He had moved the car and his bike out to make room. "We're going to set up in the garage. It should be close enough and safe from people accidentally walking in on anything." It seemed like a strangely domestic place to hold an ancient magical ritual. I guess the living room, next to his childhood pictures, would have been even stranger.

"Easier to clean the blood up off the floor too," Ryder added.

"You sounded a little too casual saying that," I said. "It was kind of creepy."

Ryder smirked and shrugged a shoulder. "It's true. I don't want your blood all over my game room."

I hadn't really thought about that. "It will be my blood won't it?"

"No. It will be mine," Hunter corrected.

I wrinkled my nose. I had been focusing on the more light-hearted part of the evening, which was the party. It was causing me enough stress thinking about intentionally dropping my shields to soak up as much energy as possible from the crowd. The gruesome mechanics of the actual ritual was something I had been actively avoiding.

"Tell me that's not what you're wearing?" Jessie's voice came from behind me, and I turned to see her closing her car door. She sauntered up to us in a short skirt and oversized blue sweater that hung off one shoulder. The heels on her boots were high enough I wasn't sure how she was going to walk all the way to the clearing in them, and she had a shiny, oversized bag slung over her shoulder.

"Hi, Jessie." I smiled.

"You're doing some epic magical shit tonight, and you're wearing a T-shirt with a panda on the front?" she scolded.

I looked down at my shirt. The panda was hugging a heart. "What's wrong with my shirt?"

"Nothing. If the only thing you were doing today was laundry."

Ouch. "Who woke you up on the wrong side of the broom this morning?"

Jessie rolled her eyes. "Come on, let's go see what other things you have to wear that you think pass as clothing."

"You're bossier than Vincent today," I said as she dragged me back into the house by my elbow. I looked back at Hunter, who gave me an apologetic face as he shook his head. He didn't even pretend to try and save me.

"I'm disappointed in Vincent if he's already seen you today and allowed you to wear that," she replied, then yelled at Katie. "Katie, you too! I brought some things in my bag."

"Is that why you're carrying the fashion week version of an overnight bag?" I asked as Katie jumped up to join us.

Jessie looked over her shoulder at me and smiled. It was the kind of smile that implied I wasn't going to like what she was thinking.

I turned to Katie and asked, "Should I be afraid right now?"

Katie laughed. "Probably."

When the three of us were alone in Hunter's room, Jessie started digging through my bag. She pulled out my black jeans and threw them at me, then grabbed a small, black piece of fabric from her bag. "Put these on."

I held up the strapless tube of fabric. "Where am I supposed to put this?"

"It's a shirt," Jessie said.

"According to whom?" I asked.

"Put it on," she demanded.

"Are you going to start telling me what panties to wear, too?" I muttered as I walked toward the bathroom.

I heard Jessie ask Katie, "What is she talking about?"

"I'm not really sure," Katie said.

I switched my jeans first. I didn't mind changing from the ones I already had on to the black pair—they were basically the same thing, just a different color. When I went to change the shirt, I had to take off my bra to be able to wear the sweetheart cut tube top Jessie had handed me. It was a nice fabric, minus the fact there wasn't nearly enough of it.

When I came out of the bathroom, I asked, "Why do I have to wear this again?"

"I don't really know how the ritual goes, but you're sharing blood, right?" Jessie asked.

I nodded. I actually didn't know what I was doing, and for once, I didn't pester Hunter for details. This was one of those situations where I did not want to get my anxiety up about anything sooner than necessary.

"This is easy access to your neck and wrists, and it's black just in case anything spills," she said.

I blinked at her. "I... did not expect that logical of a reason."

"Everything I wear is with purpose. You should know that by now," she chastised.

Sure. Hiding blood stains just didn't strike me as something she was usually strategizing around. I looked down at the shirt. "Alright, you win," I said.

"We need to put your hair up too, to keep it out of the way," she offered. Then Jessie handed Katie a black drape of fabric. "Your turn!"

Katie made a squealing sound and rushed past me to the bathroom. I don't think I'd ever seen her act so girly before. "What's with her?" I asked.

"Ryder almost kissed her yesterday. Now get over here so I can do your hair."

I laughed. Katie and Ryder had been alone most of the day in the basement, and he only almost kissed her. I was really glad he wasn't like Vincent at sixteen—or Hunter, for that matter.

Jessie tossed Hunter's hoodie on the bed and brought the chair to the center of the room. "Sit."

I did as she commanded. "You seem more pushy than normal. Everything okay?" I asked.

Jessie eyed me as she pulled a large makeup bag out of her purse. "Ian's not coming."

I raised my eyebrows. I had been wondering about that particular relationship dynamic. Jessie didn't date, supposedly. Yet, Ian had been attached to her side for weeks. Now she was upset that he wasn't around. That sure sounded like dating to me. "Any particular reason?"

"He had 'something to do tonight.'" She scowled as she started brushing my hair. "So, you're going to sit here and let me do what I want until I feel better."

If the worst thing I had to do to cheer Jessie up was let her brush my hair, it was a small price to pay for her happiness. "Do you want to talk about it?" I asked.

"No," she said sharply.

Okay, then.

"What do you think?" Katie asked from the door. She was smiling from ear to ear in a short, black slip dress with thin straps. The fabric was clingy and short, and she looked fabulous. Will was not going to like it.

"Not going to lie, you look amazing, but aren't you going to get cold in that?" I asked. It was still warm enough with the sun out, but we were getting very close to autumn, and at night it was chilly up here.

"Ryder will just have to stay super close," Jessie said smugly.

Katie's smile got even bigger. "Do my hair next?"

"Like I'd let you borrow that and go out half-finished."

I sat quietly as Jessie pulled my hair up into a hair tie, wrapping and doing who knew what with it. When she was done, she dug in her bag for eyeliner and came back over, leaning in front of me. "Close your eyes," she said. I did. When she finished and went to grab the mascara, she smirked at me. "Are you going to share about your day in bed with Hunter, or do Katie and I have to keep guessing?" she asked.

Katie bit her lip as I narrowed my eyes at her. "Did you text her about me and Hunter?" I asked.

"You told me to keep her in the loop." She shrugged, her palms up in an apologetic gesture.

"I meant about Jonah and the ritual. Not my sex life," I said.

"Your sex life is more interesting," Jessie said.

"How is that possible?" I asked.

"You're having sex with Hunter. Which, no one else I know has successfully managed. So, spill. And look up," Jessie demanded.

I stared at the ceiling as she spread mascara on my eyelashes. "I am not talking to you about Hunter," I said. My face was completely flushed from the conversation.

"He brought her food in bed," Katie added.

Okay. That was part of the day I didn't have an issue discussing. "He did feed me and make me tea."

"Of course, he did," Jessie said, followed by a sigh. "That sounds exactly like the kind of sweet gesture he would make."

I smiled before I could help myself. Hunter wasn't great at communicating his emotions—or anything, really—but he did often show them with actions. He knew my favorite foods, the music I was most moved by, and always went out of his way to make sure I was comfortable. Everything he did, from how he ran Not Right Now to planting pink roses in his yard, was centered around what he knew about my preferences and trying to please me. The fact I didn't like flowers in this lifetime was my issue.

Seeing my sappy expression, Jessie smiled mischievously at me. "Although, he was probably just trying to keep you from getting up and getting dressed."

Katie giggled as I scowled at Jessie. That was also closer to the truth than I was comfortable with. "Am I all done?" I asked.

She swatted at my shoulder to let me know I could leave the chair. I went to the bathroom to see what she had done to me. Whenever I put my hair up in a messy bun it looked exactly like the name suggested. Jessie had somehow made an intricate knot on the top of my head, with every piece of loose hair looking deliberate. I shook my head. The girl was gifted.

When I came back out of the bathroom, she was pulling Katie's hair up into a similar style. Without Katie's hair hiding her shoulders, the dress seemed that much more revealing. Will was going to murder me, and I bet he knew exactly where to hide a body. Katie looked delighted sitting there though. No amount of make-up or clothes could make her facial expressions anything less than sweet. It helped tone down what Jessie was trying to do, but only barely.

"Salut!" Chris's voice carried down the hall.

"We're in here!" I called through the door.

When they opened the door, I was greeted with the bright ener-getic aura that only Chris managed to maintain at all times. "Hey, Chris." I smiled.

"What are you all getting up to?" they asked, then looked Katie up and down before moving to me. Their eyebrows rose as they took in my top. "Should I run?"

I laughed. "I'd save myself if I were you. Jessie's in a mood."

Jessie snorted as she applied something to Katie's eyelids. "Chris knows how to dress themself."

I looked at Chris's outfit. They were wearing cropped, wide-leg linen pants and what looked like a vintage T-shirt tucked only in the front, with some band I didn't recognize on it. Sockless bright lace-up sneakers completed the outfit.

"Why do they get to wear a T-shirt?" I asked.

"Because Chris knows how to properly wear a T-shirt," Jessie countered.

Chris just smiled at her. "Merci." Then, turning to me, Chris made a wave motion with their hand. "This looks nice. I think you pull off T-shirts just fine though."

I laughed. "Thanks. Come on, I'll help you set up the drinks."

"We're right behind you," Jessie said, adding, "I can't wait to see Ryder's reaction."

I could. In fact, I did not want to be anywhere near either of them or their hormones the rest of the night. "I'll watch from a nice, safe distance," I said. "If you're smart, you'll make sure to get it over with before Will gets here. That's probably not a first reaction he should see."

Katie blushed bright red and hunched her shoulders. I was guess-ing she had forgotten she was going to be parading in front of her older brother all night, too. That got a smile and knowing look from Chris, who offered, "I'll keep Will busy for you."

"Thanks!" Katie beamed.

Chris shook their head and put an elbow out to me. "Shall we?"

I laced my arm through theirs. "We shall!"

CHAPTER 23

W HEN we walked out the back door, we were greeted with the warm, piney smell of the fire pits blazing. Katie and Jessie giggled quietly behind us as we made our way toward the clearing.

"Did Hunter tell you anything about tonight?" I asked Chris quietly.

Chris side-eyed me before answering, "I'm to keep everyone outside and away from the house—which should make it easy to keep my promise to Katie. Will's going to have to help me with that. This crowd is bigger than we usually permit, and they're excited after we took time off this summer."

I felt a pang of guilt. It was a minor thing, but yet another side effect of Jonah ruining stuff because of me. "Sorry that you had to cancel all your parties."

"No worries. They would have been less fun without all of you anyway," Chris offered.

Chris was always easygoing. It may have just been that, or the fact you couldn't help but soak up some of the pure happiness they always radiated, but they always seemed to make me feel better. "How are you so content all the time?" I asked.

Chris continued to watch me, then cocked their head to the side. "I will give you the advice someone I care deeply about once gave me."

"And what advice is that?"

"Accept who you are and stop apologizing to everyone about it. The rest of us love you. You should too," they said. Chris smiled at me and patted my hand as Jessie rushed past us with Katie, dragging her through the trees toward a table in the clearing. Somehow, Jessie had absolutely no trouble running in her heels. Again, gifted.

The two of them immediately started pulling cups out of the plastic wrappers. Chris made a nervous sound, then said, "I better hurry. Jessie might start mixing the punch without me. I don't want her trying to taste test it."

I laughed. "Need me to do anything?" I asked.

"Just be you." Chris squeezed my arm before leaving to join Katie. As predicted, Jessie was already trying to open a container of red punch to pour it into a cooler. I shook my head as I watched Chris chide her, then take on the role of instructor as they explained the ratios of alcohol to sugary punch mixture.

A dog barking caught my attention, and I turned to see Aelina sauntering toward me. She was in a cropped, low-cut top and shorts. She managed to look casual and beautiful with her hair down. Dry, it flowed in much softer curls. Vincent was strolling just behind her, watching her as she walked. A second later, a large dog bounded toward me, running in circles around my feet.

"Hey, pup!" I called, kneeling down to pet the overly excited animal. She whined and tried to lick my face as I laughed and held her back. She was a beautiful American Pit Bull. Her jowls stretched up happily in a smile-like expression as her tongue flopped about.

"This is Nala!" Aelina said. "I hope it's okay I brought her?"

"It's great!" I said.

"What are you wearing?" Vincent asked, looking me up and down. The corner of his mouth was tucked up into a smirk.

"Something that's pretending to be a shirt," I said as I rubbed behind Nala's ears to calm her down. She sat in front of me and wiggled her face into my lap as I scratched at her fur.

"I love it," Aelina offered.

I smiled at her. "Nala is a sweetheart."

"She's my baby!" Aelina patted at her thigh, causing the dog to draw from my lap and lope over to her. "I'm surprised she likes the two of you so much. She's usually more guarded."

Vincent reached out to pet her, and she licked his hand. He smiled as he scratched at the scruff of her neck. "She knows good people when she smells them," Vincent offered, talking more to the dog than Aelina.

"So, it is the dog you're interested in," Hunter said as he walked up next to Vincent. He was carrying a large blue cooler.

Vincent narrowed his eyes at Hunter but didn't comment.

Hunter smirked at him, then turned to me. The expression froze on his face as he took in my outfit and hair. I smiled up at him from where I was crouched on the ground. He blinked, then smiled back.

"I like pandas, but this is nice," he said, then motioned with the cooler. "I need to put this down. I'll be back."

Ryder was following close behind him, his arms full of a second cooler.

"Need help, little man?" Vincent asked.

"Thanks, man. I got it," Ryder said as he walked past us.

"Oh, this should be good," I said as I stood, turning to watch him carry the cooler over to a table next to the one the girls and Chris were working at. I made sure my shields were snapped tightly in place as I took in the show.

"What should be good?" Vincent and Aelina both asked.

I wiggled my finger at Katie. She was leaning forward on her hands on the table, peering over the cooler Chris was mixing punch in, listening intently. Normally, Katie would have just looked like her cute, curious self. I doubted she was even aware her posture was showing off that short dress to its best advantage. We all watched as Ryder caught sight of her and tripped, dropping one end of the cooler.

"Shit!" he said, scrambling to collect the cooler before anything spilled out. He was still staring at Katie as he gathered it back into his arms and carried it over to Hunter. Not watching what he was doing, he didn't quite lift it high enough to slide it onto the tabletop, bumping into it instead. Hunter looked up at him, a confused expression on his face as Ryder shook his head apologetically. Ryder finally managed to get the cooler on the table and ran his fingers through his hair.

"What the hell is he doing?" Vincent asked. His eyes squinted as he looked at Katie, trying to figure out why Ryder was reacting that way to a girl, then they went wide as the realization hit him. He took a step back. "Is that Katie?"

"Behold. The power of Jessie." I laughed.

Aelina made an approving noise. "Can I sign up next?"

"This is apparently her version of eating ice cream out of the container. So, tonight may be your lucky night—if you're serious about letting her do a makeover," I said.

"Ice cream? What happened?" Vincent asked.

"Ian had other plans of some kind. She was really upset about it but didn't want to talk. Instead, she decided to engage in a cathartic round of dress-up with Katie and me," I shook my head.

"That was kind of her," Vincent muttered, still looking at Katie.

"Maybe. I'm not sure Ryder would find us all witnessing his reaction a very kind gesture on Jessie's part," I said, watching Ryder lean against the table as he stared over at Katie. He looked afraid to approach her.

"Maybe not kind to him, but very kind to the rest of us. At least we'll have some entertainment tonight while you and Hunter are inside," Vincent said.

I turned to look at him. "What do you mean?"

"During the binding?" he asked.

"You're not going to be there?" I asked.

Vincent raised his eyebrows. "I thought you knew that. Hunter asked us all to make sure no one interrupted." He gestured toward Aelina and the tables where everyone else was gathered. "The six of us are managing the crowd with Will."

I grimaced. I didn't want to do this alone. What if something went wrong again? I suppose it was better if Vincent wasn't nearby if it did. I didn't exactly know how the ritual would go tonight. He was probably safer outside. Seeing my pained facial expression, Vincent reached out.

"Hey, love, come here." He pulled me into a hug and kissed the top of my head. "Everything will be fine. I'll be right here."

Aelina patted my back softly. "I don't understand. Why are you scared?" she asked.

Flustered, I pulled away from Vincent. It was rude of me to hug him in front of her. She didn't know our relationship well enough yet, and I didn't want to cause them issues. I turned, expecting her to be annoyed, but Aelina's hazel eyes were watching me with concern, her eyebrows pulled together.

"The last time we tried this, Benny ended up dead. I'm just nervous I'll do something wrong again," I said.

"Girl, you got this," she said firmly. "From what I understand, last time you weren't the one in charge. You know how it is. You want something done right, you ask a woman to do it."

I laughed.

"She's not wrong." Vincent shrugged.

I heard a crowd of people heading toward where we stood. "Guess we're getting started," I said. I looked at the sky. There was just a sliver of light left. By the time I walked back into the house, Benny would be up. "I'm going to go check on Benny quick. Tell Hunter I'll be right back?"

Vincent nodded.

"Let's get a drink!" Aelina said, tugging Vincent toward the table.

"As long as it's not the punch," he said. As they strode away, he turned back to me with an exaggerated smile as he made a wave motion at Aelina's body, then mouthed, "So hot."

I laughed and looked over to where Hunter had his arm on Ryder's shoulder. He was saying something quietly as Ryder nodded in agreement. Hopefully, it didn't include suggesting Ryder try dipping into the liquid courage tonight.

After making sure he was up and ready to go, I left Benny anxiously pacing the garage. I really hated leaving him there, but I needed to be near the crowd to gather up as much energy as possible for the ritual. In theory, I could do it from the house. Closer proximity made it easier though. I lit his candles for him before I left. Silently wishing they would help soothe him.

Hunter and I both stood near the outside of the gathering, watching everyone interact. It was a huge party. I was glad we were at the cabin. I couldn't imagine this not getting broken up by the police if it was in town, and Will still hadn't shown up. Luckily, Vincent was doing a good job directing attention. When it came to engineering a crowd, he and Chris were a force. Jessie and Aelina settled right into the center of it all too, perfectly comfortable with the excess of bodies around them. So many extroverts in one place should have been a cosmic imbalance.

Hunter had his arm around my waist, his fingers tracing along the bare skin on my hip. It was really distracting with our shields completely down and his spirit tingling along my skin. I leaned back into him, raising my head up to tell him to stop. He took the gesture to mean I was looking for a kiss and bent forward to press his lips against mine. It sent a sharp shot of energy into me, and I pulled away. "I'm supposed to be gathering energy from everyone else, not stealing it from you," I whispered.

"Sorry, I'll try to focus more," he whispered back, then kissed my bare shoulder. "In a minute."

I laughed and pulled away from him. His mouth tucked up in a smile on one side as he reached out to grab me.

"Hunter."

"Fine." He shoved his hands in his pockets and grinned at me. "I'm behaving."

I shook my head as I turned back to the crowd. It was easier for me. I didn't need to focus on any specific emotion like Hunter did. And there was plenty to go around. Lust, excitement, anxiety… jealousy. I paused at that last one. It left a familiar taste on the back of my tongue. I looked around the crowd to find Ryder sitting in a chair. He was hunched down, flipping his phone around in his hands as he stared across the clearing. I followed his line of sight to see Katie. She was near one of the fires, laughing with Jessie and Vincent. Another male I didn't know was getting a little overly close to her. As I made that acknowledgment, I felt another spike from Ryder.

I turned to Hunter. "You going to do something about that before he ends up in a fistfight with someone?" I asked.

"I tried. If he doesn't want to listen to me, it's a lesson he'll have to figure out on his own." Hunter shrugged.

"Some big brother you are," I said as I started toward Ryder.

"Where are you going?" Hunter asked.

"I'm going to help."

Hunter hesitated. "I don't know if he really wants that."

I shot a look over my shoulder at him. "Too bad. Whatever he's doing, he can't be doing it tonight."

He raised his eyebrows before saying, "Good luck."

I made my way over to Ryder, then sat in the chair next to him. We both relaxed there quietly, watching Katie. She was giggling and chatting with Jessie and Vincent, her usual animated hand motions assisting her descriptions. She stole an occasional look over at Ryder, but Jessie kept pulling her back into the conversation. I had a feeling Jessie knew exactly what it was doing to Ryder. It was probably part of some elaborate plan of hers.

"While I appreciate you offering up your energy for tonight, what gives?" I finally asked him.

Without looking at me, he asked, "What do you mean?"

"This is the farthest apart I've seen the two of you in days. Why are you over here, stewing in your own emotions, while Katie is over there?" I asked. I didn't think they had gotten into any disagreements, and I knew Katie's goal at the start of the night was not to be this far away from him. She looked over and gave him a shy smile, then laughed at something Vincent said. Ryder's spirit spiked again.

"Seriously. What is going on with you?" I pressed.

He looked at me out of the corner of his eye. "She doesn't need me anymore."

"What do you mean 'need you'?" I asked.

He let out a breath, then leaned forward on his knees, staring down at the rectangular phone as he continued to fidget with it. "Before, she needed to be around me. I helped with her depression. She doesn't need me to do that now, so why would she even want to be with me?"

"You're kidding right?"

He looked up at me. The look in his eyes told me he was very serious. "She's been over there the whole night. Why not come over here if she wants to be near me?"

"Probably because she's freezing in that ridiculous outfit," I muttered, then shook my head. "The only reason she doesn't 'need you' anymore is that you literally gave her your soul. You think that doesn't matter to her? Besides, would you rather a girl be with you because she has to or because she wants to?" He bit his lip and looked at her as I continued to rant. "You know she's dressed up like that for you? Not for any of the other losers here. You. She was practically squealing with delight when Jessie threw that dress at her, all over the reaction she was hoping to get out of you." I poked him in the arm.

"Okay, enough, I got it," he said. Sitting up straighter, he asked, "She really wore the dress for me?"

"Yes, really. That girl is dying for you to kiss her already," I said, motioning toward Katie. "Enough that she's freezing her butt off in a tiny piece of fabric to get your attention—which is also why she hasn't moved two inches from the fire pit."

Ryder's eyebrows raised. "I didn't know if she really wanted me to. She seems fine just hanging out, and after my mistake at the drive-in, I didn't want to ruin everything." Pausing, he looked away before adding quietly, "I haven't done this before. The last relationship I remember was an arranged one."

"Wow," I said, "and you gave Hunter a hard time over not dating for a few decades."

He grinned at me then. "Does she really want me to kiss her?"

I shook my head and put my hands up. "Uh, uh, no. No, that is not a question for me. That's a conversation for the two of you to have. Go ask her if you can kiss her."

He gave me a mortified look. "Ask her?"

"Yes. Give it a whirl."

"Won't that be awkward?" he asked, shifting uncomfortably in his chair.

I raised an eyebrow at him. "You mean, more awkward than never kissing her? No."

"You know what I mean," he said.

"Let me phrase it this way. Picture this," I said. I put my hand on my heart and leaned toward him dramatically. "Katie sees you from across the party, saunters toward you, eyes only for you. When she approaches, she stares into your face, leans forward, then whispers in your ear." I leaned into him and whispered, "Please, can I kiss you? …"

Ryder swallowed hard as he blinked at me.

"Would you find that awkward?" I prodded.

He shook his head, then stammered, "N-No."

I sat back in my seat. "Go ask her if you can kiss her. Just, please, let me get far away from the two of you beforehand."

He laughed abruptly, then said, "I can do that."

I stood to go back to my spot next to Hunter. I was on the verge of being uncomfortably full of energy, and we needed to get this show over with soon. As I started to walk away, Ryder called to me. "Hey, Sen," he said. I turned to look at him, and he added, "Thanks."

I smiled down at him. "Remember, sultry eye contact."

He gave me a big dimply smile.

I shook my head. "Or, sure, go with the big brown eyes and dimples. Obviously, that works for her, or she wouldn't have put up with a boyfriend that didn't kiss her this long."

He laughed again.

As I walked toward Hunter, I noticed his posture was tense. He was standing next to a figure in a leather jacket, their face hidden by waves of black hair.

"What the hell do you want?" I asked as I approached.

Fulton turned to me, a smirk on his face. "Good to see you too, sugar."

"Stop with the pet names, Fulton. Why are you here?"

He rolled his shoulders, shifting the jacket. "I figured you kids could use an extra hand."

"Oh, suddenly you want to help?" Crossing my arms over my chest, I glared at him.

"Look, I know you think I'm a bad guy. After tonight you won't be as angry at me, I guarantee it," Fulton said.

"Still doubtful," I said.

Hearing the commotion, Vincent wandered over, putting his hand on my back to let me know he was behind me. His bare skin on mine made a spark of energy, causing him to yank his hand away quickly. "Sorry," he said.

"That was interesting," Fulton said, his eyes darting between us.

"No one gives a damn what you find interesting, Fulton," I said.

Hearing the hostility in my voice, Vincent tensed and stepped forward, putting himself between me and the other man. "What did he do?"

Great. With everything going on, I still hadn't told Vincent about Fulton.

Before I could say anything, I heard Ryder behind me snort and reply, "That's Sen's dad."

Why did he pick now to decide to socialize with the group? "Way to repay me," I whispered to Ryder.

He squeezed his lips together and dipped his head apologetically.

Vincent looked over to me, eyes wide. "Wait. For real?"

I made a shrugging motion at Vincent. "Yeah."

"How did you not tell me this?"

"It's been a rough week," I said, then added, "Considering the stuff you didn't tell me until the last few days, I don't want to hear it."

Vincent clenched his fists.

"Nice to meet you, kid," Fulton said, holding out his hand.

Vincent turned to the other man. I watched him blink as he stared at Fulton's outreached hand. Then he looked up … and punched Fulton in the face.

"Fuck!" Fulton exclaimed, reaching up to catch the blood spurting from his nose.

Vincent shook his hand off. "Nice to meet you too, asshole."

"Vincent!" I yelled.

Fulton looked over at Hunter as he spoke through his bloody nose, "Actually, I was expecting that reaction more out of you."

Vincent huffed, aiming his own glare at Hunter. "Yeah, people have been saying that a lot lately."

Hunter's eye twitched, but otherwise, he ignored the jab.

I sighed. "Let's get you some ice for that."

Fulton smiled at me around his hand. He was squeezing his nostrils to keep the blood from spurting all over the ground. I hoped it hurt. "Thank you," he said.

"I wasn't talking to you," I said as I tugged at Vincent's sleeve, carefully avoiding his skin.

"I'm fine." Vincent pulled his arm away from me. He was still staring Fulton down, and I could feel the anger radiating off him. Most of it was at Fulton. I was pretty sure a good chunk of it was there for me, too.

I looked over at Fulton. "You want me to heal that?"

He hesitated, eyeing Vincent. "As long as that one can control himself long enough to let you near me."

Vincent put his hands up in a surrender motion. "She can do whatever the fuck she wants. It's her body."

Yup. He was definitely mad at me. I stalked up to Fulton, with my sweetest smile on display. He moved his hand out of the way, giving me access to his face. I reached up, gently grabbed his nose, and then snapped it back in place as I shoved energy into him. He winced and yanked my hand away, swallowing a curse. He wiped the last bit of blood pouring down his lip onto the back of his hand. "I may have deserved that, but it's the last shit I'm taking from you over the leaving thing."

"No deal," I said. "How about, I fixed your face, so you do whatever it is you came to do, and we call it even?"

Fulton narrowed his eyes at me.

"I can rebreak it if you don't like her terms?" Vincent offered.

Fulton pulled his head back and eyed Vincent, then gave me a slight shrug of his head. "Ready to give the rest of your soul away?" he asked.

I looked over at Hunter. He had been unusually calm through the entire exchange. "Yeah. Let's get this over with."

Fulton grunted, then elbowed Hunter. "Hope her excitement isn't too overwhelming for you."

Hunter's lip twitched in a snarl at Fulton. Rather than answer, he stepped up, putting his arm around me.

"Vincent, you got this?" I asked, motioning to the party.

Vincent made a curt nod, not taking his eyes off Fulton. Fulton just smirked at him as he sauntered past Vincent to follow us.

Ryder patted Vincent's shoulder, making a motion with his head toward where Katie and the others were watching us from the firepit.

As the three of us started back to the house, I watched Ryder walk up to Katie. A delighted smile spread across her face as she realized he was coming over to her and not returning to the seat he'd been brooding in all night.

"Wait, wait." I tugged at Hunter to stop walking.

"What?" he asked.

"Shhh." I hushed him so I could spy on Ryder.

Ryder grabbed Katie's hand. She giggled and followed him as he walked backward, tugging her away from the group. A smile spread across my face when he leaned forward, whispering something in her ear. Katie's face turned red enough I could see it from across the clearing. She nodded, biting her lip as she looked up at him. He leaned forward and kissed her, wrapping his arms around her.

"How cute," Fulton said.

I snapped at him. "Shut up!"

Hunter laughed. "Did you do that?"

"I may have instigated it a little." I held my fingers up, making a pinched measurement.

Hunter shook his head. "And you questioned why anyone would pray to you for your love blessings."

"Being a succubus apparently has its perks." I shrugged.

"It does," Fulton agreed. "Although, helping teenagers make out wouldn't be on my list. Seems like a waste of energy."

I narrowed my eyes at him. That perpetual smirk of his widened as he tilted his head, pulling down the collar of his jacket. He had an identical birthmark to mine. Not just similar, like Hunter and Ryder had, but exactly the same. "That's why Beth was nice to you. She usually has better asshole radar," I said.

"Beth?" Fulton asked.

"The server. At the diner." I shook my head. Naturally, he didn't bother to look at her nametag.

"Sure, sure. She made good coffee. Not much to look at though."

I felt my nostrils flare.

Hunter pressed his lips together and began dragging me back toward the cabin again. Under his breath, he said, "Let's get inside before you change your mind about using a sacrifice."

"How does being stuck indoors with him help with that?" I scoffed.

"Fewer witnesses," he whispered, then kissed the side of my head.

I laughed.

"Which one of us asked the other for help again? Oh right. Wasn't me," Fulton said.

"Yeah, well, it wasn't me either," I said. Fulton and Hunter both stayed silent as we navigated through the dark. It seemed neither of them wanted to continue instigating my mouth. There was a chance before the night was over, I might appreciate Fulton showing up. I wasn't feeling it yet though.

CHAPTER 24

B ENNY greeted me as soon as we walked out into the garage. He was crackling with anxious energy. "Sorry that took so long," I apologized.

He chimed in response. He was as nervous as I was about everything. I watched as his figure looked around, then he made another low sound.

"Katie's with Ryder at the party. They're all staying back to make sure no one wanders into the house. It's just us." I gave him a gentle pat as his posture fell. "I promise I will text her as soon as we're done. She'll be the first person to get to see you."

"Besides me," Fulton corrected.

Benny and I both narrowed our eyes at him, and the lights flickered.

"That's Fulton. Believe me, you don't want to know," I said.

"Why do you say that?" Fulton asked. "He might like me."

Hunter laughed. "No. He won't. He might break more things than Vincent."

I felt Benny tense beside me. "Don't worry," I assured him, "Fulton is… friendly." Fulton raised his eyebrow at me, and I added, "And if it turns out he's not, you'll be able to knock him on his ass here soon."

Fulton grunted and shook his head. "You're more violent than I remember."

"Thanks," I said.

He gave me a chuckle, then walked to the center of the garage floor. He leaned down with his hand, which was still covered in blood from his face, and started to trace symbols in the ground. I could feel the heat coming off the energy as it poured out of him and into the concrete.

"What are you doing?" I asked.

"Getting you started. Thanks to your overzealous friend, I'm a close enough proxy to a sacrifice. Plus, I'm your bloodline, whether we like it or not."

I watched as the blood on the floor brightened and radiated from the spirit he offered into it. He had gathered up almost as much as I had for the night, and he offered it all up into the writing.

I looked at Hunter. "Is it safe to let him help?" I asked.

Standing, Fulton said, "Funny that you would trust him with that judgment call."

"No amount of power would tempt Fulton to be stuck with the two of us," Hunter said, ignoring Fulton's shot at him. He joined the other man.

Fulton smirked at Hunter. "I don't know. She seems to have broken you down enough to make you tolerable."

Ignoring him, Hunter pulled a knife out of his pocket and made a shallow gash on the inside of his own palm. I guess we were getting right to it then. He began using his hand to draw a circle on the ground. I was thankful they had washed down the floor earlier.

"Do I have to do that?" I asked.

Fulton shook his head. "No, but you and Benjamin should be inside before he invokes it."

I looked over at Benny, who made a motion as if he were shrugging. I knew the feeling. We moved forward to stand inside the circle. Okay, Jessie was right. I would have felt silly doing this with a panda on my shirt. Writing a ritual on the ground while surrounded by snow shovels and toolboxes was amusing enough.

While Benny and I hovered awkwardly in the center, Hunter closed the circle around the three of us. It sealed and flared to life. I took two steps forward and held my hands up to it like warming them at a fire. It felt like Hunter. Like the crackling heat that came off him when I touched him. I wanted to run my hands along it, but I remembered well enough what it had felt like when I touched the circle Jonah had created. I kept my distance. Underneath the warmth of Hunter, there was a trace of something even more familiar. I looked over at Fulton.

"You didn't just mean you're my bloodline because of this lifetime," I said.

"Caught enough clues on that, did you?"

I inspected the energy of the circle. I could have started it myself for as much as it felt like me. "You're my biological father this lifetime, but our souls are made of the same energy. Doesn't that mean we're even more closely tied as family, outside of these bodies?" If that was the case, what was the big deal about him being my parent this go around?

Benny made an angry noise behind me.

Hunter stepped next to Benny as they both looked out at Fulton. To my surprise, Benny didn't respond to Hunter being so close to him. Guess he had someone new to be upset with.

"Family is a loose term. We're made of the same lineage, but we keep our distance," Fulton said.

"Why?" I asked. Ryder had already shared an explanation, but I wanted to hear Fulton's version … or excuse.

"Imagine the havoc and fighting several Jonah's together would create. You would have nothing but wars and death raging around you. Best case, they all fought each other for control. Worst case, they come to some agreement and create a power structure. If there are family bonds, the second is more likely. Jonah caused enough trouble on his own until his obsession with you distracted him," he said.

I heard Jonah's voice in my head saying, *"Not all of us can have your attention as our distraction from this dullness."*

Hunter reached out to grab my hand and pull me closer to him. I stood in front of him as he looked down at me. "Last chance. We can always figure something else out."

I looked over at Benny. "No, I can't risk testing ideas out on him."

Benny gargled quietly.

"I know you're okay with how things are. But I'm not." Benny didn't deserve to be stuck like this.

Hunter held the knife up to his neck and made another small incision on his skin.

Sounding surprised, Fulton muttered, "Interesting choice."

I turned my head to question him, but Hunter reached out, grabbing my cheek. He turned me back to face him. As blood welled and dripped down his throat, I swallowed. I could already feel all the spirit under his skin. "Am I supposed to drink it?"

Fulton laughed from outside the circle. "That is how this works, yes."

I wrinkled my nose. "Gross."

Hunter chuckled quietly. "If you're changing your mind, make it quick, please. I'm bleeding all over my shirt."

I put my hand on his shoulder to steady myself, then leaned in tentatively. Hunter wrapped his arms around my waist as I braced myself. I looked over at Benny, who was levitating as he anxiously watched. "Could you turn around, please?" I asked.

He made an indignant chirp.

"Because this is uncomfortable. Turn around." The last time Hunter took blood from me, I passed out. I wasn't certain what was going to happen, but based on that experience, I didn't want witnesses.

Benny spun around, and he made sure his motions were exaggerated so that I knew how silly he thought I was being.

"You, too," I said to Fulton.

Fulton gave me an eye roll and turned away.

Hunter smiled softly at me, then closed his eyes, turning his head away. I appreciated the gesture. It didn't really help, though, since it was his blood I was about to drink. It's the thought that counts though, right?

His pulse sped up as I moved to close my mouth on his neck. I closed my eyes as I took a deep breath, then pressed my lips to him. The metallic taste on my tongue almost made me pull away, but then I felt all the spirit inside of him rushing toward me in a wave.

I don't know why we call it feeding. When you're hungry, you feel it. It's a nagging feeling. It's uncomfortable. Then you sate your appetite with whatever craving, and it goes away.

This was not food.

All the power Hunter had been holding poured into me. I thought I had pulled as much into myself as I could take at the party. Somehow his spirit, and everything with it, filled an empty space in my soul I didn't know was there. It was warm and good, and I could have stayed like this forever. There would never be enough of him to make me want to stop. I had the faintest awareness as Hunter's hand reached out and circled my wrist. He lifted it to his mouth, placing a kiss on the inside of my wrist, then whispered, "Mi flerthrce." As the words left his mouth, all the energy between us swirled. It blew out around us, crashing into Benny and shattering the circle to pieces.

I pulled away enough to see Hunter's beautiful blue eyes watching me with concern. Then a searing pain shot through my head, and I gasped as my knees buckled. Hunter held me, lowering us both to the ground.

"You can't keep this up, Jonah," I said, reaching for him.

He looked over his shoulder at me, the anger on his face burning into my core.

"I know why you're here. I won't be manipulated by you."

Lights flashed behind my lids as my mind shifted through images.

I sprawled on the blanket in the grass, staring at the clouds. I twirled the rose Hunter gifted me between my fingers.

Hunter smiled down at me. "Will you be cross with me if I kiss you?" he asked, leaning toward me.

"Is a kiss what you want?" I asked.

"More than anything," he said.

Hunter's face blurred and was replaced with the image of a woman standing in front of me. Her silver hair was piled on top of her head. Even with her age, her skin was soft and beautiful.

"Everly," I called.

The layers of her skirt swooshed as she turned, a smile on her face. Her gray eyes shimmered with happiness at the sight of me. "The journey wasn't difficult, I hope?"

I shook my head as I approached her. I reached out to embrace her, and the image shifted again. My hand hit a teacup, knocking it off the table.

I watched the fragile porcelain fracture on the floor and kneeled down to clean it.

When I looked back up, Hunter was kneeling next to me as we watched the priest talking. An ornate cathedral surrounded us. The light shining through the brightly colored stained glass painting colors on the ground.

"I want to remember this one, always," I whispered.

Hunter's hand reached over and enveloped mine.

All the images were flickering so quickly, I couldn't process what I was seeing. My head hurt. Really hurt. I squeezed my eyes tight as I pressed my hand to my temple. I felt sick like I was on an amusement ride and couldn't get off.

I stared into a woman's face. The black eyes that peered back at me weren't human.

"Do you comprehend what you're offering?" she asked.

"Yes."

After a pause, she nodded. "You will bear the consequences if you fail."

A familiar voice came from behind me, "She won't fail."

"What have you done?" The woman's face faded at the sound of Everly's panic searing through my head. I held Benjamin's hand. His shirt was damp from sweat, but he was awake now.

I turned to see Everly standing in the doorway. Benjamin sat up, ready to come to my defense, but Everly put a warning hand up at him. She hurried forward, taking my face into her hand. "We must hide you. They cannot discover you like this."

Then, as quickly as it had come on, it stopped. I held my breath as I slowly opened my eyes. Hunter was brushing my hair out of my face, his hand running down my cheek. "Sen?" His blue eyes were full of concern as he peered at my face. He was always handsome to me, but this version was very nice. This version?

"Hi," I said, reaching up to run my fingers through his curls.

He let out a nervous laugh. "Hi, beautiful."

His words made me smile, and I pulled him down for a kiss. He let out a relieved breath as he pressed his mouth to mine, and I closed my eyes at the feel of him. I missed him. Which didn't make any sense as he hadn't gone anywhere.

"Could the two of you stop necking?" a voice called.

My eyes snapped open. "Benjamin?"

I looked up to see a familiar face scrunched up with disgust at Hunter and me.

"Benjamin! You're here!" I pushed away from Hunter as I moved to stand.

Benjamin smiled warmly at me, his expression softening at my excitement. I smiled back at him. My heart was happy to see this face I never thought I'd look into again. His brown hair fell in waves to his shoulders. His bare shoulders.

"Why are you naked?" I asked.

Benjamin looked down at his body. "Well, that's just perfect, isn't it?"

I tried to not laugh as I turned away, putting my back to him. I didn't need to see this.

"I'll get him some clothes," Hunter offered. He kissed my cheek, then jumped up, jogging into the house.

"I'd ask if I can turn around yet, but it sounds like I don't want to," Fulton said.

"Probably not." I chuckled. "Nice of you to risk your neck, Fulton."

Fulton made a dismissive grunt. "I owed you."

"Are we not angry with him?" asked Benjamin.

I eyed the back of Fulton's head. My mind was still categorizing my memories. It would take a few days before I was fully sorted out. It was disorienting, but he was right, I was fine with his choice to not stick around and pretend to raise me. I didn't understand it, but he had taken a risk tonight, offering up his own blood and energy to help. It didn't seem like a big deal, but a part of my brain was surprised. It went a long way. "No. We're not angry with him."

"I think perhaps I will make that decision for myself, thank you. You do trust the worst men," Benjamin said.

"Hey," Fulton called over his shoulder, "don't blame me for this situation."

My phone started vibrating, and I looked down to see a mess of messages from Katie and Vincent, both asking if everything was okay. Apparently, they could feel the ritual from the clearing. I quickly typed back at Katie: *Hunter's getting Benny some clothes. Hurry up to the house!*

"Katie's on her way." I smiled.

"Dear heavens. She's not going to find me like this?"

Hunter laughed, and I turned to see him walk through the door, a pile of clothes in his hands.

"Here," he said to Benjamin.

I kept myself turned away and listened to the sound of fabric moving as Benjamin fought his way into the unfamiliar fabric. Hunter came to stand in front of me, a smile on his face as he ran his hands down my arms.

"Benny!" Katie's voice echoed into the garage as she ran through the door. I turned just in time to see her slam into Benjamin. My mind corrected me. *Benny.* He had managed to get the jeans on but only had one arm inside of a T-shirt as he wrapped his arms around her in a hug. His body flickered as she came in contact with him.

"What was that?" I asked.

Katie pulled back from their embrace, her eyebrows laced together as she looked at him. "Benny, you're not alive."

He looked down where she placed her hand over his heart, and his skin rippled with energy.

"No. It appears I'm not." He looked over at Hunter. "What a surprise, you botched it up again."

"Nothing went wrong with the ritual," Fulton said. "This is an unprecedented situation. It's one thing to heal a small flesh wound, but it's another to create an entire body."

I raised my eyebrow at him defending Hunter, then I realized he probably took Benny's comment personally since he helped. He was right though. The ritual was never going to be powerful enough to manifest an entire vessel for Benny. It was impressive enough that he was as corporeal as he was. I wouldn't have thought that possible.

Benny took Katie's face in his hands and looked her over. "How are you, Katie?"

"I'm great," she said, smiling up at him.

His eyebrows furrowed as he searched for something. "You do seem abnormally happy."

"Benny, what have you been up to?" I asked.

His cheeks flushed.

"You've been feeding off of her," I said. Of course, he had. Katie had been perfectly calm and content for days, despite everything, because Benny was siphoning off any negative emotions before they could settle. "Benjamin, you shouldn't have done that. Katie needs to process her feelings without so much intervention."

He wrapped his arms around her and shook his head. "I can't bear her suffering."

Katie wrinkled her forehead in confusion. "What are you talking about?"

"What's up, Benny?" Vincent called from the entrance. He was standing behind Ryder, who was frozen in the doorway, alarmed at seeing Katie still wrapped in Benny's half-naked hug.

"Benny, you should put your shirt on," I said.

He looked down, the expression on his face giving away his embarrassment. "My apologies, Katie. That was utterly inappropriate." He pulled away from her and tugged at the shirt awkwardly until he had it on. As he looked down at it, he said, "This is barely better than being naked. I can't believe you go out like this."

Katie giggled as she wrapped her arms around him for another hug.

"You'll get used to it," Hunter offered.

"I don't need advice from you, serpent."

"Benny," I scolded.

"The murderer's opinion is worthless," Benny said.

"I was not trying to kill you." Hunter sighed.

"Oh. My mistake. Am I the only person to die at your hand?"

I started to protest, but … well, he had a point. Hunter wrapped himself around me from behind. He pulled me close, then leaned down to kiss my neck, but he kept his eyes pointedly on Benny.

"Don't antagonize him," I whispered.

Benny pulled away from Katie and crossed his arms over his chest as he glared at Hunter. Vincent motioned at Ryder to move into the garage. Based on his body language, he was anticipating a fight between Benny and Hunter. I wondered who he would side with if they started throwing blows. Probably Benny.

Ryder took Katie's hand in his, pulling her back gently against him. He wrapped his arm around her, mimicking Hunter's body language. Oh good. Benny was making them both uncomfortable.

"You always had terrible taste in suitors," Benny snorted.

Vincent laughed.

Raising his eyebrow, Benny nodded his head toward Vincent. "Case in point. I'm sure Vincent wouldn't kill someone," he said.

Vincent pressed his lips together in amusement. I think if he wasn't enjoying Benny dragging Hunter, he might have disputed that statement.

"Vincent is also a human," I added.

"Even better," Benny said. Then he leaned toward Vincent. "I was rooting for you, pal."

Vincent whispered back, "I appreciate you recognizing I'm superior boyfriend material, but not everyone wants to date your sister."

Benny smiled. "She *is* a bit of a handful."

"Trust me, I know," Vincent said. He put a fist up at Benny, who eyed it curiously, then imitated the motion. Vincent bumped his knuckles to Benny's.

"Oh right, yes. Comradery." Benny nodded approvingly at the gesture.

"Benny, we should really work on updating your vocabulary," Vincent said. "You sound like Sen's grandpa." I smothered a laugh. He really did sound like my grandfather. Benny was only nineteen when he died, but he had been dead a while. Not being able to communicate verbally all this time, he hadn't had a chance to make a habit of current speech patterns. "You should lay off Hunter a bit too. He's been good to her," Vincent added.

Both Hunter and Benny made surprised sounds at Vincent's comment. Benny then narrowed his eyes. "I expected better from you."

"Who do you think convinced me to date Hunter this time?" I asked, causing Hunter to raise his eyebrows.

Scowling, Benny opened his mouth to respond, but Fulton interrupted him. "As much fun as this family reunion is to witness, I'm going to be on my way."

"I appreciate the help," I said.

"Sorry about your face, asshole," Vincent added and dismissed Fulton with a wave.

"What did you do to his face?" Benny asked.

"Broke his nose."

"I'm sure he deserved it," Benny concluded.

"Sure, *he* assaults someone, and you blame the other person." Hunter shook his head.

Fulton smirked.

Ignoring Hunter, Benny appraised Fulton's face. "He doesn't seem injured. Are you certain it broke?"

"It broke," Vincent said. Nodding at me, he added, "*She* fixed it."

Benny shook his head at me, then said to Vincent, "She used to bring home stray animals too, you know. Couldn't get through a day without tripping over some mangy alley cat she decided to feed."

Vincent and Katie both laughed.

Hunter made a motion toward the door. "We should take this into the house," he said.

"Speaking of houses," Benny went on, "you never once thought about where I wanted to live. I would like my own room."

"Benny, I couldn't see you until recently. It wasn't on purpose," I chided. Maybe I should have left him as a ghost. He may never shut up now.

"There are extra rooms here," Hunter offered.

"I'm not making a deal with the devil."

"Then you can sleep on the sofa in the basement again," Hunter quipped.

"Naturally. You're putting me under the floorboards, like a dog."

"Hey, I sleep in the basement," Katie said.

"No insult meant, darling." Benny reached out and chucked her chin. She gave him a full, dimpled smile.

Ryder's eyes twitched, but he just turned quietly away, pulling Katie gently toward the door.

Vincent watched Ryder put his body between Katie and Benny while they all shuffled into the hallway. "It's obvious he's related to you," Vincent said to Hunter, then he shook his head and followed them.

"Don't know what you're talking about. I'm not like that," Hunter said. When I looked up at him, he winked and smiled, holding his hand out toward the door.

I laughed.

After walking Fulton out, Hunter headed into the basement. As the rest of us began following him down the stairs, Vincent grabbed my arm. "Hey, I'm going to get back out to the party, make sure Chris is holding it down."

"Did Will ever show up?" I asked.

"Yeah, he's out there." He nodded. "You should have seen Katie take off when she got your text. Ryder and I couldn't even keep up. I think Will would have been here with her if we hadn't beat him to it. Someone had to stay behind to keep the herd in check."

"I'm glad someone is excited about Benny." I chuckled.

"I'm excited. Benny likes me."

"That's because he doesn't know you well enough."

"That hurts." Vincent smiled.

"Tell Chris and Aelina I'll see them in a bit?" I asked.

He nodded.

Once I made it down the stairs, Benny was arguing with Hunter.

"Why am I being hidden in the cellar? I want to go to the celebration."

"You're still dead. You can't be around people," Hunter reasoned.

"You're a demon, and you're around them. Which one of us do you think they would prefer to toast with?"

"Neither of you, if they knew the truth of it," I interrupted. "Benny, you understand you're a Nephilim now too, right?"

Katie happily announced, "And me!"

Benny said, "Thank you for reminding me. I almost forgot I had that to hate him for as well."

"That was not my fault," Hunter said.

"He's right, that one's on me," I said.

"I'm certain he was somehow involved," Benny shot back.

Clearing her throat, Katie offered, "Why don't we stay here and watch movies? They're streaming the sequel we were waiting for." She plopped onto the sofa, patting the cushion next to her invitingly.

Ryder excitedly joined her, putting his arm across her shoulders. "I'm good with staying here," he said.

Benny regarded them for a moment, then strolled over. "I don't think so," he said to Ryder. "You can sit on the other side of me."

"What?" Ryder asked.

"You heard me. Scoot." Benny wiggled between them.

"This is my house," Ryder protested as he was forced over to the edge of the sofa.

"That's very nice for you."

"Benny..." Katie started softly.

"No." He shook his head. "The last time I allowed someone I cared about alone without a chaperone, I ended up dead," he said dryly, eyeing Hunter.

"Great, I get to watch scary movies with your ghost instead of my girlfriend now," Ryder grumbled at me.

"Don't fret. If you get scared, I'll let you hold my hand," Benny said to Ryder.

Ryder snarled his lip and shifted away from Benny. He then looked up to Hunter for help.

Hunter put his hands up. "Me getting involved will not benefit you in any way, I can promise you that."

Benny snorted. "That's for certain."

Ryder looked at me, his eyebrows raised. "Sen?"

I took a deep breath. "Benny…"

He cut me off with, "No. If you continue, I'll separate the two of you tonight as well. Don't think I won't."

I shrugged at Ryder, making Katie giggle. At least she wasn't upset.

My phone started to vibrate. As I reached for it, Hunter's went off in his pocket.

"Everything okay?" I answered.

"I need you. Ian showed up, and Jessie's having a meltdown." Vincent was trying to be quiet despite all the noise in the background. "I can't get her to calm down." Of course, Jessie would be the center of some disruption right now.

"I'm on my way," I said. I was barely finished speaking, and he hung up on me. "I need to go help with Jessie."

Hunter nodded. "Chris was just texting me about it," he said.

I turned to Katie. "I'll text you if I need you, but can you keep Benny company for now?"

"Shall we?" Benny asked her, clicking the remote. While he apparently didn't like jeans or T-shirts, he did love technology. Katie snuggled up against him. He smiled and put his arm around her. When Ryder made a disgruntled noise, Benny lifted his arm up, offering to let Ryder cuddle up to him too. Ryder did not look amused.

"Try to not get into a fight before we get back," I said.

"Hurry," Ryder urged. His brown eyes begged up at us, making me smile. He was as sweet-tempered as I remembered. The thought was mine but not mine at the same time. I shook my head, my hand reaching up to rub at my temple.

"Are you okay?" Hunter asked quietly as he reached out to place a hand gently on my lower back.

"Yeah. A little confused still."

He nodded. "It might take a few days."

I nodded back.

CHAPTER 25

W E made it out to the clearing just in time to see Jessie splash a cup of punch in Ian's face. I was going to have to talk to Chris later about letting her get into the alcohol. She was already angry with Ian, so adding drinking to her emotional state was a poor decision. Ian, for his part, looked very apologetic. He didn't even seem angry that she'd doused his white shirt in a drink that was probably fifty percent red food coloring.

"Hey!" I exclaimed, putting myself between them. Ian had been trying to pull Jessie into a hug, which resulted in her slapping wildly at his arms.

"Jess, I'm sorry," Ian apologized.

"Let her go, Ian," I said.

"I just want—"

I interrupted him, "Don't care. She doesn't want you touching her right now. You can apologize when she wants to hear it."

His eyebrows puckered as his shoulders fell, then he nodded in agreement.

"Thank you," Jessie said. She was talking to me, I think, but she glared at him as she said it.

"Come on," I said, ushering her away from Ian and the crowd of onlookers. People love drama when it's not theirs.

Vincent made a wide gesture with his arms. "Who wants a very special Vincent original cocktail?" he yelled. There was wooing and cheering as he shuffled everyone away. Or as he would say, herded them away.

Ian hesitated where he stood, watching longingly after Jessie. I just shook my head at him. If he tried talking to her now, I would never get her calmed down again. Hunter took my lead and tapped Ian on the shoulder, nodding his head toward the table where Vincent was tossing a bottle of something in the air and smiling at Aelina. She had her arms crossed and rolled her eyes, seemingly not impressed by his dexterity.

I put my arm around Jessie and walked her over to a set of open seats. She let out a huff as she dropped herself into one. I sat next to her. "I can't believe he thinks he can just show up like that."

I took the almost empty cup away from her. There was only a gulp left, but any amount was more than she needed. She let me take it without complaining. "Did he bring another girl with him?" I asked.

"No," she scoffed.

"So, why are you upset?"

"He said he wasn't coming. Then he just *did*." She scrunched her nose up and made a wave motion at him as if that explained everything. It didn't. Jessie was difficult sometimes, but this was illogical, even for her.

"What really set you off at Ian?" I asked.

"I don't know. He thought he was being funny, sneaking up behind me to surprise me that he made it. He let me go the entire night thinking he ditched me. I don't like feeling like that." She scowled, then continued, "I was thinking how frustrating that was, then I just wanted to hit him."

"Why was he late?" I asked.

"He had to go to dinner with his nana."

I raised my eyebrows. "Nana?"

She nodded. "He said he does it once a month. He didn't want to rush her, so he told me he couldn't make it."

"Did you know that's why he wasn't coming?"

"No! I wouldn't have been upset all night if he would have just told me that to start with."

"You're pretty intimidating, Jessie. I think he spends an awful lot of time worrying about how cool he looks to you."

"Whatever. It was selfish of him, leaving me not knowing what he thought was more important," she said. She wasn't settling, and Ian's behavior wasn't the terrible offense she thought it was. Not even a little.

"Jessie, give me your hand," I demanded.

"Why?"

"Just do it," I said, holding my palm up at her. She didn't ask any more questions, but she made a point to roll her eyes and let out an exasperated breath as she did. As our skin connected, her furious spirit spiked out at me. She was angry. Angrier than she should have been. Furrowing my eyebrows, I tugged at the energy in her, trying to help cool her down.

"Why are you doing that? I want to be mad at him," she complained.

"No, I don't think you really do," I said as I soaked up her temper. It was the feisty, poppy attitude of Jessie until I got to the very bottom. At the core of her spirit was something dark, vicious, and not her at all.

"Feel better?" I asked as I absorbed it into myself.

She side-eyed me. "Yeah. Yeah, I do."

"Sounds like he was trying to keep you from waiting for him all night if he couldn't make it, instead of being a selfish jerk," I said softly.

Jessie looked over at him. Ian was watching us nervously from one of the fire pits. Hunter was saying something to him, probably trying to keep him from coming over and begging Jessie for forgiveness, again. "Yeah. I guess it does."

"Going to give him another chance?" I asked.

"Ugh. This is exactly why I don't date."

I laughed. "So, you are dating then?"

"Ugh." She waved her hand at me, then smiled sheepishly over her shoulder.

I grinned tauntingly at her, then looked over to Ian, motioning for him to come back. He nearly sprinted to us.

"Hi," he said to me, smiling as he approached.

"Nice to see you, Ian." I smiled back as I stood up, leaving my chair empty for him.

He looked at Jessie. "Can I sit?"

She nodded at him. She was relaxed as could be now, but she wasn't going to make this easy on him. I doubted she was even going to apologize for overreacting. I shook my head at her.

Ian smiled at me. "Thanks."

I smirked at him. "Welcome. Say 'hi' to Nana for me next month, will you?"

His face fell, making Jessie laugh next to him, dropping her façade of irritation.

Looking back to where Hunter was standing, engrossed now in a conversation with Chris, I felt a tugging feeling. I knew what had set Jessie off. It might have started with Ian making her feel insecure that he was gone all night, but she would have forgiven that quickly enough when he told her the real reason. I turned and headed west through the trees.

In the dark, my eyes were useless. The music was so loud my hearing wasn't enough of a sense to help with where I was going, either. Carefully treading through the trees as I distanced myself from the party, I stretched my spirit out, looking for that familiar pull.

A second later, I found him. Standing in a circle of pine trees, Jonah was staring up at the open sky. The moon made the angles of his face softer and his expression gentle, but the hatred piercing through the dark reminded me it was nothing more than a trick of the light.

"Jonah," I greeted, folding my arms as I came to a stop in front of him.

"I'm surprised you came alone."

"I don't need protection from you, Jonah."

He looked down then, his eyes roaming over me before one side of his mouth settled into a smirk. "Are you sure?" He stepped forward and began to circle me. I let him walk behind me, out of sight, as he stalked like a large predator.

"Pretty sure. Aren't you getting a little old for playing mind games with teenage girls?"

He laughed. "Ah, she was an easy target. I couldn't help myself."

"Figures. Always taking the easy route."

"Only for bait," he said. "I prefer my playmates a little more challenging."

"Stay away from Jessie. You've done enough damage to her."

Jonah tilted his head to the side. "A minor lover's spat isn't so bad. Are your pet humans that frail?"

"Are you really going to act like you've forgotten all those girls you murdered?" I asked.

"Are you referring to Nathan's playthings? You should know by now I wouldn't waste all that effort just to feed off such simple things. I was just indulging his tendencies." He stopped pacing to stand in front of me. "Was she one of them? He was so sloppy, it's no surprise he let one get away."

I crossed my arms over my chest. "It was her sister. You took away the most important person to her."

"Ah well, casualties," he said. He reached out, running a finger down my arm. I felt the prickle of his energy along my skin as he tested my spirit. I was hoping to drag this out a little longer before he figured out what Hunter and I had done. So much for that.

"You..." Seething, he grabbed my shoulder, turning me to him. He knew I had closed the ritual without him. His energy was scolding hot, and I had to press my barriers in place to force it back. Noticing how easily I cast him out, he growled in frustration, tugging me toward him. "How did he convince you to do it?"

"You left me no choice," I said softly. "You tried to trap Katie. You're meddling in ways you shouldn't be. You have no business being here, right now, in this body. You know that." The words were mine, but they came out with an authority that wasn't. That pounding in my head intensified as my consciousness fought to merge the Jonah of my memory with the version in front of me. I knew Jonah. I was terrified of him, but I wasn't.

He scoffed and released me roughly. I took a step back to gain my balance. "No choice. No choice." He shook his head and continued to pace in a circle around me. "What about my choices?" he asked.

"Jonah..."

"No. You thought you could make me care about you, give me scraps of your affection, and that would be enough to control me."

"That isn't fair. You were drawing too much attention. You knew there would be consequences if you didn't alter your behavior, Jonah. I was trying to protect you," I said. I wanted to protect him. To save him. What was I saving him from?

"Consequences." He stopped moving and turned from me, staring at the sky again through the trees. "You really believe that don't you? Has Hunter caught on that you're just here to tame him?"

"That's not why I'm with Hunter."

He made a snorting noise. "Lies."

"Why do you think I'm lying?" I asked.

He turned. Even in the dark, I could feel him appraising me. He stalked toward me again, closing the distance between us in a few quick strides. Without pausing, he wrapped his arms around me. "Because you wouldn't have chosen him otherwise. He's weak. Too weak to be worth it."

I stared up into his familiar eyes. I didn't know this face, but I knew those blue eyes, so out of place in their host. "That's not true."

"It is true. He was just an easier trap."

I shook my head. "You're wrong. I love him."

He stared at me. His temper swirling inside him. Even through my barriers, I could see him war with his feelings about my admission. He was angry and hurt. I wanted to comfort him, despite everything.

Before I could say anything, Jonah said, "I guess that's that then."

Confused by his sudden acceptance, I was caught off guard when he leaned down and bit into my neck.

I cried out in pain as he tore at my throat. I twisted, trying to push him from me, but he yanked me tightly against his body. The motion caused me to roll my ankle, which was barely noticeable compared to the feel of him draining the blood and energy from me. Shards of glass being pulled through me would have hurt less than this. I thrust my elbow into his rib as hard as I could, causing him to bite down with more force to keep me from freeing myself. He then covered my mouth with his hand, muffling my screams.

Nausea swept over me as Jonah drank me down. I couldn't focus on anything but the sound and feel of him swallowing. My vision faded to black, and I collapsed against him as he finally released me.

In the darkness, I heard Jonah whisper, "Always remember this path was your choice."

"This way," Hunter's voice coaxed me through the dim hallway.

"Where are we going?"

"Somewhere I can keep you safe."

"But Everly already has a plan." I shouldn't have agreed to meet him, but I couldn't bring myself to sneak off without so much as a farewell. I wasn't sure when we would meet again, and it was so soon to part in this lifetime.

"Have faith in me, beautiful. I've a better one," he promised.

When he came to a door, he looked behind me, listening for footsteps, then nodded and pushed it open as he gestured me inside. I walked through to find myself in a chapel. The stained-glass windows left bright colored images on the floor. Benjamin stood, speaking quietly to Jonah at the center of it all.

"Benjamin!" I cried out, rushing toward him.

He turned at the sound of me. "Senlis!"

When I reached him, he crushed me in his embrace. "I thought they had taken you already."

"Not yet but I cannot stay." Pulling back, I turned to face Jonah. He smirked as he watched over our reunion.

"It took not a quarter of a life for you to love him so deeply," Jonah said. "Does he appreciate the rarity of your affections?"

Something was amiss. Jonah was guarded and his tone caused the hairs on the back of my neck to raise. "Is it so rare, Jonah?" I asked, *cautiously. I took a step back from Benjamin, who was now looking back and forth between the two of us with concern.*

"For some of us," Jonah replied.

My brow furrowed. "What affections have I not afforded you?" That was when I noticed the dagger in his right hand. His left sleeve was rolled up and his arm smeared with blood. "Jonah, what are you up to?" I asked in a whisper, looking down at my feet. There, surrounding where Benjamin and I stood, was a circle. Only the barest section left incomplete. I hadn't noticed it due to patterns from the window reflecting upon it and had walked right into the center. Hearing a scuffling behind me, I spun around.

Hunter was kneeling on the ground, just outside of the circle.

"Hunter?" I asked.

Not looking at me, he held an identical dagger to Jonah's against his bared arm. "This is the only way to put you back together."

"No!" I yelled.

Hunter hesitated, his eyes finally flickering up to meet mine. "Please forgive me."

"I will forgive you. Yes, of course, I forgive you,"—I rambled, attempting to keep his attention—"But only if you stop. You don't comprehend what you're doing. You must stop!" He was on the wrong side of the ritual. If he closed it now, he wouldn't be part of it. Did he truly mean to bind me to Benjamin?

"I know what I'm doing. It's the only way to keep you safe. Both of you," he said, his eyes flickering to Benjamin. "It will keep us together."

Benjamin took my hand. "We've discussed it, Senlis. This is a reasonable plan."

"Reasonable? According to whom?" I asked. Benjamin couldn't possibly understand that he was agreeing to be bound to my soul for all eternity. The binding would not undo what I'd done, it would only entangle us

further. Did Hunter not know this? Benjamin's question distracted me just long enough that I felt the power well up, as Hunter spilled his blood.

"Stop!" I shouted, my hand going up to ward Hunter away from his next action of closing the circle. I lunged forward but before I could reach him, Jonah's arm wrapped around me, pulling me back. Hunter's hand hit the marble floor and as he looked up his expression shifted from sorrow to fear.

Jonah had entered the ritual circle with us.

"Jonah, what's the meaning of this?" Benjamin asked. Jonah's involvement was clearly not part of the plan.

"Jonah!" Hunter's voice rumbled with anger, as the realization that Jonah had taken his place hit him. "This was not the agreement."

I tried to maintain my composure. Hunter didn't know how to perform the binding and he was trusting Jonah. But even Jonah only knew what I had shared with him. The circle was set, yes, but he couldn't finish the ritual. He didn't have enough energy stored. I could tell that just from the feel of him. I only needed to get us freed. I took a deep breath as I reached for Benjamin and he wrapped his arms around me, pulling me from Jonah's grip.

Hunter's voice was low and threatening. "How could you betray me?"

Jonah laughed. "You are surprisingly gullible for a creature sustained on jealousy, my friend."

I turned my face to him. "Why, Jonah? Why are you doing this?"

He smiled at me, his steel eyes softening. "Don't look at me with such panic, Senlis. This is better. You'll understand once you're mine. You made the wrong choice, but you'll understand that when it's done."

"The decision is not yours to make on my behalf, Jonah," I replied.

His jaw clenched. "You don't think clearly when it comes to him." He gestured to Hunter. "We could take back everything together. You'll see."

"Jonah, I don't want—"

"I don't understand," Benjamin interrupted us. "Whatever this magic, you said it would put her soul back. What trickery have you pulled?"

As I suspected, they had lied to Benjamin. I gave his arm a reassuring squeeze as I spoke, calmly, "Jonah, you haven't sufficient spirit to complete the ritual, and no sacrifice to supplement. Stop this."

"Have I not?" he asked.

I blinked at him.

Hunter's voice came from behind me, the anger shifting to a nervous edge, "What do you mean?"

Jonah's arm shot out as I began to speak. Benjamin's body jerked, his arms around me tightening in reflex. I let out a scream as Hunter shouted, "No!"

Jonah retracted the dagger, spilling Benjamin's blood violently as it tore his throat open. The weight of Benjamin's body dragged me down to the ground with him.

I sobbed as I stared into Benjamin's slack features. Patting at his cheeks to wake him, though I knew he was already dying, as I could feel his spirit filling the ritual around us. I looked up at Hunter. His face was contorted with sadness as he watched me rock Benjamin in my lap.

"I'm sorry," he said softly, as he reached out to me.

I pulled away from him. "You did this!" I screamed.

He dropped his hand, shaking his head. "It was not my intention."

Jonah's laughter filled the air. He crouched down as he smiled cruelly, enjoying the sadness and fear welling up inside me as I stared into his blue eyes.

CHAPTER 26

THE breeze blowing across my arms was cold. I shivered, blinking my eyes open. The sound of my heart racing thrummed in my ears, and I blinked back the tears that blurred my vision. How could Jonah do such a thing? There was a sweet, earthy smell in the air. I looked around, expecting to see the remnants of the ritual on the chapel floor, yet I was surrounded by bales of hay. The lantern on the floor near me lit up the mostly empty barn. Barn?

I tugged at my wrists that were pulled behind me, but they were secured to the back of the chair I was sitting in. I closed my eyes, listening for anyone behind me or in the rafters, but there were no sounds besides my breath and the wind whistling through the crack in the door. When I opened my eyes, I finally registered what had happened. I had a flash back when Jonah fed. It was the first time one of them felt like my memory, my experience. My breath shook as I tried to calm myself. I hadn't just watched Benny die—that was a long time ago—and he was safe now.

I, on the other hand, was trapped somewhere alone and at Jonah's mercy.

I looked down. Jonah had cleaned the blood off my shoulder. If any of it had gotten on my clothes, I couldn't tell. I laughed awkwardly. This probably wasn't what Jessie had in mind for the night when she chose my outfit. I looked around again. There were no signs of struggle, no one else tied up or worse. I hoped Jonah had snatched me without incident. I had no question in my mind that if anyone had tried to interrupt, they were no longer breathing. Not if Jonah had managed to leave with me.

I shook my head. I didn't have time to think about that right now. I could worry about what else he had done after I was out of here.

Where was Jonah? There weren't many places for someone to stow away, so he must have left. But how long would he be gone? Could I untie myself before he returned? There was nothing close enough to aid me at getting my hands loose. I tugged at them with frustration. Even if I managed to get free, I wasn't sure what my next step would be. For all I knew, Jonah could be standing just outside the door. I could hide, but the only real place to do so was behind the stacks of hay bales. That would leave me trapped in a corner. At least here I was out in the open and had a better chance of outrunning him. Of course, if I stayed strapped to this chair, I had no chance at anything. Except maybe dying.

As I continued pulling frantically at the ropes, trying to loosen them, someone whispered loudly, "Stop moving."

Jerking in surprise, I yelped, "Benjamin!"

"Quiet!" he hushed me. I would have flung myself at him in a hug if I could. The ache of watching his death was still very real and I felt the pang in my chest at the sound of his voice.

"How did you know where I was?" I asked.

"If you recall, your sad excuse for a beau failed to fully bring me back to life. I'm as stuck to you as ever." He hurried to untie me.

When my arms were finally free, I rubbed where the rope had left burn marks in my skin. Benny came around to the front of me. I started to reach for him but stopped. He was still as corporeal as he was at the cabin.

And very naked. Again.

"Benny, where are your clothes?" I asked.

He looked down and made a sound under his breath that I could have sworn was a curse word. "Do you see the things I endure for you?" he finally said, scowling up at me.

The stress of the situation and relief at seeing him washed over me and I had to press my lips together to smother a laugh. I felt bad laughing at him, but it beat the urge I had to sob myself into a stupor before his arrival.

"Oh, go on, have a chuckle. I'll leave you here, and you can wait for Hunter to fail to rescue you."

His words sobered me. Hunter was alive. That meant he hadn't caught us in the woods. I let out a relieved sigh. "Is he on the way?"

"Yes. I am very cross with you for putting me in a situation where I must trust his help."

Shaking my head at him, I asked, "Where are we?"

He looked around quickly, then concluded, "A barn."

I gave him a pointed look. "Yes, I recognize that it's a barn. But how far are we from Hunter's?"

"I don't fully know. I pinpointed it for Katie on her telephone contraption, but I don't have a good sense of travel yet. She sounded like it was a doable distance to cross."

I nodded and stood. My neck was sore, and my ankle protested in pain when I tried to put pressure on it. Seeing me wince, Benny knelt down and took my leg into his hands.

"You've sprained it," he said, then a shot of energy sparked through my leg as he healed it. I sucked in a breath from the sharpness of it.

"You know, you can control how painful it is when you do that," I said.

"Should we manage our way out of here, I will allow you to teach me all the finer points of being a demon. For now, let's just work on the getting-out-of-here part. What do you say?"

I reached out and touched his cheek, and his skin wavered like the ripples in a pond. He looked up at me, startled by the gentle gesture. "I'm sorry, Benjamin. I never meant for you to have to deal with any of this. I'm sorry for everything I've put you through."

He smiled softly, then he shook his head at me as he stood. "Don't think you can sweet-talk me. I'll not forgive you so easily."

I smiled back. I reached into my pocket. My phone was missing. I really didn't expect to find it there, but I had reached for it out of reflex. "We can't just stand here waiting for Hunter to show up."

"What if Jonah's waiting outside?" he asked.

"Whether he's waiting outside or comes back in here, our dilemma is basically the same. If he catches me trying to escape, he's not likely to leave me alive a second time."

"Aren't you, as Katie would say, a fierce Nephilim? Can't you fight him?" Benny asked.

"If I'd been smart earlier and not let him drain me? Maybe. I don't know why he didn't just kill me then and there, but he came pretty damn close." I had spent so much time talking Jonah down from his violent tendencies, I'd taken for granted that he had never aimed them at me. I didn't think he would. Not even with as enraged as he was earlier because part of my soul sincerely believed he cared about me, that he loved me.

I'd severely misjudged the situation.

"You need energy, then? Is that all?" Benny asked.

I laughed. "Yeah, Benny, that's all."

"My duties as a brother are never done, it seems."

I looked at him. "No."

"Have you a better idea? I'm all ears if you do."

I contemplated our options. I couldn't physically overpower Jonah. He was shorter in the body he had stolen, but he was still twice my size in muscle mass.

"The power I fed into you earlier is part of your soul now, Benny. If we use it now, I don't know what will happen. Even a small amount and you could have any number of issues. A large amount…"

"And if we don't? He's not going to dispose of you and walk away, Senlis. His type doesn't behave that way. He's going to go after Katie, just to punish you more. I won't have it."

I stared at him. He was so resolved in his decision. He didn't have a pulse, but if he did, I still think it would have been calm. I'd avoided this reality for so long. I hadn't wanted to hurt Jonah. Not hurting him meant I dragged Benjamin, and now Katie, into the crossfire of his temper. He wouldn't just stop at Katie, either. He saw Hunter as mine now. He'd hurt him—and Ryder to get to him. Even Vincent wasn't safe. I'd successfully distracted Jonah from his broader destructive tendencies, but to what end? A perpetual cycle of tormenting everyone I loved, it seemed. Benny nodded, recognizing the acceptance on my face.

"I can't take your energy. The minute he gets close, he'll feel it, and we'll lose the advantage. You're going to have to be the one to do it."

"Thought you would never offer," Benny said. "How do I do it? And what is 'it'?"

"You'll have to bite him. You'll instinctively understand the rest when you do."

"That's disgusting," he said.

"I know."

He stared at me, nodding again. "Then I have one request."

"What's that?"

"When you retell the story of how heroic I was, leave out the part about my lack of clothing."

I raised my eyebrows and grinned at him. "But then how will I explain how we managed to catch Jonah off guard?"

"Just say he's a buffoon with no attention to detail. It's believable enough," he said.

We heard something scrape against the barn door as it creaked. Benny made a shooing motion before he faded in front of me. Well, that was just fucking cool. Probably not worth being naked in front of everyone, but it was close.

I sat back into the chair quickly and had a fleeting thought that maybe it would be Hunter bursting through the door. This lifetime had made me sappy. As I tried to reconcile what felt like my own voice talking inside my head, Jonah pushed into the barn, letting the door slam shut behind him.

"You're up," he said, striding toward me.

"Nice of you to care." My heart was pounding in my chest, and my palms were sweaty, but at least I sounded more annoyed than scared.

He stopped in front of me, his eyes traveling over my body. "You untied yourself."

"Yup," I lied.

"But you didn't run."

"If you're disappointed you didn't get to chase me, there's still time to give me a head start," I said.

He clicked his tongue. "I've had enough of that."

"Pity," I said. Why the hell was I taunting him?

Jonah's head tilted to the side as he smirked. "You're almost awake."

I reached up, running my fingers across my forehead. The dull ache was still here, but I was less foggy. "Yeah. It's going slow, and it's more uncomfortable than I expected."

"It wouldn't have been this painful if you hadn't locked yourself away so long." He kneeled in front of me. As he took my face in his hands, I realized he was guarding so his spirit wouldn't leak into me. He moved my head back and forth gently, checking the dilation of my eyes. My eyebrows furrowed as I stared at him.

"Why didn't you kill me?" I asked.

"Are you in a hurry?"

"Aren't you?" I countered.

He sat back on the balls of his feet as he looked up at me. "I haven't taken your life once. That's always been your own doing."

"Weren't you planning to this time?" I asked, remembering his comment at the waterpark.

"Only so we could start over. If it helps, I planned to join you."

"Why would that comfort me?"

His face scrunched in a snarl. "Why do you see me as villainous?"

I raised my eyebrows. "Well, for starters, you murdered someone on my living room floor."

"That was just removing an obstacle."

"How was bleeding John out removing an obstacle? He had nothing to do with me."

"I apologize for the damage to your carpet." He smirked. "When I started instigating his temper, I didn't realize you had manipulated him before. He was too susceptible to my urging. I couldn't leave him walking around after that. Not after he injured our little Katie."

I thought about the argument I had with John on their porch that summer. I had shoved Hunter's energy into John in the heat of my temper. Jonah was right, having his soul burned through once before, it made John a perfect target. After that incident, he had been doing so well—maybe in part due to my influence. I had willed him to sober up when I nearly imploded his heart. If Jonah hadn't interfered, John may have straightened out. Instead, John was dead, Katie's mom was an even bigger mess than she had been before, and Katie…

"You almost got Katie killed," I said, anger filling my voice.

"Ah, it wasn't anything you couldn't handle," he said. "And I was nearby in case you failed."

"Why do you always have to meddle in everything?" I asked.

He scoffed. "We're Nephilim. You're like a human that has fallen in love with her cattle. Yet, you behave as if I'm not doing the exact thing I was built to do."

I watched him. There was some truth to what he was saying. My soul didn't regenerate by absorbing the anger and hatred that his did. It had always made it easier for me to see humans more favorably. I tried my best to give him what he needed to turn away from his tendencies. I winced as a sharp pain shot through my head with that thought.

"Don't fight it."

"What?" I asked.

"What thoughts were you having just then?"

"I was thinking that I failed to change you." The pain spiked again. I closed my eyes.

"You're still fighting."

"I'm not." I wasn't trying to fight anything.

"The real you," he corrected.

"Why?"

"Give it a day or two, we'll find out." He stood, dusting himself off.

"What, are you planning to hide here until I finish waking up? Is that what you're waiting for?"

He just looked down at me.

I stood then, putting myself in front of him. "What do you think is going to happen when I do?" I thought about his words before he knocked me out. "You think I will change my mind about Hunter. That I'll be angry with him."

"While it will be a delight to see you unleashed on him for binding you while you slept, I have other reasons."

I narrowed my eyes as I leaned toward him. "You can't bind me to you now, Jonah. I have nothing left to offer you." I watched his pulse speed in his throat. It was the closest thing to an emotion I had seen out of him in this entire exchange. I took another step toward him, nearly pressing us against each other. "Why can't we call a truce?"

He swallowed. "You still think you can manipulate me."

His comment made me pause, realizing he was reacting to me being close to him. He watched my hand as I reached up, slowly. My fingers tentatively brushed over his neck, across his birthmark. His eyes fluttered as I pressed my hand into his neck. The skin on my palm prickled as his energy fought to travel across to me and cause my own spirit to spike and swarm against him.

"I don't think that," I said.

He scoffed but didn't pull away. My heart was pounding being so close to him. Was this going to work? Could he feel how terrified I was, or was he mistaking the shaking in my hand as something else? I felt his barrier falter. He was struggling to keep his shields in place with me this close. I pressed closer to him, my face near the bend of his neck and shoulder. He reached out, putting his hands on my hips. I really hoped Benny didn't get overzealous watching this and ruin everything.

"If you expect to undo me with your mouth, I am not Hunter," he said quietly.

He was lying. He was seconds away from losing control, and I could taste it. "You're right, this path is my choice, Jonah. You still have time to make yours."

"I am not your pet."

"And I'm not yours."

"It's true, you're no longer mine for the taking." He brushed his cheek against me, then whispered, "But I can still have my fun. There is nothing stopping me from finishing the ritual with our little Katie."

I fought my body from tensing in his arms at the sound of her name. Benny was right. No matter what, we weren't walking away from this without putting Katie at more risk. "You don't want Katie."

"It might just be enough to know you don't want me to have her," he said.

"You don't mean that."

"Oh, but I do. She's practically mine already. You didn't stop me soon enough. And once I have her, you know they'll come for me." The hatred in his voice pierced through the silence around us. He lowered his voice, "Sweet little Katie will be put down just for being bound to me, and it will be all your doing for interfering in my plans to begin with."

I knew he meant it. He would bind Katie just to get back at me. That thought was enough to make up my mind. I pressed my lips against the pulse on his neck, pressing just the slightest bit of my spirit into him to shatter his barrier. I felt his hands flex against me as his breath let out.

He let his guard down to feel me, and I took that moment. I bit into his neck, gently, not ripping at his flesh the way he had at mine earlier. He hadn't expected my willingness to offer something he craved so much, and he readily accepted the risk. I felt his knees give, and he fell to them in front of me. I didn't release him as he dropped, clinging to me. I drank his madness down, knowing what he felt was my own special flavor of feeding. His spirit as warm and thick, and eager to feel soothed by my own as it rushed out of him.

When I pulled away, I looked down into his eyes. He was drowning in anger and want of me. He hated me because of how badly he wanted to possess me. It wasn't love. He couldn't love anything. But I did love him. Even now. Because I couldn't help myself. I'd spent lifetimes letting him push boundaries because I saw him as something broken that needed fixing. I was going to miss him, but he was a dangerous, vile thing, no matter what I tried to tell myself.

I ran my finger across his lower lip as he glared at me, gasping for breath as the effect of my bite still coursed through him. He spared me because of his desire for this, to gain knowledge and power from me, and maybe even just to hurt me more. But he had violated my trust for the last time.

"Benny," I called.

Benjamin appeared behind Jonah.

Jonah's eyes flashed with rage, but he was too slow. Benjamin wrapped his arms around Jonah as he bit violently into Jonah's neck. Yelling like a man ablaze in fire, Jonah clawed at Benjamin's hands. But the other man wasn't alive, and Jonah couldn't hurt him or tear his arms away. Instead of pulling power out of him, Benjamin was pouring himself forcefully into Jonah. Benny's body flashed as the light from his spirit seeped into Jonah, causing a glow so bright under his skin that I had to look away.

I felt the current a moment before it crashed into me. Benny and Jonah's spirit collided, exploding out into the barn and throwing me several feet until I knocked into the chair and finally hit the ground. I stayed there, dazed.

After a few minutes, the ringing in my ears stopped, and I could breathe again. I opened my eyes. Jonah was on the ground.

And Benny was gone.

Lying there, hot tears sliding down my face, I stayed sobbing and frozen, unable to force myself to move. Through my blurred vision, I watched Jonah's shoulder twitch.

I gasped.

He rolled slowly onto his side toward me, then coughed as he pushed himself into a sitting position. I just watched him, dejected and broken that I had lost Benny, and it hadn't even worked. Jonah was still alive. He crawled toward me on all fours, and I didn't bother to try to move away. I didn't care.

"Was it a success?" he asked. His tone took me by surprise.

"What?"

"Where did he go?" He flopped onto his side next to me, looking over to where he had crawled from. "I anticipated a body."

I reached out to take his cheek, turning his face toward me. Two gray eyes stared back at me. "Benny! It's you!" I exclaimed.

"Did you hit your head?" he asked.

I laughed through the tears that had started back down my face and tugged him into a hug.

"Well, now, that's a proper greeting." He chuckled and wrapped his arms around me. "What's gotten into you?"

I pushed him away, smiling. "Look at yourself."

He looked down. Then held his hands up, turning them in front of himself. "I don't understand."

"You're in Jonah's host."

He wrinkled his face up. "This seems unsanitary."

I laughed again.

Before I could say anything else, the doors to the barn burst open. Will was standing there, his gun drawn but pointed at the roof. Hunter was beside him, holding the other door.

"You're late again," I called.

Will gave me a perplexed look as he sighted down his gun at Benny. "Move away from her."

"Will, it's okay."

I went to stand, holding my hands up in a warding gesture as I stepped forward. Hunter's eyebrows laced in concern as he watched me move defensively in front of Benny.

"It's not Jonah," I explained.

Will hesitated, then pointed his gun at the ceiling again. "Who is it then?"

"I don't believe we've had the pleasure," Benny said as he pushed to stand, brushing the hay from his clothes.

Hunter's mouth fell open, recognizing Benny's tone. "Benjamin?"

"That's right. You're absolutely useless. What took you so long?" Benny shook his head, tsking at Hunter.

"Will, this is my brother, Benny," I clarified, just in case the name and his pure disdain for Hunter weren't enough clues.

Will holstered his gun. "This is going to complicate things a bit."

I looked over at Benny. "Yeah. A bit."

"It would appear I'm the fierce Nephilim now." Benny beamed back at me, and I smiled. It was jarring to see his expressions on the face that had just been inhabited by Jonah, but it beat the alternative.

"Looks like it," I said.

Will shook his head. "You can fill me in during the car ride."

"It would be my pleasure," Benny offered. He flexed as he walked past Hunter, following Will out to the car.

Hunter stood in the doorway, running his fingers through his hair. "How?"

I walked over to him. "I don't really know. I'm just glad he's okay."

He nodded, pulling me into a hug. "I'm so sorry."

"For what?" I asked.

"Not being here. If it wasn't for Benny, I wouldn't have found you."

"I'm the one who ran off after Jonah." I wrapped myself around him, sinking against his body.

"Then I'm sorry you had to do this alone. I know you cared about him."

I just nodded and clung to Hunter. Jonah had violated the rules when he went after Benjamin and then Katie. He could toy with me all he wanted. It was why I was here to begin with—part of the plan. I shook my head again. "Hunter," I said, looking up into his face.

"Hmm?"

"I don't understand it, but it was not accidental that we met the first time."

He brushed my hair back from my face and over my shoulder. "I know."

"You do?"

He nodded. "I was careless and bored. Jonah's games were something to do, something different. I knew what I was bringing down on myself though. It was obvious right away you were just trying to stop us."

"Why did you let me?" I asked.

"You weren't boring."

I laughed. "Is that all?"

He squeezed me tight. "No."

"You know that's not why I'm here now, right?"

He smiled. "Yeah. I know that, too."

I pressed my cheek back against him and let him hold me a minute longer. I felt like a weight had lifted off my chest.

When we got to the car, Will had somehow coaxed Benny to sit in the front to talk to him. When I opened the door to the back, there was a pile of clothing on the seat. "What's this?" I asked.

Will shrugged. "Katie made me bring those. She wouldn't let me out the door without them."

I pressed my lips together to smother the laughter. Benny was scowling at me.

Hunter just watched the two of us.

"I'll explain later," I promised.

"You will not!" Benny snapped.

I bit my lip as I continued to laugh.

Benny reached into his pocket, pulling out my phone. "Shall I keep this, then?"

"Hand it over," I demanded.

"Not until I have your word."

"Fine. Give me my phone."

He tossed it back to me, narrowing his eyes. "I'm trusting you."

I smirked at him. "I'm surprised you still would."

He smiled. "So am I."

CHAPTER 27

I HAD sent Katie and Vincent texts, so Benny's new appearance wouldn't shock them. As soon as we pulled up, Katie came bounding out the front door, Ryder on her heels. She crushed me in a hug.

"Are you okay?" she asked.

"I am. How are you? Still feeling okay?"

She smiled at me. "Never better."

She turned to Benny then, wrapping her arms around his neck, squeezing him tight. "I'm so glad you're okay, too."

Benny seemed to tense as she pressed herself against him, but then he smiled and reached his arms around her waist. He pressed his cheek into her hair. "I couldn't miss the end of our film," he said.

Ryder watched them silently. He didn't look as relieved as Katie, but her happiness helped temper his dislike of Benny. Katie pulled away, taking hold of Benny's hand with her left, and she tugged him toward the cabin. As she passed Ryder, she reached out and took his hand in the other. I watched her happily retreat inside, nearly skipping between the two of them.

"We need to talk," Will said.

I looked over at him. He was watching after Katie.

"Now?"

He nodded. "Let's go inside."

Hunter and I exchanged a look. He shrugged at me, and we both followed Will. If he was in a chatty mood, neither of us was going to shoot him down.

Vincent was sitting on the sofa. He was anxiously rubbing his hands over his knuckles as he waited for us. Aelina had an arm around his shoulders, rubbing the back of his neck affectionately to calm him. Her dog, Nala, sat in front of them, her chin resting on Vincent's leg. Nala looked up at us without lifting her head, but she waggled her backside excitedly in greeting. Noticing her reaction, Vincent looked up, and his eyes searched frantically until they fell on me. He lowered his head and let out a quiet swear before jumping to his feet.

He strode up to me, yanking me into a hug, and buried his face against me. I wrapped my arms around him.

"Don't ever fucking do that again," he muttered into my hair.

"Sorry."

"Don't 'sorry' me. I mean it. Stop running off to fight the bad guys without me. That was fucking stupid."

I smiled. "I love you, too."

He squeezed me tighter, then let go. He then glared over his shoulder at Will. "And you. You're officially on my list for leaving me behind."

Will didn't look at all ruffled from Vincent's reaction. "I told you it wasn't safe," he said coolly. "I didn't need anyone else getting in the way. I nearly shot Benjamin as it was."

"That's quite accurate," Benjamin added. "You really should be more cautious," he chided.

Will didn't respond as he stepped over to the sofa. Chris was sitting on the other side of Aelina. They were looking Benny up and down where he stood in front of them, still holding Katie's hand and smiling down at her.

"*C'est intéressant*," Chris said.

"What's happened?" Aelina asked.

"He tore his way into Jonah's soul," Chris added, nodding at Benny.

"Huh," Aelina added, "is that allowed?"

Chris shrugged. "Seems we'll get a chance to find out."

Aelina was one of us, more or less, but I didn't know who let Chris in on everything or how they could tell what Benny had done. Will stood next to them with his arms crossed casually over his chest, no surprise at all on his face.

"Will, what's going on?" I asked.

Instead of answering, he looked over to Chris, who stood up. They closed their eyes. When they opened them, they were solid black—and not just the iris. The white of their eyes had bled to the color of an empty night sky. A sharp pain struck my temple at the recognition as I recalled the woman in my earlier flashback. I had made a deal with her that I would subdue Jonah and separate him and Hunter. In exchange, she didn't erase them from existence. At least, she wouldn't until I failed. "You're a Keeper," I said.

Chris nodded.

"Are you here for me?" Chris hadn't been the same person I had negotiated with, but they were the same sort of creature.

"I won't suppress your memories again."

Chris had been the one to take my memories?

As if he could hear my thoughts, Hunter's tone was frustrated as he asked, "It was you? Why didn't you tell me?" He stepped in front of me, and I could feel his anger boiling under the surface.

"Annoying when someone withholds information, isn't it?" I asked. My question got a laugh from Vincent.

Hunter just looked back at me. Based on his expression, he didn't find it as funny.

"You never would have trusted my help if I had been honest," Chris said softly. "I've had plenty of chances to betray you. That should be proof enough that I'm as committed to protecting her as you are."

Hunter regarded them, then nodded, relaxing. He wasn't one to hold a grudge toward someone for withholding information. He was a lot of things, but a hypocrite wasn't usually one of them.

I didn't understand Chris's adamant loyalty. If I had broken the rules they were supposed to enforce, why would they defend me? Yet, I knew in my soul the words were true. Hearing it made me feel safe, and comfortable—something that I now realized always occurred when I was with Chris. I looked past Hunter to Aelina. "What about you?"

"I'm on your side, girl. I know it's against the rules. There was just too much building around the two of you to not pique my curiosity, but I've got your back."

Will finally spoke up. "You were supposed to break up Hunter and Jonah's power base."

"Which you did," Chris clarified.

Will nodded. "Yes, but you've established your own in the process."

"I don't understand. How?" I asked.

"You created Benny, and you bound both him and Hunter to you. You've built loyalty in at least two other Nephilim." He nodded toward Ryder and Katie. He glossed over the fact I helped Ryder shift Katie into a full-fledged Nephilim, too. That omission wasn't lost on me.

"And us," Aelina gestured to both her and Chris.

Will continued, "Fulton may or may not be on that list, but he's nearby, and he helped you when he shouldn't have. It's as good as the same." Katie reached out and touched his arm. He looked down at her hand and back up. "And then I suppose there's me."

"Are they coming?" I asked.

"Probably," Will said. "If nothing else, to confirm you accomplished your goal. They don't know about Katie or Benjamin yet. You might have been able to continue to hide that, but they will trace the last body Jonah inhabited. They might not like what they find there."

Chris chimed in, "Has your spirit siloed since the ritual?"

I shook my head. I was still able to feed freely. I had more control over certain emotions, but any would do.

"They can't find that out either," Will added. "The Keepers will watch to see what you do with all of the power you're amassing. If they show up to find you're able to channel any emotion you want, and you're creating an army of our own Nephilim. Well, they may decide you're trying to overthrow the order of things."

"Then what?" Vincent asked.

"They'll send formal messengers," Will said.

"And?" Vincent pressed.

"And that would be bad," Chris added.

"Will you stay?" Hunter asked Chris.

Chris nodded. "Yes. I'll stay. She would if it was me."

The pain was back, and I rubbed my head. "How long until I can follow this conversation completely?"

Hunter put his arm around me, pressing his lips against my temple. He breathed a small amount of spirit under my skin, soothing the pain. "Soon."

"There's time to deal with this. We should let her rest," Chris said. They walked up to me, blinking back to their human eyes. Chris smiled softly. Hunter moved out of the way as Chris tentatively reached out to pull me into a hug. When I leaned in and hugged back, they relaxed. "We can talk more in a few days. Please, trust us. You have earned our loyalty."

I had no idea what Chris was talking about, but I nodded anyway.

Aelina followed after them, squeezing me tight. "Vincent's right, though. No more running off without us. We got you."

Vincent eyed her from where he stood beside us. "So, are you just here for her?"

She pulled back from our hug, smirking at him. "You're not an unpleasant excuse to be hanging around for."

He looked her up and down, tucking the corner of his mouth, then made a shrugging motion. "I can roll with that."

She laughed.

"I'll walk you both out," Vincent offered, motioning Chris and Aelina to the door.

"We should go too," Will said to Katie.

Both Benny and Ryder made sounds of protest.

"But we haven't finished our horror film!" Benny said.

Will raised his eyebrows as his eyes swept over all of them. "I need to take you to see your mom tomorrow," he was speaking to Katie, but he was still watching the other two.

"Her mom?" I asked.

"I've put Mary in contact with one of our counselors to help her get on her feet. I've convinced her Katie should stay with me for a bit until she's more emotionally stable, but Katie needs to be with her." He almost sounded sad at that last bit.

"You'll be with her tomorrow, though, right?" I asked. Katie adapted quickly to anything, and she'd taken being a Nephilim with stride, but the idea of her being alone with her mom right now still made me uneasy. Mary was exactly the kind of aura that would trigger Katie's spirit. It was difficult enough to be around someone like that, but it was another level entirely for it to be your mom, who was also mourning a death. Plus, thanks to Benny, Katie hadn't processed any of the last few days herself. It was going to be hell doing it through her mom's emotions.

"I'll be there." Looking at Katie, he said, "Come on, your bag is already in the car. And you'll finally get to see the fish tank."

Brightening, Katie grinned at me. "Did you know Will likes fish? He has a huge brackish aquarium in his living room with cute yellow fish called gobies. Gobies! Can you believe it?"

No, I absolutely could not picture Will explaining all about his gobies to someone. I couldn't even picture him saying the word goby. I laughed.

Ryder reached out and hugged Katie, planting a kiss on her cheek. "Text me?"

She nodded. Benny then put his arm around her, squeezing her shoulders. "I shall wait for you to discover the ending."

She laughed.

Will grunted and motioned toward the door. I watched as both Ryder and Benny stared after her. The obvious disappointment on their faces brought a laugh from me. If I was Will, I wouldn't have left Katie here alone with them, either.

"Looks like you two get to share the bunk bed," I said.

"I claim the top!" Benny said excitedly as he headed toward the stairs.

Ryder yelled, following him, "Not a chance! The top bunk is mine unless your name is Katie!"

"Guess that leaves us," Hunter said quietly. He'd taken up his usual stance against the wall at the hallway entry. He leaned against one shoulder with his hands tucked into his pockets.

I walked over, wrapping my arms around his neck. He reached out, putting his hands on my waist as he shifted his back flat against the wall. His eyes roamed over my face, searching for something.

"Is everything okay?" I asked.

"I don't know. Is it?"

I frowned. "Why are you asking me like that?"

"You're still not upset with me?" I guess Jonah wasn't the only one who thought I was going to turn against Hunter as my memories merged. I listened for that voice inside of me. The one that had been continually barging into my thoughts all night. She wasn't angry. It wasn't Hunter we had been running from.

"I'm not upset with you. I don't think I'm going to be, either."

He let out a relieved sigh and pulled me tight, kissing me softly.

"Forgive me for disappearing for so long?" I asked.

He smiled. "I might. Depends on how you plan to make up for it."

"I have a few ideas."

"Better try all of them, just in case," he said.

"Mmm." I pressed my lips to his. I didn't fight as his spirit flowed into the center of me. Instead, I let it fill me up as I kissed him, pressing him to the wall. He slid his hands across the bare skin on my back, pulling me against him.

"I like this idea," he whispered.

"Yeah?"

"Yeah," he said, then he started kissing along my shoulder.

I pulled away, making him protest as he reached for me. I smiled at him as I unbuttoned my jeans, then began unzipping them as I backed away from him and down the hall. "How much?"

His mouth parted open as he watched my hands, then he blinked, and a smile spread across his face. "Whatever the correct answer is right now. I like it that much."

I laughed as he reached for me, curling his finger through one of the belt loops on my jeans so he could pull me against him again. "That much?" I asked.

He nodded. "That much," he said. He kissed me as he moved us through the doorway and toward his bedroom.

"Honestly, can the two of you be in the same room without this nonsense?" Benny called from behind Hunter. I looked past Hunter to see Benny shaking his head as he and Ryder wandered toward the kitchen.

Ryder smiled at us. "I'm going to help him make his first snack."

"And I don't want the experience ruined by the sound of you two carrying on," Benny warned.

Hunter called over his shoulder, "Ryder, loan Benjamin your head-phones." Then he reached for my face, pulling me back to look at him as he slammed his bedroom door closed.

I had a pang of jealousy as Hunter bent down toward me. He pressed his lips to mine, then pulled back. "Really?"

"It's his first food since he died," I said. "What if Ryder chooses something like microwavable pizza?"

He let out a disappointed groan, pressing his forehead to mine. "I love you so much." He let go of me, and I smiled up at him. Then he added, "Hurry, before I change my mind and don't let you leave."

I opened the door as I fixed my jeans. "Benny, don't touch anything until I get there!"

"They transport cheddar in a pressurized tin can!" he called back.

"Do not put that in your mouth!" I yelled. Ryder's laughter trickled out from the kitchen.

Hunter chuckled as I tugged him down the hall behind me. "Good thing I agreed to stop. You may have never forgiven me for having that in the house," he said.

Vincent walked back in as we were passing to the kitchen.

"What's going on?" he asked.

"We're making Benny a snack!" I was almost at Katie levels of excitement. I was going to have to record it for her. She was going to be so disappointed that she missed this.

Vincent looked over at Hunter and smirked. "You see, this is why I bring her food and not flowers."

Hunter scoffed. "She loves roses."

I laughed. I was eventually going to have to tell him the truth about the flowers.

EPILOGUE

I LAID the cooled cloth across Benjamin's head. He was still unconscious, and his cough was worsening. I needed to get him into a cold bath to try to bring the fever down, but I couldn't move him myself.

"I'll return in a moment," I said softly, squeezing his hand.

I wrapped my shoulders and took the bucket from the floor near the door. It would take several trips to fill the trough. I was hopeful I would have a plan for transporting Benjamin into it once it was full.

I opened the door to discover Hunter ascending the steps. Startled, he asked, "Are you off somewhere? It's a bit late."

"Oh, Hunter," I gushed, dropping the bucket. I ran to him wrapping my arms around his neck.

He hesitated before returning my embrace. Laughing, he said, "I've no complaints about such a greeting, but should we be caught like this, Benjamin may skin my hide."

I started to sob at his words. "He's sick, Hunter. I haven't been able to wake him for hours. I was going to try to cool his temperature in a bath, but I can't lift him myself."

"Shh." He ran his hands over my hair. "Go back indoors before you become ill yourself. You're not layered properly for the weather. I'll retrieve the water."

Hunter kissed my cheeks before sending me back to Benjamin's bedside to watch as he made several trips for the water. On the last trip he filled the bucket overflowing with snow.

"What is that for?" I asked.

"To lower the temperature more."

He sat the bucket on the ground, then came to the bedside. I helped roll the blanket back. Hunter wrapped Benjamin's arm around his neck and lifted him slowly but not effortlessly. The two men were not far off in size. I watched Hunter struggle to get Benjamin lowered into the trough, dropping him as he lowered him the last bit and splashing the water about.

"Sorry," Hunter said.

"It's only water," I assured him. "Thank you for moving him."

He nodded, then tossed the snow into the water. "Stay with him while I get more," he instructed.

I kept my hand on Benjamin's chest, keeping from sliding into the bath in his unconscious state. Hunter made more trips until the bath was an icy slosh. The water was cold enough I was struggling to keep my hands in it. I reached my cooled fingers up to rest my hand on Benjamin's forehead.

"He's cooling." I sighed.

Hunter perched on the stool next to me, his elbows on his knees. Concern etched across his beautiful face. "Have you offered him any spirit?"

I nodded. "I was able to keep him conscious, but I've not been out in days." I couldn't keep healing him without collecting spirit myself.

Hunter unfolded himself, laying his arm across my shoulders, placing his other over my hand that rested on Benjamin. He leaned in to press his lips gently to mine. I felt that usual fluttering in my chest, then he opened his spirit, pouring himself into me. For a moment I nearly forgot why he was making such an offering and just basked in the glow of him. Coming to my senses, I pushed the energy on to Benjamin, willing his core to cool and the fluid to expel from his lungs. Whatever this infection, his lungs and heart were taking the most of it. Even as the fever broke, I could feel he had suffered much damage from it.

Coughing, Benjamin sat forward. I kept my hands on him until his lungs cleared enough to subside into labored breathing. Squinting his eyes, Benjamin scowled at Hunter. "Have I entered hell or is this a fever-induced night terror?"

"Benjamin, how are you feeling?" I asked, pulling away from Hunter.

"Like a corpse."

Hunter laughed and reached for Benjamin to help him stand. Reluctantly, Benjamin allowed him to assist in the trip back to the bed.

"Don't think I won't remember finding your hands on my sister moments ago. When I am strong enough to right you for it, I will," Benjamin threatened.

Hunter smiled and shook his head as I grabbed a dry sleep shirt for Benjamin. "Oh, hold your tongue," I said. "You'll do nothing of the sort, Benjamin. He was merely helping me. I couldn't have lifted you without him."

"I'd rather be dead," Benjamin quipped as he changed.

I smacked his arm. "Don't say such things."

He laughed, but his laughter turned into a fit of coughing, and he had to lower himself to the mattress. When the wave subsided, his face was flush. Hunter and I exchanged glances. He was far from healed.

"Let's get you tucked in," I said. I helped Benjamin change and settle under the blanket. His temperature was down, but he was weak, and the breathing sounded worse than before he had collapsed on me.

"Rest. I should get you something to eat," I said. When he closed his eyes, I nodded to Hunter to follow me to the corner.

"I can run to town. Marie will pack some broth and ale for him," Hunter offered.

"Will you stay with him and allow me to go?" I asked. "I need energy to continue to heal him. He's not out of the woods yet."

"I can give you the spirit."

I shook my head. "Not enough with him as witness."

Hunter regarded me, then said, "If you're sure. You should take time to change before you go. I meant it when I said the weather was poor."

I nodded.

Once I was out the door, I headed to the tavern. Hunter was right, Marie would be awake and have something to help bring Benjamin's strength back. More than that, I needed the crowd. Marie's patrons would be plenty and boisterous, and I needed all the spirit I could get. Strictly speaking, what I was planning was taboo, but I could hardly sit back and watch Benjamin waste away before me. Not if I could intervene.

The moment I entered, Marie called from behind the counter, "Sweets, what are you doing about at this hour?" Marie always had a dewy glow and rosy cheeks. The perpetual flush made her seem years younger than she was.

It was a wonder she noticed me over the noise and people. "Benjamin's sick, and I was hoping I could trouble you for food. I've not had time to prepare anything." I tossed the coins on the counter for her.

"Ach, put that away, girl." Marie's husband patted my shoulder as he carried a barrel of something under his arm. "Benjamin's done enough that we can spare some food. What's he come down with?"

"He's been feverish for days. He was unconscious on me until Hunter helped me get his temperature down."

"Hunter, hey?" He chuckled.

Marie smiled. "Benjamin's lucky to have such a sister—and that she's drawn the affection of such a good boy."

"Good boy, you say." Her husband laughed and shook his head.

"Oh, off with you. Don't fill her ears!" Marie snapped a towel at him, sending him on his way. "Now, have a seat. I'll see what I can bundle for you."

"Thank you, Marie," I said.

I sat in the bustle of the candlelight, closing my eyes. There was plenty of spirit in a place such as this. I spindled all I could from the unsuspecting bunch. It wasn't as much energy as I'd hoped to gather, but without instigating people further, it was all I could manage. Now was not the time or place to try to encourage the sort of behavior that would get the amount I really needed. Not while I was here alone.

"Here you are, sweets." Marie sat a basket on the counter. "I'll check on you both tomorrow."

"Many thanks, Marie. You're an angel."

"You be safe traveling back."

I nodded and hopped off my seat.

I made my way back down the road. I had been gone too long already and decided to shorten my trip by cutting behind the mill. It seemed the better choice until I was stepping through the dark.

"Where's your chaperone?" a voice came from behind me. Before I could question the stranger, a hand grabbed my shoulder, causing me to release a scream into the night.

"Calm yourself, it's only me."

I squinted in the dark until I recognized my captor's moonlit face. "Jonah! Don't startle me so!"

"*You should be thankful it's me startling you and not another. What possessed you to be out here alone?*"

"*I was getting food for Benjamin. He has a fever.*"

"*Is that why we've not seen you for days?*"

"*Yes, now release me, I need to return quickly.*"

Jonah tilted his head to the side. "*What are you planning with all that energy you've stolen?*" *I wilted under Jonah's perception. When I didn't answer, he let out a dejected breath.* "*You should know by now I'll not tattle on you.*"

"*I'm going to heal Benjamin.*"

"*Is he that ill?*"

I nodded.

"*Have you enough?*"

I thought to myself, then said, "*I'm not certain. I didn't dare risk taking more from the strangers in the tavern. It will have to be enough.*"

He watched me a moment, then said, "*Benjamin must be quite weak if he permitted you to leave this late.*"

"*He is.*"

"*And you left him alone?*"

I shook my head. "*Hunter is with him.*"

Jonah's laughter pierced the darkness. "*You left them together? You must be truly desperate then.*" *Shaking his head, he began to unfasten his sleeve.*

"*What are you up to?*" *I asked.*

"*You'll need more if he's in as bad a turn as to have you this worried.*" *He held his wrist up to my face.*

I wrinkled my nose. "*I haven't time for this, Jonah.*"

"You want to save your precious brother? I've had my fun tonight. You'll get enough energy—and then some. It's your choice."

I eyed him. Jonah was always taunting me. He knew I didn't like feeding this way. It was unfortunate that he was right. I took his wrist delicately. "Only because I'm in dire need."

He chuckled. "As am I."

I scowled at him, nearly dropping his arm. "Jonah."

"I'll hold my tongue. Just take what you need. I'm offering in earnest to help you. Truly."

I hesitated, then lifted his wrist to my mouth. I closed my eyes, squeezing them tight as I bit into Jonah's flesh. He gasped at the sensation, then wrapped his other arm around me, pulling me against him. He lay his head against my shoulder. I'd allowed Jonah to feed from me when the occasion warranted—usually in an attempt to dissuade him from more troublesome behavior. As much as I discouraged him from taking spirit in such a way from humans, this feeling was addictive. It was no wonder why he refused to give it up.

He was telling the truth – he was nearly overflowing with energy. It made me want to inquire about what tortures he had unleashed on people earlier, but I knew well enough not to ask Jonah what endeavors he had been participating in. As I drank him down, I told myself it wasn't any of my concern, and I'd no right to question Jonah's actions considering why I was feeding on him.

When I could hold no more, I gently released his arm. "Thank you, Jonah."

He made a pleased "Mmm," as he straightened. He reached up to run his finger across my bottom lip, wiping his own blood away. "It's an offer that is always open."

"It will not be necessary again," I said, pulling away from him.

He took my hand. "Are you so certain? You didn't appear to disdain it as much as you protest."

I wrinkled my nose at him. "It was a necessity, Jonah. Nothing more."

When I turned to leave him, he laughed, squeezing my hand. "You can lie to yourself however much you desire. I'll not tell."

He continued with me as I tried to walk away, still not releasing me. "What are you about, Jonah?"

"I'm accompanying you back. You really shouldn't be alone."

I tugged my hand from him but allowed him to walk with me. We went a good while in silence. All the spirit inside me left me feeling like a cat in the night. Everything was brighter and more illuminated than it should have appeared to my eyes. We were predators, after all. I sighed at my own thoughts.

"We're almost there, stop fretting," Jonah said.

"I'm not fretting," I scowled.

He chuckled. "Is there aught else you do?"

I slapped his arm. "Enough."

"Oh, but for your delicate touch I would never stop." He laughed as I hit him again. He crossed his hands over his heart, carrying on as if I had kissed him instead.

I laughed at him despite myself. "What am I to do with you?"

"Have I sufficiently distracted you from your forlorn thoughts?" he asked.

"Oh, was that your intent?" I asked.

"Always." Even in the dark, I could see the mischievous smile cross his face. I shook my head.

When we ascended the steps to the door, I could hear Hunter's laughter on the other side. "Well, they've survived in one piece," I said. "Thank you for accompanying me, Jonah."

"I am coming in with you," he said.

"What on Earth for?" I asked.

"I want to see Benjamin."

"You mean you want to perturb Hunter," I said.

"That as well." He smiled at me, swinging the door open and making a motion for me to enter.

When we stepped inside, Hunter and Benjamin were playing cards. I watched them as I removed my outerwear and boots.

"You are a cheat," Benjamin accused.

"How could I? You're dealing." Hunter laughed.

"Do not listen to him, Benjamin. He is most certainly pulling a trick," Jonah called.

"Ah, Jonah!" Benjamin raised his hands in joy. "Finally, a decent person has arrived."

Jonah smiled cheerfully at me.

I shook my head. "Oh, Benjamin." If only you knew the truth of it, Brother.

"Join us, friend," Benjamin offered.

"I should help your sister," Hunter said.

Dismissing him with a wave, Benny said, "Fine. I'm done with being fleeced by you anyway."

Hunter joined me at the table as I unpacked and poured bone broth into a bowl for Benjamin. "Why have you brought Jonah?" he whispered as he stood beside me, nearly close enough to touch.

"He caught me and followed me back."

Hunter reached out and touched my hand. Even shielding he could feel the amount of power coursing through me. His eyes dropped to my hand as his eyebrows stitched together. "Did you..." He trailed off, then turned and looked at Jonah. Jonah made a salute motion to Hunter, making sure his wrist was visible. Hunter turned back to me. His cheeks were flushed with anger. "Why?"

"It was the safer choice. He was just helping me with Benjamin, Hunter. Nothing more."

"I said I would help you. Why would you run to him?"

"I told you, he found me. I made a decision in the moment. At any rate, I couldn't have fed from you in front of Benjamin." I took the bowl and spoon and left him seething behind me as I went to feed Benjamin. I sent Jonah to the table with Hunter, urging them both to stay out of my way as I tended him.

"You needn't nurse me like an infant," Benjamin protested as I held the spoon up for the third time.

"Be quiet and allow me to show that I love you," I said.

Benjamin smiled. He reached up and tucked my hair behind my ear. "You are a good sister." Another coughing fit rolled through his body. It was violent enough that both Hunter and Jonah took to their feet, hovering anxiously as we all watched. When it subsided, Benjamin put a hand up at me. "No more, please. I'm not hungry."

"You need fluids," I said.

He shook his head. "I need sleep." Lying back on the pillows, he closed his eyes. I took his hand in mine, and he squeezed my fingers tight. His hands were warm again. The fever was already returning.

"Forgive me, Benjamin," I whispered. He may not treasure me the same once he realized what I was. Yet, I would take his hatred a hundred times over rather than watch him die. I placed one hand across his chest, over his heart. The spirit inside me trickled out slowly at first. Benjamin didn't so much as open his eyes to the feel of it. Then, as I poured into him, seeking the weakened chamber of his heart, he let out a pained groan.

He reached up to my hand, his breath labored. "What is this?"

Rather than answer, I let the flood of it open into him. I knew well enough that this would cause him pain, but I didn't have the control necessary right now to make it more pleasant. Benjamin's back arched as he let out a yell. I felt his body knitting together, his own spirit swirling around what I offered. Then a strange sensation tore through me. Benjamin's spirit attached to mine. I'd never felt such a thing, and I started to panic as his soul searched mine out, leaving his body for my own. What was it doing? As I forced it back to him, it felt as though it was ripping away from me. I screamed at the feel of it tearing from my body. Hands were suddenly yanking me from Benjamin when all went black.

My head was splitting with pain as I opened my eyes, the sunlight causing me to wince and curl away. Benjamin was lying awake next to me. He smiled at me, perfect color in his cheeks. "You are such a lazy child," he teased.

"Benjamin!" I sat up abruptly. "Are you well?"

He laughed. "I am." His face sobered then. "You shouldn't have done such a thing, Sen."

He couldn't be too cross if he was using his nickname for me, but... "Have you any understanding of what I've done?"

"Can't say I fully grasp it all, but Hunter did well to explain what he could."

I reached out to take Benjamin's hand. His shirt was damp with sweat, but he was awake and free of his fever. It worked.

"What have you done?" I turned to see Everly standing in the doorway. Benjamin sat up, ready to come to my defense, but Everly put a warning hand up at him. She hurried forward, taking my face into her hand. I felt her pry into my spirit, discovering it no longer whole. "We must hide you. They cannot discover you like this."

"Why are you here?" I asked her.

"Hunter came for me," she said. I looked past her to see Hunter standing just inside the door. At his side was Chris. Their black eyes blinked at me, sorrow painting their features.

"Where will you take us?" I asked.

"Away," Chris said.

"Whatever we must do to protect her, we shall." Benjamin nodded, lifting himself from the bed.

"Not we," Everly corrected. "Chris will take her. Alone."

"Not a chance," said Hunter.

"I should say not!" Benjamin yelled.

Their simultaneous protests brought Everly's hand up again. "Hunter, you never should have assisted her in such an endeavor."

"How was I to know she would sever her soul?" he said.

Everly looked at me lovingly. "Because nothing is ever as you expect with her. Have you not learned this yet?" Reaching her hand for me, she said. "Come."

I walked out with Everly, leaving Hunter and Benjamin inside. If I knew Hunter at all, he was no doubt already plotting to thwart Everly's plans. I could only hope his scheme turned out to be something successful. Chris joined us on the steps. They had kept their thoughts to themselves during everyone's outburst.

Chris took my face in their hands. As a Keeper, they should have turned me in the moment Everly shared my transgression. Their protection had been all that had stood between me and the Keepers as I tried to keep my promise regarding Hunter and Jonah. Chris had allowed me so much leniency already, this was surely crossing the limits of their tolerance. "I shall have to wipe your memories. It's the only way you'll be untraceable until we can sort this out."

"All of them?" I asked.

Chris nodded.

I turned back to the door. "I won't know them."

"You won't know yourself either," they said, implying I would appear as nothing but a half-breed to other Keepers. Just as Benjamin.

My head snapped back to Chris. "Oh, but Benjamin. Won't they find him?"

"Once your trace is gone, we will bring him. It will be best to keep you together, but for you to disappear, you must abandon him for a time. He's safe. I'll see to it."

"And Hunter?" I asked.

Both Everly and Chris looked mournfully at me.

"I'll not leave him behind," I protested.

Everly touched my arm. "We shall see what can be done, but we must ensure your safety first. Even Hunter would agree with that if he could see past his emotions. Come. We must hurry before he intervenes."

I looked back at the closed door. What had I done?

I sat up in bed, gasping for air. Startled, Hunter reached for me. "What is it?" he asked as he wrapped his arms around me. When I didn't answer, he coaxed, "Sen?"

Once my eyes adjusted to the dark and reality of where I was, I whispered, "I need to call Chris."

I was awake, and I remembered everything.

Tossing the blanket from my legs and reaching over to snatch up the phone from the night table, I crawled from the bed.

"All right, let me get my phone." Hunter's voice was still raspy with sleep, but he sat up dutifully.

I touched his shoulder softly, urging him to recline back against the mattress. "No, it's fine. I'll take this in the other room. You sleep."

"Are you sure?"

"Yes. I'm all right."

Even in the dark I could see concern spread over his features, but he nodded and kept any disagreement to himself as I slipped into the hall. Chris answered before I managed to hit the back door, greeting me with, "Welcome back."

"Chris." I nearly sighed their name into the phone. "I've made a real mess of things."

"Non. Following your heart is what you are. It's never the wrong choice."

"What's going to happen to Benjamin?"

"I'm not certain. With him capturing Jonah in such a way, he'll either overpower the energy or Jonah's soul will absorb into his."

Guilt settled in my stomach. I couldn't imagine Benny feeding off anger. He had a temper, but it was more righteous indignation than anything hateful. "If I hadn't tampered with my own energy, he'd be strong enough to overpower Jonah. I left him open to this."

"You couldn't have anticipated any of this," Chris assured. I could feel the hesitation through the phone as they contemplated their next question. "Will you come clean to Hunter about intentionally abandoning your spirit's calling?"

Sighing, I said, "I just need more time to explain it correctly. I promise I won't leave him in the dark much longer."

"It's not my place to meddle either way, but you need to decide if you trust him or not. Has he not proven himself enough?"

I nodded. Chris couldn't see me, but it was all the answer I could give to that right now. Hunter *had* proven he was after more than just my spirit and what it was capable of. Now I just had to hope he would forgive me for my uncertainty of him. The worst part was not being sure if I was deserving of it. I guess time would tell on both fronts.

"What would I do without you?" I asked.

"Not something you need to worry about. We'll handle this as we handle everything. Whatever the outcome, it is what it is."

I smiled mournfully into the phone. "I've become so attached to all of them." Whatever the solution, I wanted it to end in a happily-ever-after for everyone I loved in this life. Preferably with me still a part of it.

The chiming of Chris' laughter filled my ears. "Don't you always?"

And that was the real truth.

ABOUT THE AUTHOR

K. Thomas is a human, not a talking cat.

Time to Wake was her first novel. She meant to publish one sooner but fell in love with her day job. Unlike her main character, she likes numbers and budgets, almost as much as she likes words.

Head over to **kthomasbooks.com** to find updates on book releases, book promos, social media accounts, and general shenanigans.